WORD OF THE WICKED

SILVER AND GREY
BOOK 5

MARY LANCASTER

ARE YOU SIGNED UP FOR DRAGONBLADE'S BLOG?

You'll get the latest news and information on exclusive giveaways, exclusive excerpts, coming releases, sales, free books, cover reveals and more.

Check out our complete list of authors, too!

No spam, no junk. That's a promise!

Sign Up Here

www.dragonbladepublishing.com

Dearest Reader;

Thank you for your support of a small press. At Dragonblade Publishing, we strive to bring you the highest quality Historical Romance from some of the best authors in the business. Without your support, there is no 'us', so we sincerely hope you adore these stories and find some new favorite authors along the way.

Happy Reading!

CEO, Dragonblade Publishing

ADDITIONAL DRAGONBLADE BOOKS BY AUTHOR MARY LANCASTER

Silver and Grey Series
Murder in Moonlight (Book 1)
Evidence of Evil (Book 2)
Ghost in the Garden (Book 3)
The Trick of the Treasure (Book 4)
Word of the Wicked (Book 5)

One Night in Blackhaven Series
The Captain's Old Love (Book 1)
The Earl's Promised Bride (Book 2)
The Soldier's Impossible Love (Book 3)
The Gambler's Last Chance (Book 4)
The Poet's Stern Critic (Book 5)
The Rake's Mistake (Book 6)
The Spinster's Last Dance (Book 7)

The Duel Series
Entangled (Book 1)
Captured (Book 2)
Deserted (Book 3)
Beloved (Book 4)
Haunted (Novella)

Last Flame of Alba Series
Rebellion's Fire (Book 1)
A Constant Blaze (Book 2)
Burning Embers (Book 3)

Gentlemen of Pleasure Series
The Devil and the Viscount (Book 1)
Temptation and the Artist (Book 2)

Sin and the Soldier (Book 3)
Debauchery and the Earl (Book 4)
Blue Skies (Novella)

Pleasure Garden Series
Unmasking the Hero (Book 1)
Unmasking Deception (Book 2)
Unmasking Sin (Book 3)
Unmasking the Duke (Book 4)
Unmasking the Thief (Book 5)

Crime & Passion Series
Mysterious Lover (Book 1)
Letters to a Lover (Book 2)
Dangerous Lover (Book 3)
Lost Lover (Book 4)
Merry Lover (Novella)
Ghostly Lover (Novella)

The Husband Dilemma Series
How to Fool a Duke (Book 1)

Season of Scandal Series
Pursued by the Rake (Book 1)
Abandoned to the Prodigal (Book 2)
Married to the Rogue (Book 3)
Unmasked by her Lover (Book 4)
Her Star from the East (Novella)

Imperial Season Series
Vienna Waltz (Book 1)
Vienna Woods (Book 2)
Vienna Dawn (Book 3)

Blackhaven Brides Series
The Wicked Baron (Book 1)
The Wicked Lady (Book 2)
The Wicked Rebel (Book 3)
The Wicked Husband (Book 4)

The Wicked Marquis (Book 5)
The Wicked Governess (Book 6)
The Wicked Spy (Book 7)
The Wicked Gypsy (Book 8)
The Wicked Wife (Book 9)
Wicked Christmas (Book 10)
The Wicked Waif (Book 11)
The Wicked Heir (Book 12)
The Wicked Captain (Book 13)
The Wicked Sister (Book 14)

Unmarriageable Series
The Deserted Heart (Book 1)
The Sinister Heart (Book 2)
The Vulgar Heart (Book 3)
The Broken Heart (Book 4)
The Weary Heart (Book 5)
The Secret Heart (Book 6)
Christmas Heart (Novella)

The Lyon's Den Series
Fed to the Lyon

De Wolfe Pack: The Series
The Wicked Wolfe
Vienna Wolfe

Also from Mary Lancaster
Madeleine (Novella)
The Others of Ochil (Novella)

CHAPTER ONE

S OLOMON GREY WOKE with a start as his carriage halted. He could only have nodded off for the barest instant, but it was enough to disorient him. It took him a moment to reach for the door and alight.

"Just go home," he instructed his coachman. "I'll send if I need you again."

He turned his weary steps toward the black-painted door, beside which a brass plaque proclaimed *Silver & Grey*. Although it was technically daylight, the sky was the dreary, dark gray of February and a fine, cold mist of rain fell on his face, which at least woke him up a little. He let himself in with his key.

Mechanically, he hung his hat and his overcoat on the stand beside the door and walked into his office.

"Good morning, Solomon," Constance said.

Instantly, the world brightened, as though the sun had come out. He smiled in surprise, opening his arms. "Constance."

She arrived in a pleased little rush, giving him her lips and the sweetness of her embrace. Well, they were engaged to be married, and had been for some weeks now, so it was a perfectly proper greeting, if one sadly missed recently.

The trouble was, in this new business they shared, they were the victims of their own success. Word had spread that Silver and Grey were the people who could solve the most difficult and delicate of problems, from pilfering employees to missing family members. Since they didn't like to turn anyone away—unless it was a private matter between husband and wife—they had been flooded with work all winter. Which meant that they had divided the cases and rarely worked together anymore. Solomon missed that.

When he would have hugged her closer, she drew back a little, searching his face. She touched the skin beneath his eyes and cupped his cheek, a frown tugging at her brow.

"You look tired, Solomon. Are you not sleeping?"

Not without you. "I had a few matters to sort out at St. Catherine's."

A large building on St. Catherine's Dock served as the headquarters of his other business, an empire of shipping and trade that was the source of his considerable wealth.

"Trouble?" she asked.

"No, just a few things I had neglected." Delegation was never quite complete—or right, in some cases.

She linked her fingers to his and drew him toward the comfortable chairs by the fire. On the low table was a teapot, china crockery, and a plateful of scones.

"Our new cook at the establishment is proving to be a roaring success," Constance said. "Her scones are delicious. Let me butter you one."

He watched with simple pleasure as she poured his tea, cut a scone in half, and buttered it.

He bit into it immediately to please her, and it melted around his tongue, the fruit within sharp and sweet and demanding his full attention.

"My compliments to the new cook of your establishment," he said sincerely. "Do I know her?"

Constance's establishment was *her* other business, a discreet and very expensive brothel that she owned and managed as much as a charity for desperate women as a house of pleasure.

"Bibby," Constance replied. "She had been learning from our old cook, who left us last week for one of the more expensive hotels, and she clearly has flair."

Constance was always proud of her girls who made happier lives for themselves. Solomon was proud of Constance.

It was only as he finished the scone and reached for his teacup that he noticed there were three cups and saucers and three plates on the table. "Are we expecting someone?"

"Dr. Chadwick at half past nine? The man who believes his whole village has a problem? We decided we should both see him."

"So we did." There was no point in pretending he hadn't forgotten, so he merely rubbed his tired head in the hope of restoring some liveliness there and recalled with some difficulty her current case. "Did you find the lost brooch?"

"Under her bed. Her servants are not dishonest, just lazy. I read them all a lecture and collected my fee. How is the bank fraud?"

"Solved. I have my report to write today and then I believe I am clear."

"Then we are both free to investigate Dr. Chadwick's problem," she said. "If his whole village is involved, it might well take both of us."

"I hope so," he murmured, and her eyes widened in surprise, even as a smile began to spark there. "I miss you."

Her hand went out to him, but before she could speak, a knock sounded on the door and Janey—who now worked for Silver and Grey, though she lived at Constance's establishment—opened the door.

"Dr. Chadwick," she announced briefly. With Janey, brief was best, since her language was still prone to slipping into old habits.

Solomon and Constance both rose to meet their potential new client, a well-dressed man, probably in his late forties, who walked quickly and decisively, taking in his surroundings before he shook hands with Solomon. His gaze was open and direct.

"Dr. Chadwick," Solomon greeted him. "How do you do? I'm Solomon Grey. This is my partner, Mrs. Silver."

Dr. Chadwick bowed and took the hand Constance extended.

"How do you do, Mrs. Silver? I had not realized your partner was a lady."

"I trust that is not a problem," Constance said.

To his credit, Dr. Chadwick looked surprised. "Oh no. In fact, it might well be an asset in this situation."

He sat down in the third comfortable chair, and Constance poured him tea and offered him scones.

"What exactly is your situation, sir?" Solomon asked.

"I am a physician, as I believe I said in my letter, serving the village of Sutton May in Surrey." Dr. Chadwich reached inside his coat and removed a folded sheet of paper, which he passed to Solomon. "A week ago, my wife received this in the post."

Solomon unfolded the letter, and Constance leaned closer to peer over his shoulder. A gentle waft of her perfume briefly distracted him, though the oddity of the letter quickly brought him back to the matter before them.

The letter was not written by hand but made up from individual printed words and letters that looked as if they had been cut from newspapers and magazines and glued to the page to make one unsigned sentence.

Mrs. Chadwick, return to kindness or pay.

"My wife, naturally, is upset. She is the kindest woman in the world."

"Have you any idea who sent it?" Solomon asked.

"None. Neither has my wife."

Constance plucked the letter from Solomon's fingers. "Then no one has argued with her, accosted her in the street, or made accusations against her?"

"No. Not that we have heard of, and nothing much stays a secret for long in Sutton May. It frightened my wife. I cannot have that. Even so, I told her to put it from her mind and expected to hear no more about it, my belief being that it was intended to frighten rather than actually threaten."

"The threat is there," Solomon said, "if vague. Your wife received more such letters?"

"Not my wife," the doctor replied, "but others in the village have—Mr. and Mrs. Keaton, who run the village shop, and Nolan the blacksmith. And these are the ones I know about because they told me. There could easily be others, like some poisonous outbreak."

"Do you have these other letters?" Solomon asked.

"Sadly not. Keaton and Nolan both destroyed them."

"Do you know if their letters used the same words?" Constance asked.

"More or less, I think, but to be honest, when I was told, I didn't like to ask too closely. If the sender had latched on to some misdemeanor, whether real or merely perceived, I doubt the victims want it revealed."

Solomon held his gaze. "If you are asking us to investigate this matter and find the culprit, we shall need to ask and be answered."

"I know," Chadwick replied with a faint, rueful twitch of his lips. "But you are strangers who will leave again, not the doctor in whose hands you place yours and your family's health."

"The others who received letters," Solomon said, "what sort of people are they?"

Chadwick shrugged, though his eyes were wary. "Decent. Hardworking. Nolan, the blacksmith, has a bit of a temper. The Keatings gossip—inevitably, since they hear everything in their shop—but they are good people who should not be frightened in this underhand, cowardly way, especially not in their own homes."

Solomon nodded.

"Did the letters all come by post?" Constance asked.

"No, they seem to have been privately delivered to the house."

"Did they come with envelopes?"

Dr. Chadwick frowned, as though this was something he had not thought of. "Yes… At least, my wife's did."

"Then what happened to the envelopes?" Solomon asked.

"I don't know about the others, but ours was put on the fire."

"Was it handwritten?"

The doctor's eyebrows flew up. "Actually, I don't know. It must have been, I suppose, or we would have seen at once that there was something wrong with it."

"You understand," Solomon said, "that we will ask intrusive questions? Including of your wife?"

The doctor nodded. "My wife has nothing to hide. She will answer you openly. The others might be harder work for you, especially if you inquire as to who else received such epistles."

"Half our fee is payable in advance," Solomon said.

"Your letter said so. Does this mean you will help us?"

Solomon met Constance's gaze. They were in accord. "Yes," he said. "We can come tomorrow by railway. Is there an inn in the village where we can stay?"

"Yes, there is," Chadwick said, definite relief in his voice. "I would invite you stay with us, but in truth there is little room and less peace in our house. I will let it be known, however, that you are friends of mine. I can meet you at the railway station."

⇥⟫⟪⇤

"WELL, THIS IS something new," Constance said brightly, when their new client had been shown from the premises. "We've never had threatening, anonymous letters before."

"It's not *terribly* threatening, though, is it?" Solomon said. "*Return to kindness* sounds more like an amiable vicar's sermon, and *or you will pay* is almost vague enough to be ignored."

"Unless it really means *pay*," Constance said, gazing at the slightly grubby scrap of glued paper on the table between them. "Whoever sent it might already have asked for money. Blackmail money. Dr. Chadwick wouldn't necessarily know."

"I wonder what unkindness the kindest woman in the world is capable of?"

"I suspect it's in the eye of the beholder. Some people take it as a kindness just not to be hit very hard. Others think people *un*kind if they don't constantly shower them with gifts and compliments. It will be interesting to meet the residents of Sutton May."

Solomon looked even wearier as he rose to his feet. Was it merely tiredness and too many things still to do? Or was he just not as eager as she to investigate together again? He had said he missed her, and yet unease wriggled through her, a fear that he was growing apart from her.

He said, "I had better write this wretched report and get it out of the way."

"Then, perhaps, take some time to sleep," Constance suggested. "You look as if you've been up all night." He probably had.

"Almost there," he said.

As he walked purposefully toward his desk, she said, "Sol?" and waited until he glanced back over his shoulder. It took a second. "I miss you too, but I can do this one without you if I have to."

She watched him actually consider it. She had always loved that he considered everything she said, though now it felt more like an insult. Then his eyes softened. "No," he said. "I need to come. It will be my reward."

Her heart eased and she quietly left his office for her own. Janey was in the hallway, blocking the entrance of someone Constance couldn't see.

"He's not seeing anyone else today," Janey declared. "Mrs. Silver might be able to spare you five minutes. Otherwise, I can give you an appointment for—"

"Who is it, Janey?" Constance said, concerned by the belligerence in her tone.

Janey half turned, and the man on the doorstep took off his seaman's cap.

Constance grasped the hall table for support. She had seen

him only once before, and he'd taken her breath away then too, because even with his longer, curlier hair and rough clothes, he looked exactly like Solomon—tall, lean, and dark.

"It's fine, Janey," she said, praying that it was true. "Mr. Grey will want to see this gentleman."

The sailor's jaw dropped, as though he had expected her to try harder to keep him out. Then he straightened, nodded casually, and stepped inside, leaving Janey to close the door.

Solomon was not at his best to deal with anything as upsetting as this visit. Part of Constance wanted to whisk the visitor away to her own office and make sure he hadn't come to cause trouble before she let him near Solomon.

Solomon would not thank her for that.

"This way," she said, walking back to Solomon's door and entering once more. There was no way she could make this easier for him, except by giving him an instant's warning by the tone of her voice.

"Solomon. You have a visitor."

She stood aside, and his head snapped up while the sailor walked into the room slowly, almost as though, at the last moment, the journey required more energy or more courage than he could muster.

Solomon rose from his desk as courteously as always, and the eyes of the two men, so alike and yet suddenly so different, clashed and held.

"Solomon," the sailor said in a husky whisper, as though the word had been choked out of him.

"David," Solomon returned without smiling. Pain seemed to leak out of him, and yet more than that, it was recognition.

For the first time in twenty years, Solomon knowingly faced his twin brother, who had vanished apparently off the face of the earth at the age of ten. They had met again by chance about three months ago, but there had been no recognition in David then. He had been known as Johnny the sailor and, while forced to acknowledge their physical similarity, had no memory of a brother. He remembered nothing, in fact, before an illness some nine years ago, when he had awakened in a hospital in Marseilles. Everyone there had told him he was a sailor, and so he had appeared to be.

For all Constance knew, they shared no family history, their likeness just a bizarre coincidence. Solomon had acknowledged it, too.

But that one word—*Solomon*, not *Mr. Grey*—was recognition. And so was Solomon's response. *David*, his brother.

"You said to come back if I ever needed your help," David blurted, his gaze still locked with Solomon's. "Well, I'm sorry. I need your help."

"How?" Solomon asked at once.

"I'll bring fresh tea," Constance said, meaning to leave them to whatever kind of reunion this was.

Solomon made a quick gesture toward her. "No. You are family too. You are involved. Stay."

She stayed because he wanted her to, perhaps even needed her to, but David showed no disagreement.

"You are married now?" he asked.

"Not yet," Constance said calmly. "Please, sit here."

David sat, reaching for the teapot from apparent instinct, though he checked himself, glancing from her to Solomon. "May I?"

"I'll send for a fresh tea," Constance said. "I'm afraid it's cold."

"No need." David splashed tea into the cup that had once been Solomon's. He grasped the cup around its bowl, not its handle, and drank greedily until it was gone. Then he lowered the cup to its saucer and wiped his sleeve across his mouth. "Sorry. I was thirsty, and I'm not used to manners. I'm fine now."

"What," Solomon asked, as he asked all their prospective clients, "can we do to help you?"

David's eyes were oddly unfocused, a bleak, dazed look that had not been there three months ago. "I don't know. Nothing, probably. I just felt I should try. I'm afraid I killed a man. But the funny thing is, he was already dead."

CHAPTER TWO

SOLOMON WAS REELING. With Constance's help, he had learned to accept that his brother was, in all probability, finally lost to him forever. Which had been hard, for most of his life had revolved around looking for David. And yet Constance was the reality who filled his existence, his presence, his future, his joy.

But when David walked into his office this morning, it was as if some lever had been pulled in his head. He felt the spark, a weak echo of that lost connection, because somewhere in this stranger was *his* David, not the distant Johnny his brother had become without him. David had begun to remember.

"I'm afraid I killed a man. But the funny thing is, he was already dead."

The words made no sense, but they seized his attention and forced him to concentrate.

He held his brother's desperate gaze. "What happened?"

"I was in a tavern—the Crown and Anchor," David began.

"When?" Solomon asked.

David blinked, as though distracted from whatever images were filling his head. "Last night. It wasn't late, but I'd been there for a while. Don't know why—dismal kind of a place, but I know people who drink there. Only they weren't around last night."

He had been lonely, Solomon surmised. A feeling he knew well enough. "Go on."

"I saw this fellow I knew. Couldn't recall his name or *how* I knew him, but he was...*out of place*, somehow. So eventually I couldn't stand it, and when he was alone, I went up to him and asked him his name and where we'd met before. He told me to—er…take myself off, in no uncertain terms. In fact, he was loud and offensive."

"What did you do?" Solomon asked with foreboding.

David's lips quirked. "I took myself off."

"Without a quarrel?"

"Oh yes. I'm the stranger here."

And in the Crown and Anchor—a somewhat dangerous den of iniquity—a stranger who quarreled with one man quarreled with the entire public house.

"I had another drink and tried to think of something else, but then I began to remember, as if I were seeing it all over again."

"Seeing what?" Solomon prompted him.

"How he died the first time, on the deck of a ship. Years ago. He was different, then, well dressed, with a big, gold watch on a chain. Not the ship's captain but the owner of the cargo—and maybe the ship, too, I don't know. Some rich merchant, anyway. And he caught this poor sailor pilfering his spices. Furious, he was, hit the sailor hard with a club. But the sailor wouldn't lie down. He turned on the merchant and fought back, seized the club off him and beat him to death with it."

"Did no one intervene?" Constance asked, appalled.

"Not at first. It was nighttime. There must have been someone on watch—maybe the thieving sailor, I don't know. Maybe me. The details are hazy. But the noise of the fight certainly brought people running, including the captain, who had the sailor disarmed. Too late. The merchant was dead, and the thieving sailor locked up."

"And you believe this merchant was the man you thought you recognized last night?" Solomon asked.

David nodded. "It made me uneasy. So I stopped watching him, had another pint, and decided to leave. Only when I got outside…"

Solomon and Constance both gazed at him as he stared off

into nothing, then swallowed hard.

"When I got outside," David said, "there he was again. Lying on his back with blood on his chest. He was dead. Again. I know, 'cause I knelt beside him, felt for breath or a pulse. Nothing. I tried to think who to tell, but I'd already been seen. A shout went up of 'Murder!' I ran for it. Some people seemed to be chasing someone else. Others ran after me for a bit—at least one of them was a policeman, but I kept running."

"I can see why," Constance said slowly. "You were the stranger, the dead man had insulted you, and you were seen kneeling over the body. Justice isn't always fair. But your story doesn't make any sense. How could this dead man be the same as the man you saw killed on the deck of a ship years ago?"

"And even more to the point," Solomon added, "what makes you say you killed him, when you found him outside the Crown and Anchor already dead?"

David's eyes were haunted, anguished. "Because I think I killed him the first time, too."

Solomon leaned back in his chair, staring at the stranger who was his brother. "You think *you* were the thieving sailor? Why? You described it to us as though you had watched events unfold before your eyes."

"That's how it plays in my memory. Like on a stage. But *why* was I watching if I didn't intervene? If I didn't try to stop the fight or even bring help?"

"Maybe you did," Constance said. "Maybe *you* brought the captain on deck."

David shook his head, almost violently. "That's not how I see it."

"But with the best will in the world," Solomon said, "your memory is not reliable."

David licked his lips as though they were dry again. "My *head* is not reliable," he said. "I see things, imagine things, and then I'm sure of none of it."

"What things?" Solomon asked.

David tore his gaze free, staring instead into the empty tea-cup. "For years, before my illness, I imagined I was two people. I did bad things and escaped to be someone else, to live better, happier, but I always came back to being me." His eyes lifted suddenly. "And then there was you. Exactly like me. And you are real. The bad things are real too. They appall me because of you. So, what if I talked myself into believing I didn't do the worst of it? My evil twin did it."

Solomon flicked a glance at Constance, seeing the pity and incomprehension that reflected his own.

David rubbed his forehead, his eyes. "I am a mess of a man."

"You are a confused man in shock," Constance said, and Solomon could have kissed her. "And if you have only just begun to remember what happened before your illness—"

"I haven't," David interrupted, his eyes meeting Solomon's once more. "You know I haven't. I began to remember almost as soon as I saw you. Just images at first, like dreams. On the island. Playing as children. Not being alone."

Solomon's throat ached for those times. And the loss that came after. And most of all, for whatever had happened to his brother.

"Bit by bit, it came back during that voyage after I left you here in November. In dreams and spurts, till I could make something of the whole. I remembered the idea of being someone else. Of being you. I was hiding from what I did."

"What happened to you?" Solomon no longer wanted to know. He wasn't sure he could live with it. But David had, and Solomon needed to shoulder his share of that burden. "Do you remember quarreling with me?"

David's frown flickered. "Not really. I remember being alone on the docks and wishing you were there to see the man with the puppets among all that panic and chaos of people trying to leave the island. He said I could have a puppet of my own, since I liked them so much, and I said that I needed two, one for my brother. And he said I should come aboard and choose my favorites from all the puppets. I'd begun to go with him when I realized it was a bad idea, and the ship was almost ready to sail. They were waiting to pull up the gangplank. I tried to run, but he caught me and dragged me aboard the ship."

"Then it was true," Solomon whispered. His father had pursued that rumor, and so had he. "I always feared that was you… Were you *enslaved*, David?"

Astonishingly, David shrugged. "In a manner of speaking. Not as you understand it. Not legally. But I was not free. And I had no choice but obedience…until I grew big and strong enough to fight. By then I had forgotten most of my old life. It felt like a dream, and for a time freedom was enough. I traveled the world."

"So did I," Solomon said. "And yet never once…"

"The world is big and I'm just an anonymous sailor." David shrugged impatiently. "Then I got ill and really did forget everything. Looking back, that was a good thing, but I didn't know that. It was frightening, starting again from nothing, like a newborn baby but one who can speak and read and knows enough about seamanship to get a job on any ship I took a fancy to. Anyway, that's no longer my most urgent problem. The police are after me for a murder I may or may not have committed."

David paused, drew in a deep breath, and looked from Solomon to Constance and back. "And I need your help to find the truth. I can't ask questions for myself because I'll be arrested. I'm too perfect a scapegoat for this crime."

"What will you do if we find out you're guilty?" Constance asked, and Solomon's blood ran cold.

"Turn myself in," David replied. "I won't run anymore. I'll face the consequences."

Oh, no. You've suffered enough… But Solomon would not go down that road, not yet. David's story was so unsound it was ridiculous. The investigation needed cool, hard heads, and this, it seemed, was the one thing he could do for his brother.

"In the meantime," he said briskly, "we have to find some

means of hiding you from the long arm of the law. I suppose you could hide here in the office, but that would rather make Janey complicit."

"And Mrs. Silver. And you."

"We are family," Constance said, "and don't count. But as it happens, we also have the perfect disguise at hand. You, David, are Solomon Grey."

WHILE SOLOMON RETURNED to his desk with admirable focus to write his report on the fraud case, Constance set about cutting David's hair. When that was done to her satisfaction, she took him along the passage to their little cloakroom and brought him some warm water to wash and shave with.

"There's a razor in the cabinet," she told him. "And there is a complete set of Solomon's clothes hanging behind the door."

Deciding to work in Solomon's office—he was far too tense and brittle for her to leave him alone for too long right now—she collected her notepaper and pen and returned to his room, where he barely looked up from his desk. One would not have known, from the concentration in his face or the speed of his hand gliding across the page, that he was tired to the point of exhaustion and severely rattled by emotional strain and anxiety.

Interruption would not help. So, she sat in one of the comfortable chairs and wrote out her instructions to Sarah, her lieutenant at the establishment. While she was rummaging through the railway timetables to discover where and when they could board a train to Sutton May tomorrow, she realized that Solomon would not now come with her. She understood it, and yet her heart sank for entirely selfish reasons. Another separation, another chasm opening between them, when she already missed him so badly she wanted to howl.

It had taken her some time to realize that Solomon had proposed Silver and Grey as a means of deepening their friendship, of being together, to discover where it was leading. To love, of course, if it had not already been there. Working apart had never been part of their plan.

Janey came in to clear away the tea things.

"He gone, then?" she asked, jerking her head at the sailor's cap, which still lay on the chair where David had left it.

"Not *exactly*," Constance said, just as David walked hesitantly back into the room.

Janey stopped clattering. Her jaw dropped.

"Dear God," she said, dragging her awed gaze from David to Constance. "There's two of them now? You are one bloody lucky woman."

Constance squashed back the hysterical laughter. "Keep it buttoned, Janey," she said. "You haven't seen this gentleman."

"I suppose I ain't seen his hair all over the floor, neither?" Janey retorted. "Don't need to clean it up, then, do I?"

"Sadly, yes," Constance said serenely. "But not until Mr. Grey has finished his report."

"It's done." Solomon pushed back his chair. "If he wants any more, he can ask me." He handed a fat envelope to Janey, who took it in her teeth, since her hands were full, and sailed out of the room.

Solomon and David regarded each other.

"You make a good me," Solomon said at last.

"No, I don't."

"You're right," Constance said. "You slouch and you walk like a seaman, as if the ground is rolling beneath you. Straighten your back and stride out as if you're the king."

Solomon regarded her. "I do *not* walk as if I'm the king."

"Emperor, then," she said. "Don't worry, David, no one will notice. You can go in the carriage."

"Janey's already sent a boy to fetch mine," Solomon said. "Constance will go with you, David, and make sure the servants leave you alone for the next couple of days. Jenks will keep any visitors away. If you feel the urge to go out, just don't say more than a good morning if anyone recognizes you, and never stop to talk."

"Your accents are different," Constance added. "I suppose you can't go home, Solomon, if David is meant to be you. You had better go to the establishment to sleep, because it's not exactly comfortable here."

To her annoyance, she blushed as she spoke, but Solomon did not appear to notice.

"Oh, I'm not going to sleep just yet," he said. "I'm going to the police to see what they know about the murder. David, do you have a name for the victim? Or the sailor you thought killed him on the ship?"

David shook his head. "I don't remember. I've a feeling I didn't like either of them and kept out of their way. But it's fuzzier than most of the memories that have come back to me, more like a nightmare. Likely, I had nothing to do with the merchant."

"Why would a wealthy merchant drink at the Crown and Anchor?" Constance asked, frowning.

"Even I have drunk there," Solomon said, "with my wallet sewn into my coat. Perhaps he was looking for a ship's crew or fallen on hard times. My hope is that the police have discovered his identity and are prepared to divulge it. At least that would give us a starting point."

"What if they just arrest you because you look like me?" David said uneasily.

"Oh, it won't enter their heads," Solomon assured him. "We have friends among the police. Sort of." He hesitated. "We'll be gone on another case for a couple of days, but we will set inquiries in motion and return as soon as we can."

He still intended to come.

Flabbergasted, Constance caught his eye. "Are you sure—"

He gave her no time to finish. "Yes." He nodded to David, almost as if he really were a mere client. "Good luck. I'll see you when we come back. In the meantime, if you remember anything else helpful, write. Constance will give you the address and Janey will be here at the office."

It was too difficult for him, she realized. He needed the physical distance—and perhaps the other, unconnected investigation—to be able to think clearly.

She wondered if David knew that. If he cared. Like Solomon, he was difficult to read. And he was also shocked, appalled by what had happened, and dazed, probably, by his still-returning memories of Solomon and his family in Jamaica.

It wasn't surprising that the short carriage ride to Solomon's house near the Strand passed mostly in silence.

"He lives *here*?" David murmured as the carriage pulled up at the front door. "I thought he would have some big mansion in Mayfair or Belgravia."

"No. I have one of those. Solomon's tastes are simpler. He only has three servants—the coachman, a butler, and a cook. At least you won't be disturbed by a valet."

"A what?"

The coachman opened the carriage door and handed Constance down. David landed beside her almost immediately. While she dismissed the coachman, David fumbled in his unfamiliar coat pocket and fished out the key Solomon had given him. However, if he had hoped to avoid the servants by this method of entry, he was disappointed.

Jenks materialized almost before the door was closed.

"Mr. Grey is exhausted, Jenks. Could you send up some luncheon in a little? Something cold might be best because I'm trying to persuade him to go to bed."

"Of course, madam," Jenks replied, bowing.

Somehow, Constance had won Jenks to her side—possibly because he had no idea who and what she was, but possibly because he just liked to see his master happy. And Constance was making him happy.

Mostly.

She gave her hat and coat to the butler, and David remembered to hand over his. Then she took his arm in a cozy sort of way and guided him to the main sitting room, which also served as dining room and study.

David looked about him in a baffled, curious kind of a way.

"All those books," he remarked. "*This* is Solomon."

"Even at ten years old?"

"Always." He walked restlessly across the room, examining pictures on the walls. "This is the island. Jamaica."

"Do you remember living there?"

He nodded. "I do now. In bits and pieces, like any childhood, I suppose." He shivered and drew nearer to the fire. "Why did he come here?"

Constance sat down, watching him. "To England? To make it the center of his trading empire, I suppose."

"He is well thought of," David said. "Wealthy, successful."

Interesting. David had made some effort to look into his brother. "He worked hard at it," Constance said.

"Why?"

"Largely because it was something to do, I suspect. His is a restless soul, always looking for something else."

"But now he has you." It was a statement, and yet Constance thought it was not entirely free of mockery.

"He has me," she said steadily.

"Will you live here with him?" David asked, walking to the window and looking out over the roofs to the river. "In this rather modest little house where you can still smell the stink from the river?"

"You *are* remembering your past, aren't you? No, we decided to choose a home together."

"Where is that?"

"We haven't found it yet." She felt defensive because, in truth, that failure bothered her. Their engagement had not been meant to last so long. But work, Silver and Grey, had got in their way. Was that her fault? Had she tried too hard to make this a success because she so desperately wanted to make *respectable* money? To be worthy of him?

And he had not come to her bed since that first time…

Banishing the memory, she refocused on David.

He said, "I used to know what he was thinking. I remember that. We finished each other's sentences and sometimes didn't even need to speak at all to understand. He was like my other half. And yet we forgot each other."

"Oh, no." She wasn't having that. "He never forgot you for a moment. He scoured Jamaica looking for you for the rest of his childhood. Your father scoured the other islands till he died, in search of any word, any clue. While Solomon traveled the world, making his fortune, he was always looking. He pays agents in every major port in the world to look out for you, to pass any possible word on to him. I believe he had a few hopeful lines of inquiry, but they always came to nothing. Until, quite by accident, he saw you in a photograph."

There was no malice in David's intent gaze. "Because I look like him still. I'm *not* like him, though, am I?"

"In character? I barely know you."

"But you're helping me. You don't believe I murdered that man?"

"Actually, I have no idea. But Solomon thinks if you did it, you did it for a reason that makes sense to you both, even if not to the law."

"Is that what he said?"

"No. I just know Solomon."

The long eyelashes, so similar to Solomon's, swept down across David's cheeks. But she had already glimpsed the loss.

"Are you really a bad man, David Grey?" she asked.

He nodded. "I have been. It never goes away."

"I don't believe you forgot him either," Constance said. "He was still your brother, whom you wanted to be like again. Perhaps, when you imagined being someone else, you were just remembering him. Perhaps he was your antidote to badness, because you never wanted to be bad in the first place."

A strangled, savage laugh broke from him. "An unexpectedly kind interpretation of mad and bad."

And dangerous to know?

CHAPTER THREE

S OLOMON, ON HIS way to Scotland Yard, stopped to buy the latest edition of a newspaper, but found no mention of the body outside the Crown and Anchor. Perhaps corpses at that particular establishment were so common that they did not constitute news. But at least it meant there was no general hue and cry out for David.

He suspected it also meant that David was wrong about the identity of the dead man—the murder of a rich merchant outside a dockside public house being most definitely newsworthy. But then, neither was David merely the happy-go-lucky sailor he had appeared on their first encounter. He had been damaged by his past—a past Solomon's mind kept trying to veer away from—and confused by his returning memories.

Which all meant there was much to discover in a short space of time. Determined to go to Sutton May with Constance tomorrow, Solomon could not leave David or himself in quite so much ignorance while he did so. He might have time to visit the Crown and Anchor, though he knew from experience that would be an exercise in interpreting silences and blatant lies.

He might also learn more from the local police station, but he had no friends there and was reluctant to force himself on their notice when the man they had sought last night was hiding in Solomon's house. An unofficial chat with the irritable but honorable Inspector Harris at Scotland Yard was his best start.

Unfortunately, neither Harris nor his amiable sergeant were

available, being out upon inquiries and not expected back until the end of the day.

Another name sprang to mind. "What about Inspector Omand?"

He and Constance had met and indeed helped Omand to solve the murder of Frances Niall. An older, apparently plodding sort of a man, he had proved to be both insightful and decent. Unlike his underling, Constable Napier…

"Inspector Omand is in court, sir," said the elderly constable on duty, clearly unused to visitors asking for acquaintances as though they were at a gentlemen's club.

Solomon had some sympathy with that point of view. He toyed with the idea of inquiring of the man before him what he knew of the murder at the Crown and Anchor. Then the elderly constable's eyes suddenly lightened.

"But here's his constable who works with him on most cases. Here, Napier!"

Solomon felt his hackles rise even before Napier, the ambitious young constable who no doubt still despised him, turned and walked reluctantly back to the desk.

"This gentleman's looking for Inspector Omand," the older policeman said. "Perhaps you can help him? Constable Napier, sir. Napier, Mr.—"

"I know who he is," Napier interrupted with as little respect as he had ever shown Omand, let alone Solomon. He flicked his gaze over Solomon and his lips spasmed with distaste. "What do you want?"

"It concerns a murder last night outside the Crown and Anchor," Solomon replied, since there was no point in not asking.

Napier's sneer was more pronounced now. "Come to confess, have you?"

"Not until I know who died, at least," Solomon said pleasantly.

"I hear they're looking for a black man. Where were you at eight o'clock last night?"

It was deliberately offensive, causing the desk policeman to say in shocked tones, "Here, lad, mind your manners!"

Solomon, not even surprised, said, "In my office at St. Catherine's Dock with several of my senior employees. If you know nothing, please save us both valuable time by saying so."

What Napier might have responded to that, Solomon never learned, for the elderly constable, clearly anxious to make up for Napier's unforgivable rudeness, said suddenly, "The Crown and Anchor case? I heard it was a respectable gent in disguise, had cards in his pocket, by the name of…Chase. Had a few dealings on the wrong side of the law and a bit of dodgy trading, but there, shouldn't speak ill of the dead." He eyed Napier's scowl and smiled. "Herbert Chase. That's your victim. Knife in the heart, no weapon found. Case will come to someone here, but it won't be to young Napier."

"Thank you for your help." Solomon nodded to the elderly constable and walked away.

Uneasily, he wondered what David's chances would be against such seething prejudice as Napier's, without Solomon's protections of wealth, respectability, and important allies.

⨠⨠⨠⫷⫷⫷

SOLOMON RETURNED TO Silver and Grey's offices mainly because he couldn't make up his mind whether to go home or to Constance's house. Indecisiveness rattled him, for he was used to thinking clearly and quickly and reacting accordingly. Today, bombarded by tiredness and emotion, nothing seemed clear except his desire to see Constance.

He found her in her own office, frowning over whatever she had been writing, but she greeted him with clear relief, jumping up and hurrying toward him.

"Solomon! What did you learn? Did you see Harris?"

"No," Solomon said with a rueful twist of the lips. "But I did see Napier. Remember him?"

She grimaced. "Vividly. I can't imagine he told you anything."

"No, but in spite of him, I did learn that there really was a murder outside the Crown and Anchor, and the victim was one Herbert Chase, a respectable gentleman in disguise for some unknown purpose."

"Which makes David's story substantially true," Constance said, tugging him by the hand and forcing him to sit down.

"You doubted it?"

Constance sat down beside him. "He's a bit of a mess, Solomon."

"Straws and camels' backs," he said vaguely, rubbing at his forehead and forcing his mind away from Constance's beauty to the unpalatable problem. "You think he might have committed the murder? Both murders?"

"It's what *he* is afraid of. He doesn't trust himself or his memories."

He stared at her. "Well, that would test our commitment to justice. Are we harboring a felon?"

"We're harboring your long-lost brother, who is innocent until proven guilty."

"But you don't trust him," Solomon said. "What did he say to you?"

"Nothing in particular. He needs time to adjust."

"Would you let him near your girls?"

This was Constance's acid test of a man's very basic decency. If she sensed—or knew of—physical cruelty or violence, a man was not allowed to enter her establishment, whatever his wealth or rank in the world. She was more adept at reading a man's character than anyone else he knew.

She hesitated, which caused his stomach to tighten. "I would say he's not quite stable," she said carefully. "And yet I sense less violence in him than I ever did in you. I think…from pity, I would allow him the comfort."

Startled, Solomon said, "You think *I* am a violent man?"

"It's there, under your ironclad self-control. David seems less so—unless he really is two people."

Solomon threw his head back against the chair. "I can't leave him alone with Jenks."

"He would have no reason to hurt Jenks—whatever his character. This dead man, Chase, is presumably part of his past, so I suppose we shouldn't rule out the possibility that David was involved in his death."

With relief, Solomon turned back to facts. "I went to the St. Catherine's office, spoke to some of my people. We've never had anything to do with Chase, but he is not unknown. He began respectably enough and made some good money importing on a small scale. More recently, he began to fall on hard times, and some of his business dealings are no longer quite so respectable."

"Which would explain his presence—in disguise—at the Crown and Anchor," Constance said. "It would be helpful to know whom he was there to meet."

"No one at the Crown and Anchor is going to tell us that. Nor who left the place with him. Our best chance is to find some passerby who might have seen someone running away."

"Someone who was not David," Constance said. "He did say someone else was being chased, too." She smoothed her hand over her skirts, a betraying gesture of unusual uncertainty. "Do you want to stay here tomorrow to pursue this?"

"Actually, I thought we might ask Lenny Knox to investigate Chase's place of business. And he and Janey could look around for witnesses. We do have an appointment tomorrow, though I'm hoping we can wrap up the matter of those letters without too much difficulty."

Her hand stilled on her gown. Somehow, her face lightened. She wanted him to be with her, which warmed him. How had he come to doubt this?

"In the meantime," he added, "David might have remembered more for us to mull over. I'll speak to him again tonight."

"You only have one bedchamber," Constance pointed out. "Why don't you collect your things for traveling, and stay with me tonight?"

She was not even sure he would say yes. In guilty wonder—had he been cold or thoughtless in his behavior to her?—he touched her cheek and her lips.

"I would like that," he said huskily. *God, I would...*

She turned her face into his hand in a quick caress. "Then go home, Solomon, and fetch what you need. You're dead on your feet. I'll speak to Janey and write instructions for her and Lenny."

JENKS LOOKED SLIGHTLY surprised to see him. No wonder, since he must imagine the man upstairs to be his master. Solomon almost gave in to the urge to tell him the truth, but it was important that Jenks should not be knowingly involved with harboring a fugitive. As long as the butler did not see them together, he should be safe.

Hurrying upstairs, he found David standing in the middle of the sitting room floor, staring at the door as though wondering whether or not to rush out.

Solomon shut the door. "It's only me," he said lightly. "I've come back for a few things. Are you comfortable here?"

The question seemed to take David by surprise. "Yes," he said after a distinct pause. "He doesn't bother me—the man downstairs. Jenks? Mrs. Silver told him to let me rest and just leave my meals on the table."

Pitying his brother hurt. They had been born together in privilege, and so all Solomon had should be shared with him. And yet their lives had diverged in totally opposite directions. Again, he stuck to facts.

"I think the dead man is called Chase."

David's eyes widened and he sat down abruptly. "Chase...

Yes! Herbert Chase?"

Solomon nodded, then sat opposite him, leaning forward. "When you were watching him in the Crown and Anchor, trying to work out who he was, was he speaking to someone else? Part of a large group or a small one?"

David frowned. "He was on his own...most of the time. A couple of people spoke to him—just in passing—but he didn't really want to talk. I had the impression he was waiting for someone." His eyes drifted. "Probably this one fellow I did see him with. He looked like a sailor. Sat at the same table and had a conversation."

"A friendly conversation?"

David shrugged. "Hard to tell. Seemed serious, but didn't last long."

"Did you recognize this sailor?"

David shook his head. "Wasn't really looking. It was him, Chase, who caught my attention."

"Why?" Solomon asked. "What was it about him that held your attention?"

"I—I'm not sure... Wait!" David stared at him as though seeing something else entirely. "He looked at his watch. That's what made me think he was waiting for someone. He took it out of his pocket in a secretive kind of way, and shoved it away again. People don't have watches in the Crown and Anchor, as a rule. But also, it reminded me of something. Someone. And he began to look familiar to me. I just couldn't think why—until I saw him dead again."

"And did you notice this other sailor talking to him before or after you spoke to Chase?"

"Before."

"Did the sailor stay in the Crown after they spoke?"

"I don't know. I don't remember seeing him again. But I was a bit...drunk."

Solomon let it go. "Thinking back to the previous time when you saw Chase, on the ship—how did you know he was dead?"

"Captain said so." David's eyes became unfocused again, and he rubbed them. "I think. A lot of things are still…hazy."

"Then this happened before your illness? Before you lost your memory?"

David nodded.

"Do you have any idea when it was? What year or season?"

"Not really. I…I was working on the ship, so I must have been older than fourteen." His gaze met Solomon's. "That was when I escaped and got taken on the crew of a ship called the *Curlew*."

"Was it on the *Curlew* you saw Chase attacked?"

"I don't *think* so. There were a lot of ships in between, I'm sure. I didn't like staying too long."

He was afraid of being caught again. *Dear God…*

"I *felt* older when I saw Chase," David added. Then he frowned. "Are you telling me Chase didn't die on the ship?"

"He can't have, can he?"

"I suppose not." The idea seemed to please David, for he straightened, then scratched his head. "Then why? Why tell me he's dead when he isn't?"

"I don't know yet. Unless it was something you just assumed without being informed?"

David shook his head. "No. The captain definitely told me. Everybody on board knew."

"Then you're right, there has to be a reason for that."

"I might remember," David said, more hope in his voice than Solomon had yet heard. "Things still come back to me that I'd forgotten. I thought I couldn't always trust the memories, but perhaps I can."

"The more you remember, the more we can investigate and find evidence that should help." Solomon stood up. "Just rest for the next couple of days. Make use of anything you find here, pictures, letters, books, maps. While we are away, our assistants will be looking into Chase, and any possible witnesses to the murder."

An odd expression came to David's face. "It doesn't enter your head, does it? That I could be any flimflam man just taking advantage of our similar appearance."

"No," Solomon said simply.

He left the sitting room for the bedroom, where he fished out a leather bag and began to load into it soap, razors, a comb, and a few clothes suitable for any occasion he could think of. He was in a hurry to leave, and yet part of him wanted to stay, to be with his brother, whom he didn't know anymore.

Perhaps David felt the same strange conflict.

About to leave the room, his hand already on the door, Solomon caught sight of a wrapped box in the corner. He had been saving it to give to Constance when they finally found the house that would be their home. Only they'd had no time to really look.

They had been waiting for too much.

On impulse, he picked up the box and took it with him.

CONSTANCE, HAVING MADE Janey's day on the way home by informing her of the tasks she was to undertake in partnership with Lenny Knox, retreated to her own sitting room with a heap of post and the establishment's account books. This was mostly to stop herself worrying about things she could not control, such as how well Solomon and David were getting on together without her, and whether or not Solomon would want a bath when he arrived.

Or would he, after all, choose to stay with his brother, leaving her to go to Sutton May alone? She knew she was being selfish wishing for Solomon's company.

She finished answering her letters and began noting down the welcome donations to the charitable side of her business which Solomon had helped her formalize and publicize before Christmas. It was working wonders in enabling her to pay for apprenticeships and decent clothing and medical fees and so much more.

He arrived without warning, after the briefest of knocks which she answered without even looking up.

"Come in."

As soon as he did, she knew. There was something about his very presence that seemed to make the air move. Even before the faint, unique smell of him teased her senses, she knew it was him.

He carried a large leather traveling bag and a box, both of which he set down on the floor to take off his coat and hat.

"Did no one show you up?" Constance asked in surprise.

"They pointed me at the stairs. I accepted the honor."

"How did you find David?"

"Nervous, but trying to remember, almost as if he's sorting dream from reality. He recognized Chase's name, though he's not quite sure when it was that he witnessed that shipboard fight."

"Hopefully, it will come to him."

"He also mentioned a watch that Chase looked at somewhat surreptitiously in the Crown and Anchor. Which makes me think it was valuable. It would be interesting to know if the watch was still on him when the body was found."

"It would. Perhaps Lenny or Janey could find that out, too. Do you want a bath before we dine?"

He blinked. "A bath?" He appeared to think about it. "I'm not sure I have the energy. Even to eat." He bent and lifted the box from the floor, carrying it across the room and placing it on the desk in front of her. "I bought you a present before Christmas."

"You gave me presents *at* Christmas." A ring to symbolize their betrothal, a silk shawl that was exactly the same color as her eyes. Personal gifts that touched her heart.

"This is different."

Intrigued, she cut the ribbon that held the wrapping in place and opened the box. Inside seemed to be a sea of tissue paper. She fished her way in, coming up with a round object, from which she removed the tissue paper. It was a delicate porcelain cup, so beautifully painted and unique that she recognized it at once.

"This is the tea set we saw in my mother's shop!"

"I could see you liked it, so I went back and bought it. I meant to give you it when we settled on a house."

"Oh, Solomon." She turned to him, impulsively throwing her free arm around his neck. "That was so thoughtful, so… But we don't *have* a house yet."

"I know. But it came to me that we have been waiting too much."

There was a deeper significance in his words that resonated with her. What truly mattered was not respectability or success. It was each other, being together, love.

She rested her forehead against his. "Thank you."

For a moment, his arms closed around her and she let herself bask. But exhaustion radiated from him in waves. There were other gifts she could give him. She took his hand and led him through to the bedchamber.

"How would you like a picnic in bed?" she asked.

He sighed. "That sounds like heaven. If you join me."

"I will."

He drew her down on the bed beside him and kissed her. More than warmth and gratitude, excitement ignited. He began to unbutton his coat.

"Get into bed," she said huskily. "I'll arrange for our private feast."

He was tugging off his necktie, his eyes glinting, as she tore herself away. It was enough to keep desire humming through her as she went to the kitchen and collected a tray of tasty delicacies from Bibby. Her heart beat hard, and she was smiling and breathless as she crossed the sitting room back to the bedchamber.

He had closed all the curtains and lit only a couple candles by the bedside. His clothes were in a neat pile on the chair in the corner. Solomon himself lay in bed, naked beneath the covers and sound asleep. Constance's flimsy nightgown was clutched in his hand, half hidden beneath his cheek.

"Oh, Solomon," she whispered.

He didn't wake, even when she climbed into the bed beside him. So she sat close to him and ate by herself while he breathed beside her and radiated warmth and a strange kind of contentment.

CHAPTER FOUR

D R. CHADWICK WAS as good as his word and met them at the Sutton May railway station, which was more of a brief halt with a long jump from the train to the ground. Constance, curiously refreshed after her undisturbed sleep next to Solomon, had no complaints. Solomon, fully rested, seemed much more like himself. They had talked mainly about the Sutton May case on the journey, leaving David's much more complicated matter until they returned.

"Good morning! Welcome to Sutton May," Dr. Chadwick said in his brisk yet friendly way. He shook hands with Solomon and with Constance before picking up one of the bags and leading the way. "It isn't far to the inn. How was your journey?"

"Pleasantly uneventful," Solomon replied. "How are matters here?"

"Oh, just the same, so far as I can tell. I have warned those who received letters that you would be coming and asking questions, so I expect the whole village knows by now."

"So, everyone in the village knows who has received these letters?" Constance asked.

"It seems likely, so you may receive a few half-baked theories as you investigate… The Blue Goose is the last building you can see at this end of the road, which leads out of the village and up to Mortimer Manor. The Keatons' shop is behind us, and the blacksmith's just around that corner." He pointed vaguely behind the row of the houses. "And the school and the church are over there by the green. So is the police house."

"You have a policeman?" Solomon said in surprise. "Did you consult him about the letters?"

"Well, no." Dr. Chadwick cast them a half-ashamed glance. "I hardly think the letters are a crime, as such. And to be honest, he is the biggest gossip of the lot, and quite convinced of his own infallibility."

"I don't suppose he will like our poking our noses in," Constance remarked. "Does he have a theory as to who is responsible?"

"To be honest, I doubt he knows anything about the letters. Constable Heron is the last person *I* would tell."

Constance caught his gaze. "So the village policeman is the only person who doesn't know about them?"

"Well, he probably does, by now... Here we are at the Goose."

The Blue Goose was a traditional country inn built around a courtyard, with a taproom, a common coffee room, and a couple of bedchambers above. No customers were obvious when the doctor took them inside and introduced them to the innkeeper, who was polishing the bar, and his wife, who showed them to their rooms on either side of the upstairs passage.

They did not linger, for Dr. Chadwick was waiting to take them to his house to talk to his wife.

Mrs. Chadwick, described by her husband as the kindest woman in the world, welcomed them into her parlor with a slightly embarrassed expression. She was a tall, good-looking woman with the faint frown of the constantly busy, and she was dressed neatly, though hardly in the first stare of fashion.

"I'll get off, then," the doctor said, kissing her cheek and nodding to his guests. "Let me know how things go. Good day!"

"Please, sit down," Emmeline Chadwick said, still looking somewhat flustered. "Nora will bring us tea in a moment. I feel I should apologize for my husband's involving you in this matter— it is really of no account, and I honestly don't see what good you can do."

"Did the letter in question not upset you?" Constance asked.

"Well, of course it did. One never likes to think one has been unkind—or that someone dislikes me enough to send such a letter rather than speak to me if they have a problem. I have known everyone in this village for more than ten years!" She laughed with a hint of nervousness. "Which I suppose makes me a foreign incomer by Sutton May standards."

"Then neither you nor your husband were born here?"

"Oh, no. I'm from Cambridge, where Charles—my husband—studied medicine. We moved here when he took over this practice ten years ago. But I always thought we were very much part of the community."

"I'm sure you are," Constance said. "One incident surely doesn't reflect the general view. Dr. Chadwick told us he has no idea who might have sent such a note. Do you?"

"Absolutely none. I cannot imagine who would possibly communicate in such a way."

That line, Constance thought, *is rehearsed.* Which didn't necessarily make it untrue. "Leaving that aside, has anything unusual happened in the last few weeks that might have caused someone to bear a grudge against you? Anything you have said or done that might have been interpreted—however erroneously—as unkind?"

"I honestly cannot think of anything. I am not a quarrelsome woman."

"And yet I imagine the life of a doctor's wife is not easy," Constance said. "You must be as busy as he is."

"Almost," Emmeline replied with the ghost of a smile. "I arrange his appointments, take messages, and listen to patients who *don't want to disturb the doctor.* In addition, my daughter and I call on those who are convalescing, delivering medicines when necessary. I help the vicar and his wife in their charitable works. I honestly can't think what I might have done that necessitates my *return to kindness.*"

"Has anyone treated you differently in recent weeks?" Constance asked. "Perhaps been offhand or rude? Or even given you an odd look?"

Emmeline shook her head. "Not that I have ever noticed."

There was a pause then while a middle-aged maid brought in a trolley bearing tea and biscuits.

Emmeline began to talk about the countryside. "There are some pretty walks if you care for peaceful scenery. We have a very pleasant lake that you can see on the path up to the manor house, although you should stay on this side of it to avoid the marshland…"

The door closed behind the maid again and Emmeline poured the tea.

"Do you just have the one servant?" Constance asked casually.

"Well, just Nora, who lives in. Mrs. France comes once a week to do the heavy cleaning." Emmeline met Constance's gaze. "I know what you're asking, and I have no cause to suspect either of them of being discontented in our employ, let alone of sending me such a letter."

"But you *have* thought about it," Constance said.

"Of course I have," Emmeline said tiredly. "I wonder about everyone who calls, everyone I meet in the village or speak to in shops, every patient who knocks on the door. It is not…pleasant to suspect such things of one's neighbors."

Constance nodded with genuine sympathy.

Solomon accepted his cup of tea with a murmur of thanks and spoke for the first time. "Have you considered that although the letter was sent to you, it was actually aimed at your husband?"

Emmeline frowned. "What do you mean?"

"He is upset on your behalf, which may have been the purpose. You help Dr. Chadwick, but he is the physician, the man who, without being melodramatic, holds the lives of his patients in his hands."

"Then why upset him?" Emmeline said tartly.

"Why, indeed?"

She sat straighter, a spark of hostility in her eyes. "My husband is an excellent physician."

"I don't doubt it," Solomon said. "But some things are beyond any doctor. People die, or don't recover as they should, and doctors can be blamed quite without cause. It's human nature."

Her frown deepened while she mulled that. Then she spoke with reluctance, as though the words were dragged from her. "There was the Gimlets' child over at Dravenhoe Farm. She had always been delicate, and when she caught diphtheria… The poor little girl died. There was nothing Charles or anyone could do for her."

No one could doubt the genuine pain in Emmeline's face and voice.

"When was this?" Constance asked.

"Two or three weeks ago now."

Not long before the letter, then. Interesting.

"You mentioned your own daughter," Constance went on. "Do you have other children?"

Emmeline beamed. "Edgar, our son. He is almost fourteen. He is at school just now, but you are bound to meet him soon."

"Where does he go to school?"

"Here in the village." Emmeline's smile remained but had grown slightly fixed. "For now. Mr. Ogden does his best, of course, but to go to university, Edgar will need more advanced teaching."

"Does your daughter attend the village school, too?"

"Oh, not anymore! Sophie is nineteen. She should be back from her errands any moment."

"Are your children aware of the anonymous letter?" Solomon asked.

"Sophie is, though I tried to keep it from her… Ah, here she is."

The sound of the front door closing was easily heard in the parlor, as was a female voice calling cheerfully down the passage.

Emmeline went to the parlor door. "Sophie? Come and meet our guests."

A moment later, a tall young woman came in, still untying the ribbons of her bonnet. She had merry eyes, rosy cheeks from the wind, and a perfect complexion. If her features were not quite regular enough for beauty, Constance suspected that few would notice.

The girl's eyes widened in surprise as her mother introduced them. "Are you Papa's investigators? I was expecting a couple of slightly seedy old men whom I would resent having to talk to!"

"Then we are glad to disappoint you," Solomon said, amused.

He bowed over her hand, and Constance did not miss the younger woman's swift appraisal, the inevitable acknowledgment of an attractive male. But though she flushed slightly, Sophie did not gawp, merely turned to Constance with the same air of friendly surprise.

"Is this a common thing, then? To send or receive such cowardly letters?" she asked them.

"Personally, I have never come across it before," Constance said. In her world, after all, no one cared about respectability. And until she moved to Mayfair, very few of them could write. A physical fight was more likely, even between women. "Perhaps you hear things your mother does not. Have you come across anyone who bears a grudge against her?"

"No, I have not. Nor do I expect to."

"But someone sent it," Solomon pointed out.

"Clearly. But I think it must be a one-time moment of madness that will not happen again."

Such as a parent's first terrible moments of grief?

Sophie did not speak the words, but she might well have been thinking them. She had intelligent, thoughtful eyes, their brightness seeming to come from some inner vivacity rather than the girlish giddiness of a surely much-admired young woman.

"Do you know of anyone else who has received such letters?" Constance asked.

"No. Papa told us there were a couple of others in the village, but he did not say whose. I think he imagined it would make Mama feel better. Shall I take that medicine up to old Mr. Sewell, Mama?"

"Oh, yes, if you would. And maybe look in on Mrs. Gates to see how she is." Emmeline turned to Constance. "Mrs. Gates is nearing her time to give birth, so we are keeping an eye on her for Charles. Have a cup of tea first, Sophie."

"Oh, no, I might as well go now, and then I shall be back in time if Papa needs me this afternoon." Rushing to the door, Sophie paused to throw, "Good luck!" over her shoulder to Constance and Solomon.

There was a short silence in the room.

Constance set down her teacup, ready to depart.

"Don't you think," Emmeline said quickly, "that this matter would be better left to blow itself out naturally? After all, it has not hurt me, and there is no real crime involved. It was one rude letter, sent, presumably, in a moment of frustration, never to be repeated."

"But it *has* been repeated, has it not?" Solomon said. "Several of your neighbors have received similar letters."

"Maybe they—" Emmeline began impetuously, and broke off, biting her lip.

"Deserved it?" Constance suggested.

"Not that," Emmeline said, flushing. "But maybe did something that set the sender off on this path. I don't know. I'm just not sure making it public in this way will help any of us."

"We can only try," Solomon said, rising with Constance. "Can you think of anything you and the other recipients have in common? Are you members of the same committee or club? Do you have much contact with them?"

"Well, the Keatons own the only shop in the village, so naturally we are customers. The same with Mr. Nolan, the blacksmith. My husband keeps a pony and a gig for local journeys, so we are customers there, too. Mrs. Keaton is on the same church committee as I am, but these are our only outside connections."

"Are they not also your husband's patients?"

"Well, yes, but surely that is not relevant."

"Probably not," Solomon said peaceably.

"One last thing for now," Constance said. "Have you received any demands for money since this letter came?"

Emmeline stared. "Not apart from the usual accounts from local tradesmen. You surely don't think the threat to make me pay was meant *literally*?"

"We are not ruling it out," Constance said. "And I beg you to tell us immediately if such a thing does happen."

WHEN SHE HAD seen her visitors off the doorstep, Emmeline returned to the parlor and sat by the fire, her shaking hands held tightly together in her lap. She felt cold and rattled by the investigators' questions—prying questions she should not have to answer, even to herself.

Shame washed over her, burning her face and then fading so fast that she felt dizzy. She knew herself to be a good woman, trying her best, which was all anyone, even God, could ask of her. And truly, it was not her fault that the Gimlet child had died. She had never been unkind to any of the family.

And yet she had never been to see them since… She had assumed she would not be welcome, though she had done nothing wrong.

Except make them wait for Charles's attention. He had been over the hill at the time, delivering a difficult baby at the Lances' house. He could not have been in two places at once, and even if he could, she doubted he could have saved the poor little girl.

Then why did she feel guilty? As if she deserved that accusation of unkindness, delivered anonymously, as though it was from the whole village?

She should go the shop. But she found she could not face people. Were they all whispering about her? Would they tell Mr. Grey and Mrs. Silver? And would they tell Charles?

Tell Charles what? That she had made a mistake? Indulged in a moment of frustration with a child? Put her husband before a sick child?

A doctor's wife, *this* doctor's wife, had to hold herself to the highest standards. And Emmeline had failed.

CONSTANCE AND SOLOMON went next to the blacksmith's shop, a short walk away. They found him hammering away at his anvil, the muscle of his right arm bulging and flexing as he worked. He was a large man somewhere in his fifties, with a graying beard and thick, scowling eyebrows.

"Mr. Nolan?" Constance said pleasantly from the doorway.

The man grunted, presumably by way of greeting, took three more swipes with his hammer, and laid it down. "Yes?"

"My name is Grey," Solomon said, going up to him. "This is Mrs. Silver. Dr. Chadwick has asked us to look into the matter of the anonymous letters received by several people in the village. We believe you are one of them."

He grimaced. "Stupid, pointless piece of paper. Burned it."

"Did you burn the envelope too?" Constance asked without much hope.

"Course I did."

"Can you tell us anything about it?"

"It was an envelope. Like those in Keaton's. What else is there to tell you?"

"Was it written by hand?" Solomon asked patiently.

"All in capital letters."

"Well, what about the letter itself? I gather it was composed of letters and words cut from newspapers?"

Nolan nodded, curtly, and picked up his hammer again.

"What did it say?" Constance asked.

He glowered at her. "Some rubbish I paid no attention to."

"And yet you told Dr. Chadwick about it. It must have affected you in some way," Constance said.

Nolan glared at her. "It annoyed me at the time. Doctor's got no cause to go pulling strangers in to talk about it."

"Well, it seemed a good enough cause to him," Solomon said. "And it would help us to know the wording of your letter."

"We're not here to judge the accuracy or otherwise of these accusations," Constance added. "As you say, we are strangers and it's not our business. But if we know who's sending them, perhaps we can—er...discourage them. Do you know or suspect anyone?"

Nolan sighed. "No. Not sure I care. It said something like, *Keep your fists away from the children or lose more than your temper.*"

Constance blinked. "Do you beat your children, Mr. Nolan?"

"I don't have any children," he retorted. "If I did, I'd bring 'em up with more manners than some of those little tearaways. I have to chase hordes of them out the shop some days before they burn themselves. It's not a toy shop in here."

"No, indeed," Constance soothed. She had once been quite used to the blows of the adults she annoyed, till she learned to avoid them by smiling and dodging. "Was there one particular incident when you had to do so, perhaps a little roughly?"

"Aye," said the blacksmith, hitting the horseshoe before him with more aggression than seemed necessity. "School was out, and it was pouring wet, so they all came rampaging in here. Ain't safe, is it? So I told 'em to get the hell out, and when they didn't, I chased them."

"With fists?" Solomon asked, just a little too smoothly.

"With fist, singular," Nolan snarled, showing them his left hand suitably clenched. He sniffed. "Never touched them. Never had to. But...I had a red-hot shoe in my tongs. Forgot about it, to be honest, but it certainly made the little tikes run."

"Did anyone see this happen?" Constance asked. "Apart from you and the children themselves?"

"Nope. They were all inside sheltering from the rain too."

"Then who do you think sent you the note?" Solomon inquired.

Nolan shrugged. "That's what I don't know. One of the little b—children must have blabbed to their parents, though the parents don't want their precious darlings in here any more than I do. They should be grateful to me, not threatening me."

Solomon's parting lips had a caustic look about them, so Constance barged in before he could speak and lose them whatever information Nolan might be harboring.

"That is a fair point," she said. "Which children invaded your shop that day?"

"Oh, the lot of them. The Keaton brats. Edgar Chadwick, the doctor's boy. The Gimlet lad was there, a couple of Dickies, and the vicar's twins, who're the worst of the lot, only Mrs. Raeburn will never believe it. They need a damn good hiding if you ask me, but that schoolteacher's too lily-livered to do more than look at them—!"

Nolan broke off and glared between them. "There. Know who it is yet?"

"Not for certain," Constance said, "but you have been most helpful."

"I have?" Nolan looked taken aback.

"Absolutely," Solomon agreed. "Thank you for your time."

As they left, they heard hammering start up again.

After the heat inside, Constance was glad of the cold wind to cool her face.

"Well? Who did he give away?" Solomon demanded.

"I have no idea. I just don't want him to think he shouldn't talk to us. We don't want to be clueless strangers."

"So, what are we?"

"Clueless strangers," she said, smiling amiably at the two

elderly ladies who were marching directly toward them. One swung an umbrella like a weapon of war, while the other commanded a walking stick at an impressive pace.

The ladies came to a halt in their path, forcing them to halt.

"Good day," said the one armed with the stick. This close, she seemed younger than Constance's original impression, somewhere between fifty and sixty, perhaps. She was a small, round person in well-made if old-fashioned clothing, and she bestowed an unexpectedly sweet smile upon them.

"Good day," Constance replied, while Solomon tipped his hat.

"You must be Dr. Chadwick's friends. Welcome to Sutton May."

"Thank you."

"I'm Jessica Mortimer—of Mortimer Manor, you know. This is my companion, Miss Jenson."

Constance dipped a curtsey. Solomon bowed. "I'm Constance Silver. My partner, Mr. Grey."

"How do you do?" Miss Jenson said. At first glance, she appeared to be the opposite of the first lady, being tall and almost stick thin, her expression one of brisk determination compared to the rather unworldly gaze of Miss Mortimer.

"We have been most curious to meet you," Miss Mortimer said. "You are not at all what we expected, are they, Hannah?"

The thin Miss Jenson's nostrils flared. "That remains to be seen."

"Perhaps you would care to join us at the manor house for tea this afternoon?" Miss Mortimer asked.

"Thank you," Constance said. "That would be lovely."

Miss Jenson did not dispute it, though neither did she look delighted.

Miss Mortimer beamed. "Until tea, then. Goodbye!"

CHAPTER FIVE

"**I** COULD ALMOST imagine I'd met the queen," Solomon murmured, "only a couple of decades into the future."

"I wonder what she wants with us? Keeping her eye on her kingdom, I suppose."

"Or she knows something she wishes to impart."

"That will be interesting. What shall we buy at the Keatons' shop?"

"Anything you like," Solomon replied when he had opened the door, for the shop was positively stuffed with goods, from newspapers to bedsheets, children's sweets to sides of ham hanging at the back. Constance particularly noticed a shelf full of notepaper and envelopes.

The shop seemed to go on for miles, with little space between the packed shelves to move around. Constance could see no other customers but became aware of a woman in an apron waving from behind a crowded counter of cakes and sweets.

"Good day!" the woman said amiably. "Can I help you?"

"I'm certain you can," Solomon said, gazing around him. "Is there anything you *don't* sell?"

"Fresh meat," the woman said at once. "But the ham is very popular."

"It does look good," Constance said.

"I expect you'll have it for breakfast at the Blue Goose."

"Mrs. Keaton?" Solomon said, removing his hat.

"Indeed!" The woman squeezed out from behind the counter. "Come through to the back…"

The back did not mean beneath the hanging ham, but through a half-hidden door at the side, where a middle-aged man was discovered seated at a table, munching a sandwich. He half rose in alarm as they invaded his territory.

"Ralph, my husband," Mrs. Keaton said, almost apologetically.

Solomon offered his hand. "Solomon Grey. And my partner, Mrs. Silver. I believe Dr. Chadwick has mentioned why we are here."

"Indeed," Mrs. Keaton twittered, "though it's a difficult situation and I'm not quite sure… Impossible to know what's best."

"I don't think that can be decided until we know the facts," Solomon said, while he and Constance squashed in around the table with their hosts.

Constance felt the urge to laugh as her wide skirts enfolded Solomon's legs as well as the table's. "Dr. Chadwick said you had destroyed the anonymous letter you received."

"Despicable thing," Mr. Keaton said, shoving his empty plate toward his wife. "I don't know what the world is coming to. Nor do I know—meaning no offense, Mr. Grey—why Chadwick had to go stirring things up by calling in strangers to investigate."

"I believe he hopes to stop it happening again," Constance said. "I take it you have received just the one such letter?"

"And one is more than enough," Mrs. Keaton said with a theatrical shudder.

"What exactly did the letter say, ma'am?" Constance asked.

Mrs. Keaton flapped her hands. "Oh, I don't remember exactly."

"It *said*," Mr. Keaton pronounced, glaring, "that bearing false witness led to the ruin of the accuser and we should repent. As if we don't go to church like decent Christian folk!"

"Then the letter was definitely accusing you?" Solomon said. "What was it referring to?"

The husband and wife were carefully avoiding each other's

gazes while a moment's uncomfortable silence passed.

Then Mrs. Keaton flapped her hands again. "All we can think of is an incident in the shop. It was busy at the time, and both Ralph and I were run off our feet serving different people. We had these rather pretty little shawls in stock—silk, they are. Miss Mortimer bought one for Miss Jenson's birthday, so that shows you the quality…

"Anyway, I was showing a few of them to Mrs. Raeburn—the vicar's wife, you know—and while she was making up her mind, I went to serve Mrs. Johnstone. And when I went back to Mrs. Raeburn, she'd gone and so had one of the shawls, and that Nell Dickie was standing there looking guilty with her youngest in tow. I asked her if she'd dropped the shawl—giving her a chance to make it right—and she denied it, so I asked her to leave. Told her not to come back or I'd send for Constable Heron."

"And had she stolen the shawl?" Constance asked.

"Someone had, for I never saw it again," Mrs. Keaton said with an air of triumph.

"And yet this Nell Dickie remained in the shop waiting to be served? While Mrs. Raeburn vanished? Didn't you think Mrs. Raeburn was more suspicious?"

Both Keatons looked shocked.

"She's the vicar's wife!" Mrs. Keaton exclaimed.

Perhaps her husband read something in Constance's face—or Solomon's—for he said quickly, "You have to know the local people. The Dickies are all a waste of space. It's not the first time one of them's been caught thieving. But times are hard, and Faye made the kind decision not to charge her. We bear the cost of that theft."

"I see," Solomon said. "And you think that was the incident referred to in the anonymous letter? So do you think this Nell Dickie might have sent it? One of her family?"

Keaton scratched his head. "I'd be surprised, to be honest. Not because I think it's beneath them, but because they're illiterate."

"How many of them are there?" Constance asked.

"Dickies? There's the old man, Harry—he can't walk anymore. His son, Hen and Nell, the wife—no better than a gypsy, if you ask me—and Lord knows how many brats. Four?"

"Five," said Mrs. Keaton. "I think."

"And how long was it," Solomon inquired, "between this incident of the missing shawl, and your receiving the anonymous letter?"

"A couple of days," Keaton said. "Maybe three?"

"You said the shop was busy," Constance pursued. "Did your other customers see and hear what went on between you and Mrs. Dickie?"

The Keatons did exchange glances then.

"Maybe," Mrs. Keaton said reluctantly. "I kept my voice down, and she slunk off like the guilty creature she is, grateful not to have the constable after her, but Mrs. Johnstone might have heard. And Miss Fernie, who was waiting to be served."

"There was one of those uncomfortable silences when Nell had gone," Mr. Keaton offered. "But no one said anything, even Peregrine Mortimer, who was in buying cigars at the time."

"Peregrine Mortimer?" Solomon asked.

"He's staying up at the manor. Miss Mortimer's nephew."

"Ah. Was anyone else there?"

"Tilly Gimlet, poor soul."

"The woman who lost her daughter to diphtheria?" Constance asked.

"That's her. It wasn't that long before poor little Jenny died…" Mrs. Keaton glanced upward as though to heaven.

"Do you think it could have been any of those people who sent you the letter?" Solomon asked.

"Oh, no!" the Keatons said at once, quite emphatically.

"Then do you have any idea who did?"

They shook their heads.

"None at all," Mrs. Keaton said. "Never happened before in Sutton May. I think someone's gone mad—which is how we came to speak to Dr. Chadwick about it, since if someone round here was mad, he'd be likeliest to know. And then it turned out his wife had received a letter, too. Which is ridiculous, Mrs. Chadwick being such a good woman. She goes to church, too."

"I DON'T EVEN know where to begin," Constance said as they walked back toward the Blue Goose in search of sustenance.

"Possibly without the judgment you so dislike in Mrs. Keaton," Solomon murmured.

Constance cast him a glance of disapproval, though her eyes held a rueful twinkle. "Was I that obvious?"

"Not to them."

"You're right, though. I don't know any of these people or their backgrounds. But we do seem to be collecting quite a list of suspects. Interesting that Mrs. Gimlet was in the shop to witness the accusation. It connects her to both letters."

"Maybe. We should certainly go and speak to her."

"And to the vicar's wife," Constance said.

"To accuse her of stealing a silk shawl from the Keatons' shop?"

"To see if she has received an anonymous letter accusing her of it," Constance corrected him.

"A good point worth asking." Solomon drew her hand into the crook of his arm. "But this is going to be next to impossible to narrow down. I doubt the perpetrator of the Keaton letter had to have been in the shop the day of the theft. Word of the incident would have spread around the village like wildfire, including the Keatons' account of it, because I don't imagine they kept it themselves, however discreet she claims to have been to the unfortunate Nell Dickie. Someone else we should speak to."

He suspected they would need to speak to the entire village before they were finished. And it was not going to be the quick case he had hoped for. He thought uneasily of David and the dead merchant and the police waiting to pounce—and wondered if he should have stayed in London.

IT WAS STILL morning when Janey swaggered into the Crown and Anchor, the silent Lenny Knox at her heels. The place was dark and dingy, and it stank. But at this hour of the day, it was at least relatively quiet, with only a few elbow movements in the gloom to disturb the rancid air.

"'Ere, you got a rozzer on your doorstep," Janey threw at the potman who was heaving a barrel into place behind the counter.

"Bloody peelers," the potman said bitterly. "Not my fault someone croaked outside my pub. What you want?"

"A pint and a half," Lenny said. "And have you got any work?"

"What d'you think? Course I don't."

Janey sniffed. "Wouldn't work here anyhow, with murderers and peelers all over the place. Who was he, then? Who done him in?"

"How would I know? Happened outside, didn't it?"

"Probably whoever he was drinking with," Lenny said wisely, picking up the mug that was almost slammed in front of him.

"That's where you're wrong," said the potman. "Again. 'Cause he left well before the dead cove."

"Could have lain in wait, though, couldn't he?" Janey said, and then, as the potman began to look suspicious, she added, "Where *is* there work going, then? Preferably somewhere no one gets murdered."

"Thought of Mayfair?" the potman sneered.

"Good idea," Janey said, nudging Lenny. "Fetch the carriage, James!" She went off into bawls of laughter.

"Cut it out, girl," Lenny said roughly. "Let's go. That rozzer makes me nervous."

"Maybe he's got work for the likes of you," the potman said with a grin.

"I'll ask," Janey said. "Put in a word for you and all, if you like!" She let out another shriek of laughter as they abandoned more than half their ale and lurched off out the door. She was pleasantly surprised by how well Lenny played along, even holding her up as they staggered out the door.

"'Ere!" she addressed the tall-hatted policeman. "You got a rotten job, ain't ya? That's an 'orrible place, in there. Wouldn't work there for all the tea in China!"

"Nor for the beer, neither," Lenny muttered.

"What you hanging about here for, anyway?" Janey asked the policeman with a friendly nudge.

"Doing my duty and keeping watch. Like I said, a man was killed here the other night." For a second, the policeman looked hopeful. "You weren't around here night before last, were you? About eight in the evening?"

"Might've been," Lenny lied, impressing Janey all over again. "What should I have seen? Never saw a fight, I'm sure of that."

"What about someone running away? Maybe even two people?"

"Two people?" Janey pounced, then, afraid of seeming too eager, she added, "That ain't fair, two against one."

"Murder isn't fair," the policeman said austerely.

Janey nodded sagely.

"How do you know two people croaked him, then?" Lenny asked.

"I never said they did. Just two different people were seen running away. Sailors, both of them, but one was English and one was dark."

"Together?" Lenny asked.

"Not necessarily," the policeman said grandly. "And you can move on if you've got no information."

Janey and Lenny moved on, remembering to weave as they went.

"We need to find out who the English sailor was," Janey said. "Because he was probably the one who committed the murder."

"I don't see how you work that out," said Lenny, who had never met Mr. Grey's double. "Could have been either of them. Or neither."

"Well, we know who the dark man was," Janey admitted. She sighed. "I should go back to the office. You coming?"

To her disappointment, Lenny shook his head. "I got things to look up about Herbert Chase. I'll call in later, though, if I find anything."

"Right you are," Janey said cheerfully.

It was too soon to hope for any more from Lenny Knox. In her heart, she knew he would never look at her that way, and she didn't blame him.

⇶⤜

AFTER A PLEASANTLY filling meal at the inn, which made up for their lack of breakfast, Solomon and Constance borrowed the innkeeper's gig and followed his instructions to Dravenhoe Farm to seek out the Gimlet family.

The Gimlets were, apparently, long-standing tenants of the Mortimers of the manor house. Dravenhoe was not large, although it seemed to be in good repair. In the distance, a couple of men were working in a field, part of which was already plowed. Solomon drove the gig past a few curious cows, and some sheep, before arriving at the farmhouse.

The door opened almost at once and a young woman came out, drying her hands on a cloth, her hair covered by plain kerchief. She looked tired and somehow frail.

She paused, blinking at her visitors in surprise. "Oh. Are you lost?"

"I don't think so," Constance answered. "Is this Dravenhoe, and are you Mrs. Gimlet?"

"Yes, but…"

"We're friends of Dr. Chadwick," Solomon said, with a touch of exaggeration. "My name is Grey. This is Mrs. Silver. We're hoping you can help us with something."

"Are you looking for my husband? He's over in the field."

"Perhaps later," Constance said, "but we'd like to talk to you first, if you don't mind."

"I don't mind," Mrs. Gimlet said, and Constance rather thought that she didn't. She might have been going through the motions of life, but neither her heart nor her mind shone in her weary, numb eyes.

At her invitation, they tied the horse to the fence around the henhouse, followed her into her clean kitchen, and sat at her well-scrubbed table.

"We were wondering," Constance said, deciding to start with the easier question, "if you happened to witness an incident in the village shop, maybe three or four weeks ago? The shop was busy and Mrs. Keaton was showing a selection of new silk shawls to the vicar's wife."

"Was she?"

Mrs. Gimlet probably hadn't noticed. No doubt her daughter was already ill… "One of the shawls disappeared and Mrs. Keaton thought Nell Dickie took it. She asked her to leave."

"And threatened her with Mr. Heron, the constable. I do remember that. Poor Nell. The Dickies get blamed for everything."

"With justification?"

"Maybe. Sometimes. But what on earth would Nell want with a silk shawl? It won't keep her or her babies warm, will it?"

"She could sell it or exchange it for something that would."

"She could. Maybe." Mrs. Gimlet didn't look convinced. But she didn't look particularly upset either.

"Then you didn't see her steal it?"

"I didn't see anyone steal anything. I was looking for a tincture to make my little Jenny better."

"I heard about your loss," Constance said quickly. "I'm very sorry."

"Thank you," Mrs. Gimlet said mechanically.

"Um...did you happen to hear what passed between Mrs. Keaton and Nell Dickie?"

"Not really. I heard Nell raise her voice and then Mrs. Keaton sent her out and threatened her with Constable Heron. Her little lad looked terrified."

"Are the Keatons kind people?" Constance asked. "Are they liked in the village?"

"I never thought about it," Mrs. Gimlet said with a shrug. "They're important to us—because of the shop. And church. They're charitable people. Gossip, of course, but they hear everything from everyone, and who wouldn't, in that position?"

It was the most she'd said at one time, but there was no animation, let alone strong feeling, in her voice.

"Can Nell read?" Solomon asked.

"No, I don't think so. Neither can old Harry nor Hen. The children must do, though."

"Why do you say that?"

Mrs. Gimlet shrugged. "Because they go to the village school, same as mine. Mr. Ogden makes sure they all read and write, makes no difference between any of them."

Solomon met Constance's gaze. "Interesting."

"How many children do you have, Mrs. Gimlet?" Constance asked.

"Just the one now. Richard. He's eleven. Broke his little heart when his sister died. I told him she was with God now, and he said he hated God."

"It will take time," Constance said, feeling stupid and helpless, because nothing she said could help a mother, a family, with such grief.

But the woman nodded in acknowledgment. "He hated everyone for a bit."

Very reluctantly, Constance said, "Including the doctor?"

"At first. But there was nothing Dr. Chadwick could do. She was just too ill. Maybe if he'd come sooner…"

"Did you ask him to?"

"I sent Richard to him, and he spoke to Mrs. Chadwick. Doctor came the next day, and our Jenny was dead by evening." Mrs. Gimlet stood up, unable to be still. "A cup of tea, maybe? Or some ale? We make our own—Fred says it's better than the stuff at the Goose."

"Oh, no, we shan't keep you any longer," Constance said at once.

"Just one more question," Solomon said. "I don't suppose you have ever received an anonymous letter?"

Mrs. Gimlet blinked in clear incomprehension. "A what?"

"An unsigned letter that might be insulting or threatening."

"I've never heard of such a thing," Mrs. Gimlet replied with some distaste, before the numbness drifted back across her eyes.

⇛⇛⋈⇚⇚

"I HATED THAT," Constance said intensely as Solomon drove the pony along the path from the farm.

"I know. And I doubt it will be any easier with her husband."

"I don't think she's in any state to be bothered producing anonymous letters."

"Two of them were sent before her daughter died," Solomon pointed out.

Constance turned to stare at him. "Seriously? You think *she* sent them?"

"Not really. But it's not impossible, is it? And then there's her boy, angry and grieving." He slowed the horse at the side of the hedge, and they gazed over to where the men were working. "We could make our way over there and interrupt them at work."

"Or we could wait until Gimlet notices us and comes over for a more private conversation. Or I could attract his attention by bursting into song."

"Or we could wave," Solomon said, rising from the seat to do so.

It worked. One man saw him first and called to the other, and the second walked smartly along a narrow path between furrows.

"Good afternoon," Solomon called amiably.

The farmer nodded curtly and came to a halt at the hedge that separated them. "What can I do for you?" It wasn't rude, but nor was it encouraging.

"Mr. Gimlet? My name's Grey," Solomon said. "I'm looking into an odd matter for Dr. Chadwick."

"What sort of a matter?"

"A sort of anonymous insult aimed at his wife."

The farmer made a derisory puffing sound through his lips. "That'll be women's stuff, and he should know better than to get involved. Some nice church lady'll be jealous of another's flower arranging. What's he involving you for?"

"Oh, a fresh pair of ears and eyes," Solomon said vaguely.

"Two fresh pairs," Gimlet said, his gaze flickering over Constance.

"As you say. I don't suppose you have an idea who might have done such a thing?"

"I don't even know what thing you're talking about," Gimlet retorted. "And if I did, I'd keep out of it."

"What, even if someone insulted *your* wife?"

Gimlet's eyes narrowed. "What do you mean by that?"

"Nothing," Constance said. "Merely that a man rarely tolerates his wife's being insulted."

"I wouldn't know. No one'd ever insult my Tilly, because she never gave 'em cause."

"Do you think Mrs. Chadwick might have given someone cause?"

"How the devil would I know? Look, I got work to do, and I don't think much of yours. My best to Dr. Chadwick."

CHAPTER SIX

Miss Mortimer, the lady of the manor, welcomed Constance and Solomon to her drawing room. Although it was not a particularly large house, it was well maintained and decorated and looked to be a very comfortable home.

Her companion, Miss Jenson, set aside her needlework and gave the visitors several long, assessing looks. Almost like a bodyguard, Constance thought. Or perhaps she was guarding her own position.

"I'm so glad you found the time to join us," Miss Mortimer said with her sweet smile. "Tea will just be a few moments. How do you find our village?"

"Most charming," Solomon said.

"And your commission from the good doctor prospers?"

Solomon did not blink. "We have not yet accomplished our goals."

"How foolish of me! You have only just arrived. You must tell us if we can help in any way."

"Actually, you can," Constance said. "By telling us your impressions of Sutton May and its inhabitants. Have you always lived here?"

"Yes, by and large. Apart from a few forays to school and Town, and travels abroad. This has always been my home."

"And yours, Miss Jenson?" Solomon asked politely.

"Oh, no. I grew up somewhere quite different. I only came here after Jessica's—Miss Mortimer's—mother died. As her companion."

"That was over thirty years ago," Miss Mortimer said. "I think we can call it your home."

"How did you meet?" Constance asked. "Are you related?"

"Only by interests," Miss Mortimer said. "Hannah was my teacher when I was sent away to school, and we became friends. Naturally, when my father said I should have a female companion, I thought of her." Her eyes twinkled. "I can see you are thinking it is unusual to have a lady of the manor without her lord. I never chose to marry, but I believe I have been as good a squire as my father. The estate was never entailed, you see, so I was his heir. Shocking, is it not? Would you care for a quick turn in the garden now that the sun has come out?"

Since it was February, there was not a great deal to see in the garden, apart from a few clumps of early daffodils and crocuses. Miss Jenson brought shawls, dropping one around Miss Mortimer's shoulders and offering another to Constance, who accepted it gracefully. She had the feeling the lady of the manor wished to talk to her, a notion proved right when Miss Mortimer took her arm and, with the aid of her walking stick, all but galloped around the path until a low hedge separated them from Solomon and Miss Jenson.

The old lady began without preamble. "I know you are you looking into the matter of the nasty letter Mrs. Chadwick received, so I shall tell you at once that I received one too. Here. We don't have long." She thrust an envelope into Constance's hand. "Hide it. I don't want Hannah to know."

"Why not?" Constance asked, tucking the letter into her substantial handbag.

"She worries enough. And is likely to blame the wrong person. This is between you and me."

"I will share it with Mr. Grey," Constance warned.

"But not Dr. Chadwick?"

"Not if you don't wish it."

"I don't."

"Who do you think sent it?" Constance asked.

"If I knew that, I could put a stop to it. I am placing my trust in you to find out."

"I shall try to earn that trust. When did you receive it?"

"About a month ago. I thought I was the only one until Dr. Chadwick told me about his wife and the others, and I realized something must be done."

"Do you have any idea what inspired your letter?" Constance asked.

"It's somewhat vague, as you will see. But I have not evicted anyone, held any recent orgies, or committed any crimes. I haven't even put up rents for several years, though I fear I will have to very soon. I am at a loss."

"Could the ill feeling be aimed at someone acting on your behalf? A steward?"

"I would doubt it, but again, I don't know. If you have specific question once you've read and investigated, feel free to call again. In fact, come tomorrow evening, and we shall find time to speak alone. I am holding a little card party—they remind me of my youth, and we only play for halfpennies—so I hope you and Mr. Grey will come."

"Thank you," said Constance, who had hoped for Solomon's sake to be back in London by tomorrow evening.

"It is not warm, is it? Shall we go back inside?"

Miss Mortimer performed a military-style right wheel, and they came face to face with Solomon and Miss Jenson marching toward them. Solomon's lip twitched with amusement, but he too turned with good grace, Miss Jenson on his arm, and they all returned together to the drawing room.

Tea was being laid out by the servants.

"Oh good," said Miss Mortimer. "Tell Mr. Mortimer, if you please."

"Yes, ma'am," said the footman, bowing.

"Mr. Mortimer is your nephew?" Constance asked. "Does he live with you?"

"No, but he stays frequently, I am glad to say. He is my heir, you see, and will make a much more dashing squire."

In what was clearly a long-established habit, the teapot was set before Miss Mortimer and the servants departed. While the lady of the house poured, Miss Jenson conveyed cups and saucers to the guests, along with plates and offerings of dainty sandwiches, pastries, and cakes.

"So, tell us about Sutton May," Constance said brightly. "Is Mrs. Chadwick as kind as she seems?"

"Unfailingly," said Miss Mortimer.

"And just as tired," Miss Jenson added, dryly.

"Because of her work among the sick?" Solomon asked.

"And with the doctor. It is she who organizes him while keeping the house, dealing with her unruly son and her stubborn daughter. No wonder she is exhausted."

"Her son is unruly?" Solomon asked. "He is only fourteen, is he not?"

"Oh, it's just mischief," Miss Mortimer said. "Boys will be boys, and there is no spite in Edgar Chadwick. He has just been a little overindulged."

"And Miss Sophie Chadwick is stubborn?" Constance said. "In what way?"

Miss Jenson shrugged. "She makes her own friends, goes her own way. Which is admirable, in my view—up to a point."

"What point?" Solomon asked.

"The point where her path veers from that of her parents," Miss Mortimer said.

"But she seemed so willing to please and run errands for her mother."

"Oh, yes. She is a kind girl, and very bright," said Miss Jenson, no doubt with her old teacher's hat on. "Very bright indeed."

The drawing room door opened, and the footman announced, "Miss Chadwick and Mr. Ogden, ma'am."

Dr. Chadwick's daughter swept into the room ahead of a tall, gangly young man who appeared to be all legs and awkwardness.

The girl's eyes widened in surprise when she saw Constance and Solomon, but she greeted her hostess first with a curtsey and a kiss on the cheek, a greeting she repeated with Miss Jenson, who patted her shoulder in a pleased sort of way.

To Constance, it looked very natural, a long-standing fondness between all concerned. Could Sophie's "stubbornness" be to do with the awkward youth now standing with his arms hanging by his sides, fingers flexing, as though unsure what to do with himself?

He was not an ill-looking young man, for he had bright, inquisitive eyes beneath a high, intelligent brow, a rather long nose, and a pointed chin. His mouth, with its full lower lip, might have been sulky or passionate, or just indicative of the fact that he did not want to be there. His clothes, which could not ever have been fine, were past their poor best and did not fit well, being both too loose, and slightly too short in the arms and legs.

"I brought Mr. Ogden," Sophie said cheerfully, "since I know you are always pleased to see him and hear about the children."

With all eyes now on him, the young man made a jerky bow.

"Of course we are delighted, Mr. Ogden," Miss Mortimer said. "How do you do?"

"Well, ma'am," he got out. "I trust you are both also in good health?"

"Indeed we are. And you must meet our other guests," Miss Mortimer said. "Mrs. Silver and Mr. Grey."

Ogden swiveled on his feet and bowed again. His gaze was peculiarly penetrating while he muttered, "How do you do?"

Had Sophie told him why they were in Sutton May?

"Mr. Ogden is the village schoolmaster," Miss Jenson said.

"We consider the school very fortunate to have him," Miss Mortimer added. "Do sit down, sir."

For a moment Constance thought he would insist on standing, but he did lower himself into the place next to Sophie on the chaise longue, and Miss Jenson brought him a cup of tea. While she offered the sandwiches, the door opened again and a very different young man swaggered in.

It was clear at once that he was Miss Mortimer's nephew. His coat was of the finest cloth and best cut, his posture both graceful and arrogant.

"Am I in time for tea, Auntie?" he drawled. "And how delightful! We have visitors. Miss Sophie, your devoted servant!" He bowed elaborately, his eyes dancing and crinkling at the corners in a way that might have been attractive if it had not been quite so studied. He was a handsome, charming man—and he knew it. Clearly, he was used to making the most of it.

"Mr. Mortimer," Sophie said carelessly, "I thought you were leaving us."

"Oh, Aunt Jessica persuaded me to stay for her card party— which I am happy to do, since you will be there." Mortimer's eyes gleamed with rather more malice as he turned to the schoolmaster. "Why, Oggie, is it you? I thought you had to work for your crusts?"

Ogden barely looked at him, though some of his tea slopped into his saucer. Mortimer undoubtedly saw this sign of discomfort or annoyance for his mocking smile widened.

"I don't suppose you will be imperiling your soul—or said stipend—at my aunt's devilish gaming tables."

"I shall be busy," Ogden muttered.

"Perry, our other guests," Miss Mortimer intervened gently.

Mortimer had little choice but to leave off tormenting the schoolmaster and turn to be introduced to Constance and Solomon. His eyes widened as they landed on Constance, but that seemed to be his only spontaneity. He crinkled his eyes again and let them twinkle attractively.

"Mrs. Silver. I am enchanted."

"Oh dear. Have some tea," Constance added, since Miss Jenson was approaching with his cup and saucer.

He promptly sat down between Constance and Solomon, though he lazily offered the latter his hand. "How do you do, Mr. Grey. What brings you to our backwater?"

"A little business," Solomon said.

"And you, Mrs. Silver?" Mortimer turned back to Constance, his eyes leaving hers to drift down over her chest and waist.

"The same business," Constance said.

"Oh." Mortimer's eyebrows flew up in surprise. "Are you...?" He gestured from one to the other.

"Betrothed?" Solomon said coolly. "Yes."

"I did not know that," Sophie said from the chaise longue, adding to Ogden, "They are friends of my father's."

"It isn't a secret," Constance said.

"When will you be married?" Sophie asked.

"Soon," Solomon said.

They had been saying that since before Christmas. It would be spring soon...

Constance rose to her feet. "We should be on our way, Solomon. Miss Mortimer, thank you so much for tea. It has been lovely meeting you and your friends."

"Until tomorrow evening, then," Miss Mortimer said, while the gentlemen all stood and Ogden bumped his knee on the nearest small table, rattling the china.

"I'll show you out," Mortimer said unexpectedly.

Constance suspected the courtesy was to emphasize his unique position in the household and heir to the lady of the manor, but here she maligned him. Dismissing the servants who came to help with coats and hats, he assisted them both himself.

"I hope I am not speaking out of turn," he said, almost apologetically, "but if you are friends of Dr. Chadwick, and here on his account, perhaps you are the people I should be warning."

"Warning?" Solomon said, donning his own coat.

"Well, telling. I am worried for my aunt. And sending anonymous letters is exactly the sort of low, underhand sort of trick that old witch would perpetrate."

"Old witch?" Constance repeated.

"Hannah Jenson," Mortimer said quietly. "My aunt's so-called friend and companion. Hah!"

"Why do you say that?" Solomon asked.

"Because she has always worked to cut my aunt off from her family and friends. She's after the old girl's money—as much as she can lay her hands on. I'd watch her very, very carefully."

"Thank you for your information," Solomon said politely. "Good afternoon."

He opened the front door himself, since Mortimer seemed to have forgotten about it, and Constance sailed out in front of him, allowing the young man a regal inclination of her head.

She felt his hot eyes on her, though, as Solomon assisted her into the gig.

Only as he flicked the reins to get the horse to move did she let her breath out in a rush.

"Now, *there* is a young man I would not let near my girls," she murmured. "At least not without a character reference and a few long conversations in the salon."

"You think he's malevolent?" Solomon asked. "Or just a typical young man who likes women a shade too much?"

"There's no respect there. He has his aunt wound round his finger and treats both Sophie and me as if we are conquests he has already won. The only person he is even prepared to respect is you, and I doubt he's made up his mind about that yet. He clearly despises the schoolteacher."

"He is certainly an arrogant young cub," Solomon allowed. "Do you think he said what he did about Miss Jenson because she's one of the few females he can't cozen?"

"Possibly. Though I doubt he's cozened Sophie Chadwick either. He just doesn't know it yet." Constance leaned her cheek briefly against Solomon's shoulder, needing the closeness. "Can you see him taking the time to compose our anonymous letters?"

"No. Nor can I see his caring about anyone's kindness or false accusations against poor Nell Dickie—though it's true he was in the shop at the time."

Constance straightened and opened her handbag. "Which reminds me, Miss Mortimer *did* receive a letter, and hers is in an envelope without a postage stamp."

"So, it was hand-delivered, too," Solomon said.

"It would seem so." The direction was hand-printed in capital letters, presumably as the others had been. And inside, the letter was clearly of the same type, with glued bits of newspaper attached to notepaper. "The envelopes and the paper look to be the same kind the Keatons sell in the shop."

"What does it say?" Solomon asked.

She smoothed it out in her lap.

You are responsible for them all. It is you who will pay.

Solomon gazed at it while the horse trotted on without any guidance. "*Could* it be a warning from her faithful companion?"

"I don't see how it helps Miss Jenson gain power over her, let alone inherit a lot of money. And if it's a warning—wouldn't she just speak to her? She's not really subservient, is she?"

"She doesn't say much," Solomon remarked. "But if they are such good friends, why has Miss Mortimer not confided in her?"

"To stop her worrying, or so she says."

"Or because she doesn't trust her?"

Constance frowned. "I would say she does. They certainly seem to understand each other, communicate without speech, like old married couples and young siblings." She glanced at him, for she hadn't meant to bring up the subject of David just yet, but since she had, she said, "Did *you* do that? You and David?"

"Yes. I think so, anyway." His throat moved as he swallowed, and she leaned against him once more. "Now he is a stranger I don't know if I even like. I don't know what happened to him, what it did to him."

He had told her once that he'd had nightmares about such things as a child. Now he was afraid again that the nightmares were true. And she could not tell him that they weren't.

"It hurt you too," she reminded him. "And he is strong, like you. We'll sort it out. Meanwhile, he is safe."

He shifted his gaze from the road to her face, and she was relieved to see the smile in his eyes. "Where would I be without you, Constance Silver?"

"Reduced to merely raking in thousands of pounds from trade," she said flippantly, "without any fun at all. Or you might have traveled the world as you were going to before I hauled you off to rescue Elizabeth Maule."

"I still wouldn't have enjoyed it. Where shall we go for our honeymoon?"

She smiled, just because he was speaking of marriage again. And he had bought her the tea set. "Venice."

"Why not? I've never been there…"

CHAPTER SEVEN

"FRED GIMLET," SOLOMON said over dinner at the inn's otherwise empty common room, "was very certain that our letters are the work of a woman. Is that fair? Or is he trying to point us away from himself?"

"Without noticing that it might lead us to his wife instead?" Constance chewed thoughtfully and swallowed. "His grief has not numbed him, as hers has. He could well bear anger against Mrs. Chadwick for not sending the doctor more urgently to his child. He could have heard of Mrs. Keaton's accusation against Nell Dickie and considered it unfair. And he is Miss Mortimer's tenant—there's bound to be a grudge somewhere in their history."

"If not in their future, since she is going to raise the rent. But what has he got against Nolan the blacksmith?"

"He has a farm horse, so he must be a customer. And his son, Richard, was one of those Nolan chased."

Solomon frowned. "Would an angry father not storm in there and have it out with Nolan? Gimlet did not strike me as a timid man. Then again, wouldn't he be angrier with his son for causing trouble? Sitting down and painstakingly cutting out and gluing a lot of bits of newspaper to form a vague message to send anonymously to a neighbor he could easily speak to face to face?"

Constance sighed. "It's not a natural reaction, is it? I can't see either of the Gimlets doing it, even maddened by grief. But—" She broke off and slowly lowered her knife and fork to the plate.

"Isn't it a rather childish thing to do? A game with the letters that also makes a powerless child's sense of injustice plain to an adult? Richard Gimlet must have had his parents' grievances as well as his own, and his own mother admitted he hated everyone when his sister died."

"He might even be a friend of the Dickie children."

"Or it could be the other way round, and a Dickie child is the culprit." Constance shoved her plate away from her. "Or any of the children in the village, come to that. They could even have banded together to teach the adults a lesson."

Solomon's smile was twisted. "We're not exactly eliminating suspects, are we? What about Sophie Chadwick, who seems to be always out and about, delivering medicine and good cheer, and making friends like Ogden, the downtrodden schoolmaster."

"Stubbornly going her own way," Constance said. "We don't know her well enough, I suppose, but I can more easily imagine her scolding people for unkindness, false accusations, or whatever. Wouldn't the sender of our letters be more timid and downtrodden?"

Solomon raised his eyebrows. "Like the schoolteacher? I'm not sure he *is* downtrodden. Socially awkward, yes, despised by Peregrine Mortimer, yes, though not, apparently, by Miss Mortimer herself."

"His eyes are sharp enough," Constance said. "But he doesn't meet one's gaze for long, if at all."

"Something to hide? Devotion to Sophie?"

"I don't see Mortimer regarding Ogden as much in the way of competition."

"He was sniping at him," Solomon pointed out.

"Like a bully picking on the one he sees as powerless… Solomon, would *Mortimer* send such letters? Despite the effort involved?"

He shrugged. "I can't see his noticing the things the letters point out, let alone caring about any of them."

"Oh no, I'm sure he doesn't care. That wouldn't be his purpose. But…a bit of stirring for amusement's sake, with the primary aim of blaming the letters on Hannah Jenson?"

"His aunt's friend and companion," Solomon considered, "who might interfere with his inheritance. I could believe that. He might take the trouble for so much gain. Plus…" He caught Constance's gaze. "How does he know about his aunt's letter? You said she hadn't told anyone but you."

"That," Constance said, releasing her breath in a rush, "is a very good question."

They discussed the case further during the rest of the evening, and Constance made up a neat little chart showing the timing and contents of each letter, and the witnesses of the incidents that seemed to have inspired them. After which, they both knelt on the floor and stared at the document with some discontent.

"Nothing leaps out at me," Constance said.

"Nor at me. Come, let's take a walk before bed and begin afresh in the morning with the school and the notorious Dickie family."

"I suppose it was never going to be as easy as all that." Constance gave him her hand and allowed him to draw her to her feet.

It seemed a long time since they had spent so much time together. An ache he had barely acknowledged began to ease within him as they walked as so often before, her hand in his arm, her skirts brushing his legs. This sense of deep companionship he had only ever known with her had once taken him by surprise— frightened him, if he were honest—for he hadn't been prepared to lose himself in love. And yet it had been exciting and wonderful to let it happen, to *feel*. To be happy.

He had never been a passionless man, but he had been a very controlled one. He cared for causes and justice and for finding his lost twin. Urges of the flesh had been separate and often inconvenient, indulged with care and a fondness he now recognized as mild. Because now there was Constance.

Constance his friend, whom he loved with a passion that only grew, and whom he had taken to bed only once and missed there ever since.

He forced himself to stop thinking and just absorbed her presence, her light, arousing scent, her warmth, the sound of her low, slightly husky voice. As they walked the length of the village street and turned left to the square bordered by the church and vicarage on one side, and a schoolhouse on the other, it didn't matter to him that the evening was dark, cloudy, and slightly damp, with a wind that cut like ice. Until he felt her involuntary shiver, when he turned their footsteps back toward the inn.

The taproom was busy, judging by the noise that greeted them as they passed the door, but the common room was empty, save for a maid polishing the tables who cheerily wished them, "Goodnight!" as they made their way toward the stairs.

When they were married, there would be no necessity of *goodnight* to each other. For the merely betrothed, in a respectable house, it was a requirement.

When he took her gloved hand from his arm, she was tense, as she had been too often over the last few weeks, during their too-infrequent encounters. She missed him, as he missed her, and yet…

He bent and kissed her lips. "Goodnight, Constance."

There was a moment's silence while she gazed into his eyes. Their candles flickered, as if someone had breathed on the flames. She seemed to be waiting. Her lips parted, and in spite of his determination to be good, his heart beat faster.

Her breath hitched, and then she stood on tiptoe and kissed him back. "Goodnight."

Just for an instant, her alluring softness pressed against him. Desire surged.

And then she was gone, whisking herself into her own room. The door closed behind her with a small click that seemed to break the spell. He walked the few paces to his own door and went inside.

Somewhat mechanically, he lit the lamp from the candle

before taking off his coat and his necktie and dropping them on the chair.

He was not really alone. She was no more than a couple of yards away, on the other side of the wall, and he wanted her very badly.

There was no wrong in that. When had he become such a conventional prig that he was bowing to false respectability rather than making himself and his beloved happy? He smiled, imagined the sweep of joy and excitement over her face if he went to her now…

His smile faded.

There had been a reserve in her since that first time she had admitted him to her bed. The happiness of that night and the morning after had got lost in work and in some kind of personal uncertainty. As if she were no longer sure.

And yet he had given her pleasure. He knew enough to be well aware of that. But her past was a checkered one where men and women traded, and he was afraid he had slipped into that category for her. Had he lost her in that act—those acts, plural, for it had been a long and glorious night—of love? Or did she imagine it was all he wanted of her—a warm, willing, and beautiful body in his bed?

He found himself facing the wall that divided them. Almost involuntarily, he lifted his hand and spread his fingers against the whitewashed plaster as though he could reach through it and touch her.

When she was ready, she would tell him.

CONSTANCE TOUCHED THE wall between their bedchambers, aching for him. She had tried to tell him, to invite him to come to her, but she had been afraid to speak the words in case he rejected her, whether for foolish respectability or, worse, from lack of desire.

She knew she was a kind of unholy grail for men, because it was the role she had chosen to entice men to her house. She had made herself desirable and unattainable. Only she knew her lack of skill, and yet she had made Solomon happy.

Once.

Perhaps he was not as happy as she had imagined. And having known her once, was that enough? It had not been deliberate seduction. He was not the kind of man to make notches in the bedpost. But the distance between them now… Was he having second thoughts?

Why does he not come?

Her breath caught and her hand fell away from the wall.

Why do I not go to him?

To resolve this one way or the other, it was the only thing to do.

She crossed the room and snatched up the candle again. And paused.

They were in the middle of a case—two cases, counting David's problem. This was not the time to risk personal emotions.

Was it?

"Oh, damn you, Solomon, why don't you talk to me?" she whispered. Although even then she knew she was being unfair. Because she had not talked to him either.

"Sophie?"

To her annoyance, she had no sooner closed the front door behind her than her mother emerged from the dim parlor.

"Yes, of course," she said lightly. "I hope you were not waiting up. Mrs. Lance sent me home in their carriage."

"I thought she would. I just worry until you are home. I'm the same with Edgar and even your father."

"You worry too much, Mama. Do go to bed now, or you'll be exhausted tomorrow."

"So will you."

"But I am young—as you keep telling me."

"And I am not yet in my dotage, thank you! How are things over the hill?"

The Lances' estate was called Chettering, but in Sutton May, it was always referred to as *over the hill*. Even though the hill was barely a bump in the landscape, it stood out in the unrelieved flatness of the surrounding countryside.

"They all seem well. They are going to Miss Mortimer's party tomorrow night, as we thought."

"Excellent. I own I am looking forward to it—aren't you?"

"Yes, of course." Except, of course, that Perry Mortimer would be there too with his hot eyes and wandering hands. And *he* would not be there.

"Edgar says you went to Miss Mortimer's for tea," Mama said casually.

"She is always at home on Wednesdays."

"Was Peregrine there?"

"Sadly, yes."

"Why sadly?" her mother demanded. "Any other girl would be flattered to have such distinguished attention, which you appear to delight in thwarting!"

"Trust me, there is no delight," Sophie said. "I do not like him, and I very much doubt that his attentions, as you call them, are honorable."

"Sophie!" her mother said, genuinely shocked.

"He already sees himself as lord of the manor. And trust me, the daughter of a country doctor is not the bride he will choose."

"You cannot possibly know that. He is merely a gentleman of deep feeling, which you would recognize if you spent time with people of your own class."

"I count Netta Lance as my dearest friend," Sophie said patiently, although she knew exactly whom her mother was referring to. "And she is very much a gentleman's daughter."

"Was Ogden there?"

"At Chettering? Oh no." She met her mother's gaze. "He was at the manor this afternoon, though. Teaching is considered an honorable profession by most people."

"I suppose he will be there like a lowering black cloud tomorrow night, too."

"No," Sophie retorted. "Nor do I blame him when he has to face down snobbery like yours."

"How dare you speak to me like that?"

Sophie dropped her gaze. She did not really want to fight. Or not yet. "I'm sorry. I know you aren't really snobbish. It's just that you never used to be like this."

"Like what?"

"Unkind about people who might be a little…different."

A strange look came into her mother's eyes. A mixture of horror and fear that made Sophie feel instantly ashamed.

"Are you suggesting I *return to kindness*?" Mama said unsteadily.

Sophie swallowed. "Perhaps I am." She brushed past her mother to the stairs. "Goodnight, Mama."

IT HAD RAINED during the night, so the path to the Dickies' piece of land was somewhat muddy for the inn's horse and gig.

According to the innkeeper, the Dickies had always owned that same square of land, back through the centuries, maintaining their independence in the face of powerful landowners and occasionally unfriendly villagers.

"They make a living," the innkeeper had told Constance and Solomon with a shrug. "But only just. It was touch and go in the forties—though everyone was hungry then, weren't they?—and they're certainly not well off now. But they seem happy enough."

"Is there ill feeling against them in the village?" Constance had asked.

"Not really. Some tenant farmers like to pretend they're better because they farm more land—but Hen Dickie just laughs and points out he *owns* his. They're a bit of a ragtag bunch and get the blame for any poaching or thieving, but it's just like a habit. No one's ever laid any charges against them in my lifetime."

"I understand it came close," Solomon had said, "in the Keatons' shop a few weeks ago."

"I heard about that."

"Could Mrs. Keaton have been right?"

"She could have been, but more likely, she made a mistake. What would Nell Dickie want with a silk shawl? She's hardly going to wear it to church."

And at first glance, the muddy yard, which contained a ramshackle little house and a couple of outbuildings with hens and a pig, certainly did not seem the right environment for silk. A ball and a couple of other battered old children's toys were scattered in the mud.

No one answered Solomon's knock on the door, but in the field beyond the house, a man and a woman were laboring with spades and hoes, turning the soil ready for planting. The couple clearly saw them, for the woman called something to her companion and began to walk down the field toward them.

"Mrs. Dickie?" Constance said as she approached the gate. "My name is Constance Silver. This is Mr. Grey. Could we possibly have a word with you?"

"What for?" the woman asked suspiciously. She was still young, not much more than thirty, despite her five children. And she was pretty in an untidy, careless kind of way that made Constance think of Lady Grizelda Tizsa. Beneath a square of cloth, her hair was escaping from its pins. There was a streak of dirt across her nose and one cheek, and her once brightly colored clothes had faded with too many washes.

"We're friends of Dr. Chadwick," Constance said, since the

connection seemed to soothe people.

It seemed to work, for Nell opened the gate and came into the yard. "Nothing wrong with the doctor, is there?"

"Not with his health," Constance said, watching the frown clear from the other woman's brow. "You are another of his friends."

Nell shrugged. "He's been good enough to us. Came when the little 'uns were sick and never dunned us for payment. Not many like that around here."

"Is his wife kind, too?"

"You should know, if you're his friends."

"Well, she's kind to us," Solomon said. "That doesn't mean she's kind to everyone. In fact, the doctor is concerned because someone insulted her."

"Yes? Insults ain't sticks and stones," Nell said. "They won't hurt her—I should know."

"Someone insulted you, too?" Constance asked.

Nell laughed. "Would I notice?"

"I heard Mrs. Keaton implied you had stolen from the shop."

"*Implied?*" Nell mimicked. "Accused, tried, and convicted me, more like. She still spreading that around? I can't even go into the shop now. I'm afraid to send the children in case she has Heron chain them up, and Hen don't have time to go. I've got to wait for the market every week and get what I need then. I don't care. Market's cheaper anyway."

"Someone pointed out to Mrs. Keaton that she shouldn't bear false witness."

"Good," said Nell, glancing up at the sky.

"Is it just you and your husband working?" Solomon said. "No children around to help?"

"They're all at school." For the first time, there was an air of pride about her. "Even Tommy, our youngest, and he's only five. He's another good man, that Mr. Ogden. He sees the brightness in the kids and makes it shine brighter. If you see what I mean."

Constance nodded sagely, although, in fact, she didn't really see the clumsy, silent young man as much of an inspiration to scholarship for wild boys and girls. She imagined he was more likely ridiculed, in much the same manner as Peregrine Mortimer had mocked him yesterday.

"You never went to school yourself, Mrs. Dickie?"

"Nah, nor Hen neither. But the world's changing and I'm glad ours will have chances we didn't. Not enough land here to provide for five in the future. They'll have to make their own way—the girls and all, though I know there's some against educating females."

"I'm all in favor of it myself," Constance said. "I didn't go to school either, though my mother taught me to read and write."

Nell looked at her with more interest. "You done all right for yourself, then, ain't you?"

"I hope so. Thanks for your time."

"Pleasure," Nell said, puzzlement in her voice as she turned and strode back into the field.

As they walked back toward the gig, Solomon murmured, "Look at the window."

A white-whiskered old man watched them from the small window beside the door of the house. Presumably Hen Dickie's father Harry.

"Upstairs," Solomon said, and then she saw what he had. A patch of newspaper had been tied across the tiny, broken attic window.

The adults might not read, but they certainly had uses for newsprint.

CHAPTER EIGHT

As Constance had suspected would be the case, much hilarity was emanating from the village schoolhouse. It was a long, single-story building, which might once have been two cottages knocked together perhaps at the turn of the century. There were two doors, so presumably the schoolmaster lived in one part and the classroom occupied the other.

Exchanging glances with Solomon, Constance followed the laughter and gently pushed open the larger door. An adult male voice spoke, not mingling with the laughter as she'd half expected, but talking between bursts.

And the children were loving it.

Constance and Solomon stood in a cloakroom filled with coats and hats, boys' on one side, girls' on the other. A half-glass door provided a window into the classroom, through which they could see Mr. Ogden standing at the far end of the room, leaping from place to place between bursts of talk, and more bursts of laughter. Sometimes he asked an obvious question and the children shouted out the answer.

At the desks in the front few rows were children ranging in age between about five and ten. Moving position, Constance could see a row of older children with open books who clearly were meant to be working on something else but were grinning as they too watched the antics of their teacher.

It took Constance several moments to realize that Ogden was giving a grammar lesson by pretending to be two different people. One was calm and poised and just a little supercilious, and spoke correctly. The other scratched his head a lot and lumbered, saying the same things incorrectly. The teacher moved from place to place—and character to character—with one great leap of his long legs. It was so comical that Constance found herself smiling.

Then Ogden caught sight of her. Instead of looking shame-faced or jumping to attention, or even bolting to meet them at the door, he ignored everyone but the children.

Crouching down between the youngest two pupils, he gave them quick instructions and they reached obediently for their pencils.

Then he walked between the desks behind and spoke clearly. "You boys and girls, I want to write a story using as many as you can of the verbs we've been talking about. Your story can be as funny or as serious as you like, but your grammar should be perfect."

Still smiling, the children opened their books and quietened down.

Ogden glanced at the older children, whose grins broadened, though they bent immediately to the work they'd been neglect-ing. The classroom was not deathly quiet, but everyone was busy. And comfortable.

Only then did Ogden walk to the classroom door and step outside. He closed the door behind him and swiveled so that he could see his pupils through the glass. There was nothing remotely awkward about him. This was his territory, his place, and he was comfortable in it.

"Yes?" he said.

"We met yesterday," Solomon reminded him. "At the manor house."

"Yes," Ogden said again.

Constance tried a little flattery, though she suspected it was not so far from the truth. "You appear to be a gifted teacher. With unconventional methods."

Solomon cast her a curious glance, as though wondering

when she'd had time to observe any methods of education.

Ogden gave a shrug. "Children remember more when you make it funny. Or different. Do you want something?"

"I suppose we want your view of the village," Constance said. "As an educated man. There has been some…unpleasantness."

Ogden, apparently, had nothing to offer to that.

"It crossed our mind," Solomon said, "that one of your pupils might have something to do with it. One who felt strongly about certain things."

"What things?" Ogden asked, frowning.

"Some delay to the medical treatment of Jenny Gimlet, an accusation of theft made against Nell Dickie, the blacksmith's chasing a crowd of children away from his forge while wielding a red-hot horseshoe, even some lack of responsibility by Miss Mortimer or her estate people."

"Making sentences from newspaper cuttings seems quite…childish," Constance said.

Ogden looked at her, then his eyes slid away. "The accusations you mention are not childish. And these are good children."

"I heard some of them were a little wild."

"Of course they are. They're children. And most of them are too poor to buy the paper and envelopes you're talking about."

"I don't recall talking about paper and envelopes," Solomon said mildly.

Ogden's lips twisted into a smile. "There are secrets in this village. That isn't one of them. Excuse me."

"One more thing," Constance said before he could push open the classroom door again. "How well do you know Sophie Chadwick?"

This time he did look alarmed. A storm of color swept over his face, but he didn't answer, merely bolted back into the classroom—where he once more transformed into the calm, authoritative teacher.

"WHAT AN EXTRAORDINARY young man," Solomon said when they were walking around the square toward the church. "Would you let *him* near your girls?"

"Yes," Constance said, "but I don't think he would accept. I can see why Sophie likes him. He's...different."

"Different enough to send the letters? He certainly seemed to know all about them."

"I'm not convinced other people's lives impinge on him to that degree. He was certainly defensive of the children."

"But was he telling the truth that none of them did it?"

"Would he know?" she countered. "Even parents aren't always aware what their children are capable of. He's probably correct that most of them wouldn't be able to buy paper and envelopes, but some of them probably could—Dr. Chadwick's son, Edgar, for example, and the Keaton children, whom we haven't met yet."

"But possibly not the Gimlets or the Dickies? The paper could be stolen or provided by friends. Or the children could be in alliance."

Constance groaned. "How would we ever find that out? We cannot go about interrogating other people's children."

"It was just a thought," Solomon said mildly. "And we haven't yet met anybody's children. Does the vicar have any?"

"He's bound to."

They found the vicar inside the village church, which was a small, rather charming old place with pews very close together. He wore his vestments, which bunched around his legs as he strode down the aisle toward them.

"Good morning," he said in surprise, coming to a halt. "Might I be of assistance?"

"I hope so," Solomon said. "My name is Grey. This is Mrs. Silver. We are friends of—"

"Of Dr. Chadwick," the vicar said. "So I heard." He thrust out his hand. "Luke Raeburn. Vicar of this parish."

Constance became aware of a lone woman sitting at the very end of the front pew, her head bent in prayer. Behind them, the church door opened again.

Shaking the vicar's hand, Constance said, "Could we talk in private, Mr. Raeburn?"

"Of course, of course. Come back to the vicarage!"

The vicarage was a rambling house, probably built in the previous century, just outside the churchyard. "Come in, come in," Mr. Raeburn said hospitably. "It's lovely and quiet at this time of the morning, since the children are all at school!"

Constance pounced on the subject. "How old are your children?"

"Fourteen, twelve, eight, and seven," the vicar replied proudly.

"Do they attend the village school?"

"They do indeed, and they are all getting on very well. Even the girls. And I have hopes my eldest will follow my footsteps into the church."

"Then he will go to university?" Solomon said. "Will he need to go to a different school first?"

"Oh, no. Mr. Ogden is an excellent tutor. Odd sort of a fellow, but nothing wrong with his intellect. Got a double first at Cambridge, you know. I did wonder just at first if the children would mind him, but they do... Come into the study, and then when we've talked, my wife will give us tea. Sit down! Now, how can I help you?"

The vicar's study was a comfortable room where he clearly spent a good deal of time. Books lined the walls and cluttered the large desk in the window on which a long sermon—or perhaps some theological paper—appeared to be half written.

Mr. Raeburn indicated two winged armchairs by the fire and pulled over another chair from his desk to join them. After poking the fire into life and adding another log, he sat down and smiled.

Behind round spectacles, his eyes sparkled with interest.

"Perhaps you are aware of Dr. Chadwick's concerns," Solomon began.

"About his wife's nasty letter? Yes indeed, he told me. He was concerned that others in the village might have received similar letters, but I could not help him there."

"Because of your duty of confidentiality?" Constance asked. "Or because you had heard of no other letters?"

The spectacles winked in a passing beam of watery sunshine through the window. Mr. Raeburn shifted position to avoid it. "People can be…ashamed to receive such missives, not just because of the objectionable content and accusations that may or may not be true, but because someone they know dislikes them enough to send them such a thing. To say nothing of the fear that secrets or lies might be revealed to the whole community."

"I can understand those fears," Constance said.

"Some people need someone to talk to," the vicar said, "and that, in general, would be me. To others, I would be the last person to confide in just because of my calling and the shame they might feel in front of me."

"I see," Solomon said, holding the vicar's gaze. "Perhaps you can tell us how many such letters you are aware of?"

Mr. Raeburn blinked rapidly, as though debating if this were a permissible revelation. "Two."

Solomon's eyebrows flew up. "And yet you would appear to have a knowledge and understanding that goes far beyond a mere two letters."

"I do, as it happens, but most of my experience is not from Sutton May. When I was a very young curate in the north, our parish was plagued with a spate of such spiteful letters. They caused a lot of ill feeling, a lot of fear and distrust, even tragedy. To be frank, I find it hard to forgive such plain nastiness."

There was genuine distaste and an echo of old anger in his voice.

"Did you ever find out who sent them?"

"Oh, yes, eventually. A spiteful spinster who had constituted herself the arbiter of parish morals."

"What happened to her?" Constance asked.

"Once she was unmasked, everyone turned their backs on her. She left the area soon after—to live with family, I believe. Though whether she truly repented her sins, I do not know."

"Do you think that is what would happen here? If the culprit is ever discovered?"

"My hope is that my next sermon will deter any further letters and lead the perpetrator into shame and repentance. And there will be no more letters."

"Given your experience," Solomon said, "and your knowledge of the community, do you have any idea who might be responsible here in Sutton May?"

The vicar steepled his fingers. "I have thought about it a great deal and prayed. But no one comes to mind. I would say it is almost certainly a woman—women being in general less powerful and resorting to such methods that men do not need to. Women bear grudges that men do not even notice. Generally against other women."

Interesting, Constance thought. *He doesn't know about Nolan's letter. Is he even aware that the Keatons' letter was addressed to them both, or is he just making assumptions?*

Solomon said, "What can you tell us about the women in Sutton May? Who might constitute herself the arbiter of village morals?"

The vicar's wife, Constance thought suddenly.

"It is so hard to judge," Mr. Raeburn protested. "Our northern culprit did not reveal her spite in any other way until she was caught, literally, with her hand on the letter she was delivering. She was merely nosy and full of gossip. Like many women."

"And men," Constance said mildly. "Who is the biggest gossip in Sutton May?"

Mr. Raeburn shifted in his chair again. "I could not say. We are all guilty of it to some degree, are we not? There is a fine line between interest and gossip."

"What of Mrs. Gimlet?"

"Less of a gossip than most. Poor creature. Despite her grief, I am sure she would not lash out in such a way."

"Nell Dickie?"

The minutest curl twitched at the vicar's lips. "I scarcely know her. The Dickies rarely come to church. Except to have their children baptized."

"Are the women friendly?" Solomon asked.

"Mrs. Gimlet and Nell? Not particularly, though they must know each other."

"What about the other women? Are there feuds? Even those you and I might find ridiculous. Say, between Mrs. Keaton and someone in the village?"

"I really could not say."

He *would* not say. "What about the men?" Constance asked. "Are there particular enmities or ill feelings?"

"Good grief, no. None that would lead to such spiteful letters."

"Really?" said Solomon. "I have heard disparaging remarks against Mr. Dickie. And against Mr. Ogden."

"The Dickies tend to be scapegoats," Mr. Raeburn admitted. "Ogden doesn't drink at the Goose or attend parties when he's invited, but I never heard of ill feeling toward him."

"Not even from Peregrine Mortimer?"

"Ah, well, that's probably jealousy on Perry's part, and Perry doesn't live here officially. He is a mere visitor and doesn't appreciate Ogden's value to the village. Perry judges a little too much by appearance."

Constance certainly agreed with that. "What is he jealous of?"

The vicar smiled. "Now that *would* be gossip!"

"Sir, our confidentiality is as rigid as your own," Solomon said with one of his rare hints of hauteur. "It has to be."

For the first time, the vicar looked uncomfortable. Constance couldn't work out if that was in his favor.

"Mr. Mortimer admires Miss Chadwick," he said at last. "And as a suitor, he is favored by her parents. Well, he is heir to Mortimer Manor, besides being a handsome and charming fellow. Sophie, however, appears to prefer the company of Mr. Ogden."

And who could blame her? "I see…" Pushing that aside for future mulling, Constance moved on. "One thing that struck us is the simplicity of the letters' language, and the way they are formed. Could this simply be children's mischief? They might not fully understand the kind of trouble they are causing. There is a certain childishness about the accusations."

Mr. Raeburn's jaw dropped. *"Children?* I hardly think…" He broke off, his expression momentarily unguarded and yet unreadable. "But the letters are sent to adults, not other children. So far as I know."

"Do all the children play together?" Solomon asked. "Or do their friendships tend to separate along class lines?"

"I hardly—"

"From your experience, of course," Constance added. "Who are your children's friends? Do they go out and play all together?"

"They play more according to age," he said. "My eldest son is friends with Edgar Chadwick and the oldest Dickie boy, among others. But they don't get up to mischief."

"Then they were not among those Mr. Nolan had to chase away from the forge a few weeks ago?" Solomon asked, although he knew from Nolan that at least some of them were.

The vicar closed his mouth. "Perhaps you should be talking to my wife. She has more to do with the children, while my vocation—"

"Of course," Constance said. She was eager to meet Mrs. Raeburn.

MRS. ABIGAIL RAEBURN was also eager to meet her husband's

visitors. She had seen them arrive from an upstairs window and knew at once who they were. Strangers in Sutton May tended to stand out, and in this case, the couple were both attractive and almost exotic.

Even looking down from the window, Abigail could see Mrs. Silver's beauty—in fact, she was, possibly, the most beautiful woman Abigail had ever seen, which made the woman inherently untrustworthy in her eyes. None of the men would be safe.

As for her companion, he was too dark complexioned to be a proper English gentleman. He might have lived abroad, of course, and he certainly walked with all the elegance and self-confidence of royalty, so she would defer judgment. Surely Luke would bring them to meet her for morning tea?

Which meant she had little time to change…

She wore the new gown, which, though of muted colors, as suited a vicar's wife, she knew to be flattering. Perhaps it would make the Silver woman feel overdressed for the country.

Abigail knew—as most of the village knew—that they were looking into the anonymous letter received by Emmeline Chadwick. Not that Emmeline wanted anyone to know. No wonder. She liked to play the good doctor's wife to the point of martyrdom, did Emmeline, but the woman clearly had feet of clay. She was a little too free with her opinions at the Christian Women's Circle and tended to forget the natural order of precedence. Even Hannah Jenson, the old biddy who thought her connection to the Mortimers gave her special privileges, had had to put Emmeline in her place.

And goodness, only think how impossible the woman would be if her even more opinionated daughter actually married Perry Mortimer! She would be lording it over everyone! By far the best match for Perry—should he wish to choose a local girl—would be found in the vicar's family. In a few years, of course, when Perry was ready to settle down. He and her own daughter Bessie were of the same class, at least. No matter what the Chadwicks thought, a country doctor was *not* a true gentleman.

Not that she had anything against Chadwick. He was a good doctor, and he worked hard. But he let the women of his family too much into his inherently unladylike profession. Even Sophie. One shuddered to think of an unmarried girl attending lyings-in and grisly injuries…

Abigail shuddered and examined her reflection in the glass, patting her hair in a satisfied manner. Still no gray strands there. Whenever there were, she pulled them out at the roots. It was not vanity, of course—she merely had a certain position of respect to maintain as the vicar's wife.

She went downstairs to the parlor, most curious now to meet Luke's guests. What on earth could they be talking about for so long?

Oh, the letters, of course. She rang the bell and Alice the maid appeared quickly, drying her hands on her apron. "Tea, ma'am?" she asked cheerfully.

"Indeed. Inform Mr. Raeburn in his study, and make sure his guests know they are invited. Oh, and give the fire a poke, would you? It feels cold in here."

"I'll put another log on," the girl said.

She was a good creature, was Alice. Never questioned, or gave herself martyred airs like her mother, Mavis—despite her fall from grace. Mavis had once been the late Mrs. Mortimer's personal maid and seemed to imagine this gave her the right to monopolize the vicar. She haunted the church at all hours of the day especially to instruct him. A trial to Luke's patience, poor man.

Alice was a much more comfortable person than her mother. Mind you, she was not so good with flowers. Sighing, Abigail went to rearrange the daffodils in the vase on the windowsill and was still there when she heard Luke's voice approaching.

She turned quickly, glad to see him ushering in the lovely Mrs. Silver, who was indeed stunning close up, and the elegant Mr. Grey.

Unexpectedly, it was the latter who deprived her of breath.

She had graciously given Mrs. Silver her hand and found her friendly, appraising gaze overbold. This woman was not one who could be easily intimidated. Abigail slipped her hand free and smiled into Mr. Grey's eyes.

It felt almost like blow, like when she had fallen off a horse as a girl and been winded. Deep, compelling eyes gazed back at her as though seeing into her soul. His brow was broad and intelligent. His full lips seemed to denote both humor and passion. And yes, he was a most handsome man in an excitingly dark kind of way. She just hadn't expected to be so overwhelmed by...what? Awareness? Some presence that went beyond rank and wealth and position? It felt like recognition. Fascination.

And she must be staring like the village idiot.

"Mr. Grey," she managed, forcing a smile. "How do you do? Won't you both sit down? Alice is bringing tea."

"Our friends have just asked me a question I can't fully answer," Luke said, handing Mrs. Silver into Abigail's favorite chair. "About the children's friends."

"*Our* children's friends?" Abigail asked in surprise.

"If you could give us an idea," Mrs. Silver said.

"Sherridan spends a lot of time with Edgar Chadwick and Ned Lance from other the hill, though perhaps Ned is more Timothy's friend."

"What about the Gimlets and the Dickies?" Mr. Grey said.

"They know each other through school, obviously," Abigail admitted.

"But not outside school?" Mr. Grey sounded so surprised that Abigail knew he must have heard something different.

"Children can never tell when someone is unsuitable," she said. "We don't encourage it, but Richard Gimlet and Joe Dickie do turn up occasionally. Even Bessie, who is most particular, insisted on having Jill Dickie to her birthday party—along with Maria Lance, can you imagine it?"

"No," Mr. Grey replied, gratifyingly, although he immediately qualified it by adding that he knew nothing of any of the children. "Are they wild? Do they trouble shopkeepers or make a lot of noise? Give insolence to adults? Get into fights?"

"Well…Richard Gimlet and the Dickies might get out of hand occasionally—they have never been taught manners, you understand. Even Edgar Chadwick has been known to bully a bit, though to be fair, Mr. Ogden seems to have weaned him off that. Why do you ask about the children?"

They would be looking for reasons and motives, of course, for Emmeline's nasty letter. A matter that certainly did *not* concern Abigail's children. They asked a few more questions— Mr. Grey had the most beautiful voice, like melting chocolate, so she was more than happy to answer just to hear him speak again.

Until she caught an odd glint in Mrs. Silver's eyes—half cynical, half understanding—and pulled herself up. She was the vicar's wife, not Bessie in the throes of yet another infatuation!

"More tea, Mrs. Silver?" she said graciously.

"Thank you, no. I'm afraid we have we have kept you both too long already. I believe we shall meet again at Miss Mortimer's card party this evening, so we shall be on our way. Thank you so much for your help."

"Then we *have* helped?" Abigail asked, hiding her unease beneath a hopeful smile aimed at both visitors.

"Indeed," said Mr. Grey. "And we are grateful."

At least she would see him again at the manor…

❧ ❈ ☙

CHAPTER NINE

"WHAT IS THE vicar hiding from us?" Solomon asked as they walked through the churchyard.

Constance took his arm. "At best, something unsavory about his parishioners. At worst, that his wife sent the letters. Or he is afraid that she did."

"Do you believe that?"

"Not absolutely," Constance admitted. "But I do find Mrs. Raeburn the likeliest culprit of everyone we have met so far. She is very judgmental and convinced of her right to be so."

"Would she not be more inclined to speak her mind to those concerned than send letters in such a way? Would she really go to such lengths to remain anonymous?"

"That is the part I don't understand. What would make her feel she had to?"

"If saying something to someone's face might adversely affect her children?" Solomon suggested. "Though I admit I don't quite see how it would."

"She would not want to make an enemy of Miss Mortimer," Constance said. "That was the first letter she sent. Perhaps she liked the feeling of power it gave her, so she sent the others to lowlier people, too." She sighed. "No, I don't quite buy that either, but then, I don't really understand the mind workings of anyone who would send such letters. It's interesting that the vicar has come across such things before. We should…"

She trailed off as someone hurried out of the church and

walked toward them. A tall, thin woman in respectable if dull garb, apart from an unexpectedly bright hat decorated with artificial flowers.

"Is that not the woman who was praying in the church?" Constance murmured.

"It must have been a long prayer."

"Indeed…" Catching the woman's eye, Constance smiled. "Good afternoon."

"Good afternoon, ma'am, sir." There might have been the faintest dip of a curtsey, as if she had once been in service, but Constance could find no sign of obvious servility in her manner or her direct, assessing gaze.

Constance stopped in front of her. "Did we not see you in the church a little while ago?"

"You did."

"It is a very fine old church, is it not?"

"The little bell tower goes back to the fifteenth century, so the vicar says."

"Then I suppose it must. I look forward to the Sunday service here."

The woman's eyes might have lightened a fraction in approval. "Mr. Raeburn preaches a fine sermon."

"I felt sure he would! I'm Mrs. Silver, by the way. This is Mr. Grey."

Her gaze flickered from one to the other as Solomon politely touched his hat. "Mavis Cartwright. I suppose you have just come from the vicarage?"

"We have."

"You'll have seen my Alice, then. She is parlor maid there."

"She is your daughter? A very smart and polite girl. You must be proud of her."

"I could not be prouder. Some think she should be working up at the manor house like I did, but I say she could not do better than be in the service of our own vicar."

At something of a loss, Constance nodded in what she hoped

was a sage manner.

"Have you always lived in Sutton May, Mrs. Cartwright?" Solomon asked.

"Born and bred here."

"Do you find the village has changed much over the years?"

She blinked as though surprised by the question.

So was Constance.

"Not really," Mrs. Cartwright said at last. "Mostly the same faces, new generations of the same families... Apart from the vicar, of course. And Dr. Chadwick. And the shop is bigger. They sell all sorts of things now that you'll never need! Things the Mortimers and the Lances used to send to London for."

"Is that not a good thing?" Solomon asked.

Mrs. Cartwright shrugged. "It's a *different* thing."

"Was it Mr. and Mrs. Keaton who expanded the shop?" Constance asked, catching on to the line of Solomon's questioning.

"And changed its name," Mrs. Cartwright said. "Used to be Corner's, not Keaton's. Her father had it, you see, and his before him. Then suddenly Ralph Keaton came to the village from nowhere and married Corner's daughter. Inherited the shop, and now..." She flapped her hand toward the main street. "Well, as you see! I suppose it does well enough, and Faye Corner's certainly done very well for herself—more new gowns than Miss Mortimer herself, though she's only the grocer's daughter. Well, must get on. Good day!"

"What," Constance murmured as they walked on, "was all that about?"

"I was thinking, vaguely, about hostility to or from outsiders," Solomon said.

"Well, Mrs. Chadwick is an outsider, as is Ralph Keaton. I doubt Nolan is, though, and Miss Mortimer certainly isn't."

"No. But there has to be some reason for hostility to those particular people."

"Mr. Raeburn believes the culprit is a woman, probably a spinster who has set herself up to judge. It certainly doesn't appear to be someone trying to make money out of knowledge. I still don't see what the perpetrator is getting out of these letters."

"Perhaps that is because you've never cared for public opinion."

She turned her head slowly toward him. "Except I do now, because of you. Has something changed recently for someone in the village, that the letters are now their only means of scolding?"

"If so, I can't yet see what that is. Perhaps we need to look at the letters again, and go over what exactly each of them said."

"The trouble is, we don't know *exactly* what half of them said. We only have Mrs. Chadwick's and Miss Mortimer's."

"Then those must be our starting points."

Constance nodded emphatically. "They're the only real evidence we have. And then... I'd quite like to see how all these children behave once they're out of school."

FOR DAVID GREY—IT was becoming more natural for him to think of himself by that name—being cooped up between four walls did not work well.

For one thing, it caused horrific memories to resurface too often, memories of the early days of his abduction. For another, in the nine years since he'd awoken in that French hospital, he'd grown used to going on deck whenever he wished to, seeing the endless sky and far horizons. The comfort of Solomon's house did not make up for that. Even opening all the windows and sleeping with the curtains and shutters open was not enough.

He needed to go out before he went mad or punched a hole in Solomon's elegantly papered walls.

At first it had not been too bad. He'd felt safe. And it had been interesting learning about Solomon from all the books and maps and mountains of correspondence about business—business that seemed to involve eye-watering amounts of money.

His brother was a very rich man. Which made David feel alien and disconnected, and yet the memories were there, misty and warm, of running around the large plantation house, rooms filled with sunshine, open fields and rolling, forested hills in the distance.

Half of that estate was *his*. Though he surely had no claim to all that Solomon had built from that beginning. It struck him more than once how trusting Solomon was being, leaving a stranger in his home to rob him or do whatever he chose. A stranger who could easily be guilty of murder.

The servants did not bother him. He had only seen one, a bald man who brought him food and wine without being asked. David had only ever nodded curtly to him. He had no idea whether or not one was supposed to thank servants. His parents did, but then, they were odd, and the servants of his childhood had probably been slaves.

He could not think of that now. He could not even think about the body he had stood over—twice, it seemed to him. No, however many memories seemed to be coming back, he could not trust them.

And he would go mad pacing the space between the walls of this house, without even the creaking of a ship to remind him there was open air and expanse beyond.

He strode through to the bedchamber, examining himself in the mirror. It could have been Solomon looking back at him. Apart from the fear and desperation in his reflection's eyes.

I was not always like this…

He had a sudden image, so vivid it felt like longing. Walking beside Solomon, even running, in the hot countryside of their youth—only they were adults now. They weren't speaking, but they didn't need to. They were happy.

Was that really how it had been? How it could have been if he had not been taken? After twenty years spent so far apart from his brother in every conceivable way, he didn't see how it could ever be that way again. But Solomon had given him the means of freedom if he chose to take it.

David no longer looked like the fugitive seaman who had run from the hue and cry at the Crown and Anchor. He looked like Solomon. A gentleman, waited on by white people.

David went to the wardrobe and took out the overcoat, hat, and gloves he had been wearing yesterday. Donning them and lifting a cane from the stand, he walked past the mirror. He adjusted his shoulders, lifted his chin, and imagined himself swaggering down the street with Constance Silver on his arm. Damaged but undeniably beautiful goods.

And she was kind.

God, I need out of here...

He went, almost creeping down the stairs to the front door. Listening to the silence of the house, he eased open the door and strode into the street with a massive sense of relief.

He doubted he'd ever go back.

AFTER A LIGHT luncheon at the inn, during which they picked the innkeeper's brains as to who drank with whom of an evening, they repaired to Constance's room to re-examine and update her lists.

"It seems to be more or less as you'd expect in a small community," Solomon said, throwing himself into the comfortable chair with a sense of discontent. "They all drink amiably together with a certain amount of egalitarianism, but more private discussions are also accepted. Such as the doctor drinking with the vicar, young Mortimer, and the Lances from 'over the hill.' Gimlet and Nolan appear to be friends. Dickie occasionally causes trouble but picks on no one in particular and never gets barred for more than an evening when someone always takes him home. There seems to be no *enmity* among the men of the village."

"Apart from Mortimer and Ogden," Constance pointed out.

"Is that enmity? Ogden never fought back."

"Unless Mortimer too has received a letter and simply didn't tell us."

"Do you believe that?"

Constance sighed. "No."

"We haven't actually spoken to the policeman yet, either. Heron."

"True. I think we need to…" She trailed off, frowning at her lists. "Miss Mortimer's letter arrived just over four weeks ago. Then the following week came the Keatons' and Nolan's. Then there was a gap until Mrs. Chadwick's, just over one week ago."

"Is that significant?"

"Well, the first three were sent in quite a flurry, weren't they? And then she—or whoever the sender is—seems to have given it up, either because it's ineffective or because she's afraid of being caught. And then she can't help herself sending one to Mrs. Chadwick because of the tragedy of Jenny Gimlet."

Constance spread out the two letters they had and Miss Mortimer's envelope, which Solomon picked up.

"It looks like an adult hand to me. Not a child's."

"It could be an older child," Constance argued. "We're missing something. Perhaps we'll need to catch someone actually putting the letters under someone's door, like Mr. Raeburn's previous experience."

"So when is our culprit doing this?" Solomon said. "Is it someone who has easy access to all those houses? Or do they shove the letters under the door in the dead of night?"

Constance sat up straighter. "It comes back to children again. They run from house to house all the time, looking for playmates, or just playing some game. Or running errands for their parents."

"The village children wouldn't be able to just wander into Miss Mortimer's front hall, where, presumably, her letter was found."

"True. Though we don't actually know the precise timings of

each delivery. Perhaps we should walk home from the manor house this evening and see who is out and about."

Solomon's lips twisted. "Most of the village seems to know what we're about. They're hardly likely to go sending more anonymous letters while we're poking around."

"Perhaps we should just behave badly and hope the culprit will send a letter to us!"

"It may come to that," Solomon said with some frustration. "It all seems rather…trivial."

She met his gaze. "I think we probably need to observe everyone at Miss Mortimer's party this evening. But I think tomorrow morning you should catch an early train back to London and see how things are."

He didn't want to leave her. But she was right. Part of him needed to assuage the guilt of leaving David. Again. He needed to know. "I can come back the same day."

Her lip twitched. She knew he had already checked the railway timetable.

"You won't do anything outrageous while I'm gone, just to inspire a letter?"

"I might. If something springs to mind." She gathered up the papers and shoved them in the drawer of the rickety desk. "Come on, let's go and skulk around the policeman's house and the school."

Constance was right about needing to observe the children. Even if none of them were directly responsible for the letters, they could easily be part of the motive. Parents would do anything for their children, even things that would not otherwise enter their heads. And here in Sutton May, there seemed to be too many conflicting views of them.

They had been lively and attentive in school, but certainly not rowdy. Nolan the blacksmith told a very different story. Depending on who one spoke to, Edgar Chadwick was a studious boy or a bully. Wildness was blamed on the Dickies, or on the Gimlets, whose own son was angry for understandable reasons, yet still seemed to be friends with Edgar.

Strolling down from the policeman's house—he had not been at home—Solomon and Constance were in time to see Ogden opening the classroom door and allowing the neat if chattering line of his pupils to emerge into the schoolyard. The smallest ones came first. One or two of them lurked in the yard, waiting for older siblings, while others surged out of the gates, vanishing in all directions with waves and shouts to friends. The younger children were taken in hand by the older, a couple marched along the road leading out of the village, and then across fields, the others scattering with their fellows.

Ogden closed the door and went back inside.

Solomon and Constance followed the biggest swarm of children down toward the Keatons' shop. One small girl ran around her big brother to put him between her and the blacksmith's.

"Best part of the day?" Constance said lightly as they caught up with a group of lads.

They all grinned at her. One or two tugged their caps. "Always is!" one said.

"Don't you like school?"

"Like it better than we used to," the biggest boy pronounced. "Mr. Ogden's not so bad."

"Has he not been your teacher very long?"

"Few years. We had Miss Fernie before that." He shook his head, and there was a good deal of muttering against poor Miss Fernie.

"She lives over there," one of the boys said, pointing to a neat little cottage, where a curtain twitched. "Still comes out and tells us off if we're too noisy, tries to make us go straight home."

"Nothing to do with her anymore," another muttered. "She just can't stop interfering."

"Well, we were in her garden once," the first boy said reasonably. "Though she was furious mad about that."

Someone else to look at? Solomon almost groaned. He felt they were sinking deeper into this case without achieving anything. But then, he always felt that.

"You're Mr. Grey, aren't you?" said one of the biggest boys. "My father's friend?"

"Ah, you must be Edgar Chadwick," Solomon replied. "Pleased to meet you at last." He regarded the boy beside him, who was a bit smaller, though his clothes were rougher and just a little too short.

"Richard Gimlet," this boy said, shoving his cap to the back of his head and grinning in a swaggering kind of a way, though his eyes, meeting Solomon's gaze, were almost challenging.

"I met your mother this morning," Solomon remarked. "Aren't you going in the wrong direction for home?"

"Not going home. Yet."

None of them seemed in a particular hurry to go home. Two older girls stood at one corner, chattering while a smaller boy tugged at one of their hands. A few boys were playing tag up and down the road, trying to involve other children as they went, to occasional cries of "I'm not playing!"

"Who else is who?" Solomon asked. "Which are the Keaton children?"

"The twins?" Edgar said, nodding toward a boy and girl, walking backward toward the shop, still calling to their friends. "There. Paul and Petrina. She's talking to Jill Dickie." Who clearly wasn't on the road going immediately home either. "Paul's arguing with Timmy Raeburn the vicar's son and Jack Lance from over the hill."

The shop door opened just then, and the Keaton children stopped talking to stand aside for a woman to come out. It was Mavis Cartwright, the mother of the vicar's parlor maid, and she did not look best pleased to find herself surrounded by so many noisy children.

The Keaton children greeted her politely. Some of the others, more distant, were nudging each other as she sailed around the corner toward the square, her nose in the air. A couple of the children followed her, mimicking her while their friends laughed. Mrs. Cartwright spun around, and the mimickers walked on with perfect innocence as their friends laughed harder.

"The Lord will judge," Mrs. Cartwright exclaimed, and marched on, her head high.

"And so will she," Constance murmured beside Solomon. She had been walking among some of the girls, who were now on the other side of the road along with Edgar and his companions. "The children don't like her."

"They don't like their old teacher either," Solomon noted. "Which may or may not be interesting."

CHAPTER TEN

BOREDOM ALONE WOULD have made Peregrine Mortimer look forward to one of his aunt's extraordinarily dull parties. In this case he added the attraction of cards, where he might just make enough money to get himself back to London, and of course flirtation, not merely with the charmingly respectable Sophie Chadwick, but also with the mysterious beauty Mrs. Silver—who, for some reason, he suspected was not respectable at all.

With such prospects for the evening ahead, Perry actually whistled as he ran downstairs from his bedchamber to greet his aunt and her parrot-faced companion in the drawing room.

He stopped whistling to stand in the doorway as though stunned, his arms spread wide. "Why, Aunt Jess, how lovely you look! Just like that painting of you as a girl!"

"Oh, get along with you," Aunt Jessica said, smiling—moved not by any truth in his assertion, he knew, but by the fact that he bothered to lie to please her.

Old Hannah Jenson did not quite snort, though her face managed to convey a silent if undoubted derision. Perry was in too good a mood to answer her in kind, so he merely smiled at her too.

"A most becoming gown, Miss J!"

Her expression changed to one of suspicion, which was so amusing that Perry smiled some more. The ringing of the doorbell interrupted this unprecedented courtesy, and he solicitously aided his aunt to rise from her chair in order to greet her approaching guests. In a moment of malice rather than manners, he offered his other arm to Miss Jenson.

"No, no, stay seated, Hannah," Aunt Jessica said impatiently. "Perry shall assist me."

That didn't please the old companion, though it certainly boosted Perry's mood even further. He hoped his warning words to Dr. Chadwick's inquiry people would bear fruit. If not, he was sure he could invent enough suspicion so that between them, they could see the Jenson woman cast off. In any event, it would be fun trying.

Slightly to his disappointment, the first guests were not Mrs. Silver and Mr. Grey—did they have to come as a pair, or would he find the means to separate the delectable lady? Instead, it was Mr. and Mrs. Raeburn, the vicar and his wife, who walked first into the room.

Mrs. Raeburn was not a bad-looking woman, though an arrant snob. Her husband was amiable enough—except on Sundays, when his sermons tended to the fire-and-brimstone type. When Perry inherited the manor, he'd see the fellow toned it down a bit. Enough to give a jolly fellow nightmares sometimes…

At his aunt's side, Perry greeted them both with hostly bonhomie, and turned to welcome Miss Fernie, the old schoolteacher who came hard on their heels—Friday-faced old thing. He wondered who had displeased her since the last time he'd had the misfortune to run into her. Why did the school always seemed to be staffed by half-wits—daft old ladies or laborers' sons too foolish to be good for anything else? Mind you, at least Ogden didn't talk to him, or pretend to be of the same class, as Miss Fernie always did.

The Chadwicks arrived next. Sophie looked particularly pretty in an ivory gown with pink rosebuds. He was sure it was the same one she'd been wearing at Christmas, but since it suited her so well, he forgave her. Unlike her mother, she greeted him in a very offhand kind of way, which she probably thought alluring. Perry was amused and would have teased her for it, had not Mrs. Silver entered then, escorted by the tall, lean Mr. Grey.

She really was a stunning woman, casting every other female into the shade. While he offered his hand to Solomon, he kept his gaze on her as if he could not draw it away—a trick that had worked well for him in the past, though one haughtily raised eyebrow was Mrs. Silver's only reaction.

"I'm so glad you could come," he murmured, taking her hand. "You brighten the room, as if the sun has come out."

Her hand, which he would have retained a second longer, gave an odd little twist, sliding free of his grasp, and she would undoubtedly have made her escape had he not latched on to the couple behind, surely the last of his aunt's supposedly genteel guests.

"Ah, you will not have met Mr. and Mrs. Lance from Chettering House? Allow me to present you. Mrs. Silver and Mr. Grey are distinguished visitors to Sutton May."

Somehow, Grey was between him and Mrs. Silver as he greeted the Lances, and Perry was forced to offer his aunt his arm back to her chair, while all the guests were served sherry, wine, or brandy, according to their tastes.

At least Perry was able to stay by his aunt and flirt with Sophie Chadwick, which was a pleasant enough way to pass the time before the games started. Sophie and Netta Lance were as close as one could come to a young lady of quality in Sutton May, and of the two of them, Sophie was by far the prettier. It amused Perry that she kept starting toward Netta, some distance away, and then all he had to do was to say something to her—anything, however outrageous, or even mundane—and she felt obliged to answer. The benefits of a well-brought-up young lady!

Not did it escape his attention that Mrs. Silver's gaze landed on him frequently. His blood heated as their eyes met. He barely noticed that Sophie slipped away from him, for Mrs. Silver suddenly seemed not only attainable but *necessary*, urgently so.

She smiled, and her lips fascinated him. They seemed to have an extra little curve, and he could just imagine the pleasure they could give...

"Shall we play?" Aunt Jessica suggested, rising with the vicar's assistance this time, since Perry was already prowling across the room, almost magnetically drawn to the beguiling Mrs. Silver.

"Say you will play at my table," he breathed.

"This table," she said, seating herself at once. Annoyingly, it was a table for four rather than two.

"Only if you promise your next game to me alone."

"We shall see."

She is playing hard to get, he thought, amused, for he knew he would catch her this very night, one way or another. He caught her watching him much too often for indifference. And she saw him win. Tonight was going to be so profitable in so many ways...

He pocketed his winnings graciously as he rose—and he did not even need to follow her, for she remained at his elbow as they stood alone while others continued playing or milled around.

"Are you ready for our game?" he asked, smiling into her eyes.

"Why, no, I merely wanted a quick word," she said, and her low, musical, and yet slightly husky voice sent delicious thrills along his nerves. "I hope you won't compel me to expose you."

The shiver, suddenly, was unpleasant. And it was she who held *his* gaze.

"You cheat, Mr. Mortimer," she said softly. "And you do not even do it well."

She moved away, accepting a glass of wine from the footman and smiling at Mrs. Lance and Miss Fernie, who had just risen from another table.

Perry was left alone, his heart thundering in his breast so hard that his ears sang. For although he despised his company, he realized suddenly that their poor opinion of him would be devastating. Not just for his cachet among the yokels, but for his aunt's inheritance. She was not compelled to leave him anything at all.

Mrs. Silver could ruin everything with one word that would spread like wildfire in high wind—around the room, around the village, around Society…

CONSTANCE'S INSTINCTS ABOUT men were rarely wrong, so she was not surprised that her initial opinion of Peregrine Mortimer had been proved right from the beginning of the evening. His pursuit of the clearly uncomfortable Sophie Chadwick smacked of social bullying, while cheating his supposedly lesser friends and neighbors at cards was arrogant, contemptuous, and curiously entitled. He had even seen Constance watching him, and yet not taken the hint, assuming instead that she could not take her eyes off his manly charms.

She had encountered far too many Peregrine Mortimers in her life not to recognize the type. She only hoped her warning would work, for she wasn't prepared to give another.

Solomon was playing cards with the vicar's wife. Mrs. Lance, who seemed a pleasant lady, joined a game of whist, leaving Constance alone with Miss Fernie, one of the people she particularly wanted to speak to, since she had once been the village schoolteacher.

"A game of piquet, ma'am?" Constance suggested.

"To own the truth, I can't see the cards as well as I used to. Staring at them gives me a headache. I believe I shall sit out the next game and instead enjoy a few choice morsels from the buffet."

"What an excellent idea."

Constance had not even noticed the buffet being laid out at the far end of the drawing room, but it was clearly meant for casual nibbling between or even during games. Since they were currently alone picking at this feast, Constance said, "Actually, I am glad of this opportunity to consult you, Miss Fernie, since you must know the village and especially the children very well. Are you a native of Sutton May?"

"My father was the vicar here, long before the Raeburns came, obviously. And I was brought up to be useful, so I eventually taught at the school—being educated, you understand."

"Eventually?" Constance repeated.

Miss Fernie smiled, almost preening. "Oh, I had my Seasons in London, you know. My father was the younger son of a very prominent family. I have traveled the world more than anyone else in the environs of Sutton May. You come from London, do you not?"

"I do."

"I'm sure I knew a Silver family when I was young… I still correspond with my family who have a house there. I even visited them last spring. Town has changed so much, I find. The lines of Society are no longer what they were. Perhaps that is a good thing. What is your first name, my dear?"

"Constance." She replied with some misgivings, for her name was certainly notorious in some circles. However, a maiden lady of good family was hardly likely to have heard it, and several people in the village knew her Christian name by now.

Besides, Miss Fernie had already moved on.

"My father founded the school, you know. Until then, no one taught the village children. Some still chose to remain in ignorance, of course, as if education was a waste of time for any but gentlemen."

"Yours was an enlightened family."

"Oh, indeed we were. I like to think I still am, although, of course, things can be *too* enlightened and then standards drop. Our first teacher was our curate, you know. A most clever gentleman of excellent family. And then the son of one of my father's friends took over. A very fine, upstanding man, but sadly of indifferent health. I began teaching merely to cover for his unavoidable absences, and then I took over altogether. I like to think the school ran perfectly when I was in charge. The children read and wrote and counted and learned how to behave. Now they run wild, like mannerless little animals, but what can one expect with such a man in charge?"

"Mr. Ogden?" Constance said in surprise. "I have heard him very well spoken of."

Miss Fernie wrinkled her nose. "An example, sadly, of Society changing too far and too fast. I understand he is a clever man—though one would never think it to speak to him—but honestly, what is the son of a laborer even doing at Oxford? Or was it Cambridge?"

"I expect he was well taught by someone like you," Constance said lightly.

"Indubitably, and inevitably a charity case, but the results are before us all. He cannot maintain discipline and has no idea of manners or morals."

"Tell me," Constance said, "about the local families. The Dickies, for example, and the Gimlets…"

"FORGIVE ME," MISS Jenson murmured, sidling up to Solomon as he gathered the cards after his game with Mrs. Raeburn, "might I have a word?"

"Of course." Half standing. Solomon watched her slip into the vacant chair. Her slightly beaky face expressed discomfort.

"It's about Mrs. Silver," she confided. "I would hate her to be taken in by Mr. Mortimer's—um…playful manners."

Solomon glanced around, almost involuntarily. Constance was turning away from Mortimer, smiling at Mrs. Lance and Miss Fernie. It was Mortimer himself who looked discomfited, blinking rapidly, his half-smile rigid on his lips.

Solomon returned his gaze to Miss Jenson. "I believe Mrs. Silver is the least likely person to be taken in by Mr. Mortimer. Do I take it you do not trust him?"

"He cheats," Miss Jenson said bluntly. "At cards and love. Jessica—Miss Mortimer—won't hear a word against him, of course, but I felt as strangers amongst us, you and Mrs. Silver should be warned."

"Thank you," Solomon said. He had the feeling she had more to say and was struggling with the impulse.

"You will think me foolish," she blurted, "or even jealous, but my fear is that no one takes him seriously. And I'm sure he is."

"You're sure he is serious?" Solomon said, trying to uncover her true meaning.

"About Jessica? Oh yes. He wants her money very badly. Needs it, in fact. I'm fairly sure he's living off his expectations as it is, and I don't know how long he can go on doing that. She has bailed him out several times already—boys will be boys, she says with foolish indulgence—but he doesn't want to keep begging her for tidbits. He wants it all. Mr. Grey, I'm afraid she is in *danger* from him."

Solomon's hands stilled on the cards, his attention all on Miss Jenson, whose color was changing rapidly from pink to white to pink again.

"Did you write a letter to warn her of this?" he asked.

She blinked. "A letter? I told her to her face, but she laughs at me for a silly old fool. She probably thinks I am jealous. And he has probably told her *I* want her money."

He had certainly told Solomon and Constance that.

Solomon shuffled the cards. "Forgive me, but what is your position in Miss Mortimer's will?"

"I don't know," she said impatiently. "What does it matter? I'm five years older and likely to die before her. But I do know *he* will inherit virtually everything, and he is too impatient for that to happen."

His previous words seemed to come back to her, for she

broke off quite suddenly, staring at him, though he could not read her expression. "Letter? You mean Jessica has received one of those nasty letters?"

"I did not say so." He set the pack of cards on the table. "Would you blame him for that if it were true?"

"For hers? I wouldn't put it past him, to frighten her or convince her to give him what he wants now… But I can't see his annoying the Chadwicks with such a thing. After all, he wants their goodwill so he can seduce their daughter!"

"Then he does not seek Miss Chadwick's hand in marriage?"

"As the master of Mortimer Manor, he probably imagines he can snare an heiress. I don't think he has any idea how little an estate of this size produces in terms of profit. Even well run as it is. *He* will run it into the ground and have nothing to pass on to his own children, God help them."

"I see."

"Do you?"

"Would you like me to speak to Miss Mortimer?"

"She might listen to a stranger more than a friend. Thank you," she said suddenly, smiling brightly as Dr. Chadwick approached. "A little refreshment would be lovely."

It was clearly said to prevent any suspicion that their conversation had been serious, but obediently, Solomon rose and went in search of some wine and food for her.

En route to the buffet table, he encountered Constance.

"Miss Fernie is unhappy with both Ogden and school manners," she murmured for his ears alone. "She likes to be charitable but has no egalitarian leanings. She is, on the other hand, a busybody. And the walking definition of judgmental."

"What did she tell you?"

"That Alice the vicar's maid was born out of wedlock, and her mother Mavis no better than she should be. Mavis is never out of the church, apparently, because she has every reason to beg the Lord's forgiveness."

"I see. Did she say anything about Mortimer?"

"Neither of the Mortimers in a critical way, nor even Miss Jenson, whom I think she regards as impoverished gentility. Why?"

"Miss Jenson is afraid for Miss Mortimer's life at her nephew's hands."

Constance blinked. "Seriously?"

"I think she has been getting a few ill feelings off her chest, but there may be truth in it. What is your impression of him?"

"Well, he cheats his aunt's guests at cards. He is also young, too convinced of his own charm, and much too entitled. But I would have thought self-preservation alone would prevent his actually harming anyone. Do you think Miss Jenson might have sent the letters?"

"She certainly keeps her eyes open and judges," Solomon said. "And though she denied knowing about Miss Mortimer's letter, I could not be sure whether she was acting. But my impression is she would tell someone their faults to their face, not disguise her identity in such a way."

"Miss Fernie seems much the same in that regard. And I suppose they both fit the vicar's theory of a judgmental spinster with too much time and too little power. Who is your next conversational target?"

"Miss Mortimer herself, to please Miss Jenson."

"Then perhaps I shall speak to Mr. Lance from over the hill. Unlikely to be involved on *this* side of the hill, perhaps, but his children do attend school here."

"Good luck," Solomon said, as she strolled on her way.

Approaching Miss Mortimer turned out to be easy, for she had stopped beside her companion at the little table where Solomon set down the plate and glass.

"Mr. Grey," his hostess said, smiling at him, "I trust the luck of the cards has been with you?"

"I believe I am breaking even. Might I escort you to a table or bring you some refreshment?"

"What exquisite manners you have," she replied, taking his

arm. "Come to the fireside with me and let us talk."

"Gladly," Solomon said. Deciding his hostess would appreciate bluntness, he settled himself on a pouffe beside her and said at once, "Miss Jenson is concerned for your safety—and your nephew's desperation."

The old lady sighed. "Hannah is a silly old thing. As if I don't know my own nephew. On the other hand, he does snipe at her verbally, which I have told him off for, so she is disposed to think the worst of him. He is undisciplined and a shocking hedonist, but truly, there is no harm in him. And if she is thinking of him as the writer of these letters—"

"I don't think she is." He searched for a tactful explanation of Miss Jenson's fears. "Her concern is more that his need for money may overset his good sense and family devotion."

"Well, she needn't worry about that. How do your inquiries progress?"

"Slowly," Solomon admitted. "The trouble is, we do not have a lifetime's knowledge of these people, their histories, grudges—everything you, having lived here for so much of your life, will have absorbed over the years without noticing."

"Ask me whatever you wish. Any loyalty I feel to Sutton May, which is considerable, must be balanced by the harm these foolish letters are doing. Suspicion and fear can quickly become intolerable, and that is when true tragedy occurs."

He lifted his eyebrows. "You sound as if you speak from experience."

"I am an old lady," she said tartly. "Experience is not something I lack simply because I have chosen not to marry."

Chosen not to marry. "Why did you make that choice?" he asked, because it appeared to be relevant. To her, if not to him.

"My mother did not have an easy life," Miss Mortimer said, "which gave me, perhaps, a somewhat jaundiced view of marriage as an institution. And yet I have enjoyed my life and have, I believe, done some good in the world. At least in my little corner of it. Who is it you really want to know about?"

"Busybodies," Solomon said. "Tell me about Miss Fernie. Are you friends?"

"Of a kind. We grew up together, the only girls of genteel family in the neighborhood at that time. Of course, her birth is better than mine, as she never tired of telling me, since her family is titled, and mine never was. On the other hand, mine is landed and my home my own, while hers lost the right to live in the vicarage when her father died."

"Is that why she became a teacher?"

Miss Mortimer's lips twitched. A sardonic gleam lit her eyes. "No, I think that was a favor she elected to bestow upon the children of Sutton May. To be fair, she really did teach them to read and write and count. But her pupils could recite poetry without feeling or understanding of the words. They could tell you the names of countries without knowing anything else about them. They could recite chunks of the Bible like automatons, with as much accuracy and as little feeling as they did their multiplication tables."

"She taught by rote?"

"*Only* by rote."

"Is she judgmental by nature?"

"I would say so, and not always rightly. But no, you are quite wrong if you imagine she would send me or anyone else an anonymous letter. She imagines her presence adds more weight to her pronouncements."

"You don't like her."

"I find her a hypocrite." Miss Mortimer smiled wryly. "But then, so am I, for I still invite her to my parties. The habits of childhood stay with us."

Sensing more here, Solomon leaned forward. "Hypocritical rather than simply misguided?" he suggested.

"Oh yes." Miss Mortimer lowered her head, her voice dropping further so that he could barely hear. "We had to retire her from the school for appropriating the funds for books, writing materials, and school outings. That is when we got Mr. Ogden in instead."

Startled, Solomon cast an instinctive glance in Miss Fernie's direction. She was playing cards, but her gaze was on Constance.

"Who knows this?" he asked with inexplicable urgency.

"Just Mr. Raeburn and me. We contrived it so that she resigned voluntarily and traveled for her health. I was surprised when she came back, but I suppose Sutton May has always been her home. And I, it seems, will always be her friend."

But will she always be yours?

CHAPTER ELEVEN

*C*ONSTANCE SILVER. CONSTANCE *Silver…*

Where had she heard that name? It kept repeating in Helen Fernie's head even after they had stopped conversing and she was playing cards with Sophie Chadwick and Abigail Raeburn.

She knew why the young woman was asking all those questions, of course. She was nosing around for Dr. Chadwick and his silly wife. The daughter was even sillier, by all accounts, though Helen knew better than to believe in village gossip. Still, she had seen Sophie with Ogden—the girl even visited him at his house, which was utterly improper. And nothing to do with Constance Silver.

Where *had* she heard that wretched name? She was sure she had not met her in London. She was far too noticeable to forget. She was also far too well dressed to be a woman in need of work to live. And Mr. Grey was not her husband, whatever else he was.

Solomon Grey. Did she know that name, too? When she went home, she would go over her letters from her family in London. Wait, though, was he not one of those benevolent, wealthy men of this new world? Made his first fortune in Jamaican sugar and cotton and built another in shipping. A surprisingly young man who preferred seclusion to Society and was therefore sought after by all.

Oh yes, it was coming back to her now. Could this man really be *that* Solomon Grey? His coat was certainly well enough cut for wealth, but why on earth would such a rich man be ferreting out squalid information for the likes of Dr. Chadwick? *Eccentric*—was that not another world flung around about Solomon Grey? And some kind of scandal written in a letter by her shocked cousin, something to do with his being snared in matrimony by an infamous courtesan.

Her breath caught. *Constance Silver! Of course!*

As if she couldn't help it, Helen's gaze sought and found the woman, so pretty, so charming—and so false. How dare she masquerade as a decent woman, tricking poor Jessica into accepting her as a guest, introducing her to the respectable people of Sutton May!

The jezebel was laughing over her shoulder at something Mr. Lance said to her, then she stood up and left the room.

She must be going to the retiring room.

And Helen was just outraged enough to follow. She was halfway across the room with a poor excuse thrown to her fellow players before she realized her own foolishness. And her own possibilities. What *was* her best move here?

THE FOOTMAN IN the hall directed Constance to the staircase at the end of the passage. "The first door on your right is for the use of ladies."

"Thank you."

The room was easily found and brightly lit. As she dealt with her own comfort and examined her hair in the glass for wayward strands, her mind flickered from guest to guest. As in most communities, secrets and ill feeling seemed to seethe beneath the surface of neighborliness, most of them trivial. She could not actually imagine anyone present here this evening sending those anonymous letters. None of them, she felt, would see the need of anonymity. Unless it was Sophia Chadwick, afraid her youth gave her less gravity than a pasted-together letter of complaint?

She sighed. No, that did not really work either. Constance could not imagine her treating her mother or anyone else in that way, no matter how unjust she felt their actions to be.

But what if the culprit was not in her or his right mind? Everyone in the village seemed to be eminently sensible and even likeable people—with the exception of Peregrine Mortimer.

Mr. and Mrs. Lance from over the hill were also amiable and impressed with their children's school progress under the auspices of Mr. Ogden. They knew of no trouble amongst the children or their parents in Sutton May, and pronounced Helen Fernie "a funny old thing" with no harm or malice about her.

Mr. Raeburn's theory of female spite did not seem to work in this case.

Emerging from the retiring room, it took Constance a moment to realize that the landing was now in total darkness. A glow filtered up from the foot of the stairs, but it seemed very dim. Surely all the lamps and candles had not gone out at once?

Constance stood very still, trying to get her bearings, but she could not even see the top of the stairs, only the faint light below. Feeling idiotic, she put out both her hands and shuffled slowly forward, groping for a wall, or the balustrade that bordered the stairwell.

Her flesh crawled. She was sure she heard someone's breath—though it might have been her own, erratic and shallow. Something moved at the corner of her eye, a swirl of air and shadow, and she whirled abruptly toward it.

Nothing but darkness.

With relief, she found the post at the head of the staircase and grasped it, shuffling forward until she could feel the drop of the first stair under her foot. She slid her hand from the post down to the banister, but before she could grip it, two hands shoved her hard in the back and she tumbled forward into darkness.

So much for trivial and harmless…

SOPHIE CHADWICK HAD the uneasy feeling that things were coming to a head. Part of that was no doubt due to her own guilty conscience, and the shocking, uneasy suspicions that had begun to plague her. And she had been only too aware all evening of Mr. Grey and Mrs. Silver, circulating and asking questions.

When she saw Mrs. Silver leave the drawing room, it even crossed her mind that the woman had gone to poke around Miss Mortimer's or Miss Jenson's private things—though why on earth would she suspect such kind and respectable old ladies?

Miss Fernie slipped out a few moments later. Everyone needed to deal with calls of nature…

And yet when Mr. Mortimer went out too, a quite different suspicion hit her.

Had Mrs. Silver made some kind of assignation with him? They had seemed rather friendly during the first game, and afterward had appeared to exchange some intense conversation. But surely Mrs. Silver did not know what he was like. That he lurked in dark corners and imagined women liked to be handled like…

She left the drawing room yet held on to the door handle for a moment. The footman had vanished from his post, perhaps even sent away from it by Mortimer. Worse, the stairs and the landing above were in darkness. Someone had put out the lights to the retiring room.

Hastily, Sophie picked up the branch of candles that stood on the table outside the drawing room and strode purposefully to the stairs—too late.

Something thudded in the blackness above and fell like a bouncing ball to lie in a dark heap on the half landing.

With a cry, Sophie leapt up the stairs, the candle flames flickering wildly. It was Mrs. Silver, her eyes wide open and staring at Sophie.

"Oh, ma'am, what happened? Can you move?" Sophie sank down beside her, placing the candlestick on the step above.

"I… I think so," Mrs. Silver said, much to Sophie's relief, even though her voice was unsteady. She cleared her throat. "I think I saved my head. For once… Though my arm hurts like the devil. Sorry, that isn't very ladylike, is it?" She smoothed her hands over her skirts as though to be sure she was decent—or perhaps feeling for injury to her leg.

"Let me help you to sit up," Sophie said. "Slowly, now."

Mrs. Silver sat, wincing as she took her weight on her arm. "I believe I am fine."

"What happened?" Sophie demanded. "Why are the lights out?"

"I can only imagine someone put them out. It was perfectly bright when I entered the cloakroom."

"Was…was anyone else up there?" Sophie asked.

Mrs. Silver glanced up at the dark landing, then refocused on Sophie's face. "Can you guide me somewhere private for a few moments until I recover?"

"Of course. Let me fetch my father. And Mr. Grey—"

"No," Mrs. Silver said flatly. She smiled slightly, "Not yet…"

With Sophie's help and holding on to the banister, Mrs. Sliver stood and took a step forward. Sophie snatched up the candlestick and told Mrs. Silver to lean on her. In this way they made their way slowly to the foot of the stairs and to the small antechamber beside the drawing room. It was in darkness, but the branch of candles soon lit it up well enough. Sophie eased Mrs. Silver into one of the two armchairs, then went and closed the door before joining her.

"Give me your arm," Sophie said, and was pleased when Mrs. Silver raised it unaided. She felt her way along the bones, asked her patient to bend her elbow and wrist, then wiggle her fingers and move her shoulder. Fortunately, all seemed to be in working order. "I think it's just bruised, but my father should really have a look."

"I will consult your father tomorrow if it's not better," Mrs. Silver said with a sort of forced lightness in her voice. She was not going to give in this evening, though her reasons were not at all clear.

"What happened?" Sophie asked again. "Did you miss your footing in the dark?"

Mrs. Silver, still rather white and tight-lipped, held her gaze. "I'm afraid I was pushed. I didn't see by whom, but at least I know it wasn't you, since you came *up* the stairs toward me. No one else has come down."

"No, but there are two other staircases they could use. And I know who left the room after you did."

Mrs. Silver pounced. "Who?"

"Mr. Mortimer."

Oddly, Mrs. Silver showed no surprise. She even nodded. "I told him off earlier in the evening. Is he really so vindictive?"

"He has a temper. And he doesn't like to be made to look small. Or to feel small, probably."

"Was he the only one who left the room after me?"

"No. Miss Fernie did, too, but I can't imagine *she* would push you or anyone else down the stairs!"

"Not without a good reason," Mrs. Silver said thoughtfully.

Sophie blinked. "You are taking this remarkably in your stride, as if such things happen to you every day."

"Not every day. But someone obviously doesn't like my questions... Is Mr. Grey still in the drawing room?"

"When I left, yes. Shall I...?"

"No. No, I just need to be sure he is safe. Has my hair come loose?"

"Only a little," Sophie said. "Let me see if I can repair it for you."

Mrs. Silver nodded, and Sophie retrieved a couple of hanging pins, plus a few spares from her own reticule. "You think it was Mr. Mortimer who pushed me, don't you?"

"Well, I don't like him," Sophie admitted.

"May I know why not?"

"Oh, every reason. He is smug and insulting and thinks he is so charming, when he is just entitled, like a child with too many toys."

"And hands?" Mrs. Silver suggested.

Sophie wrinkled her nose. "That too. To be fair to him, though, I suspect my parents encourage him. They would like me to marry him and be the lady of them manor one day."

"That is not your wish?"

"*He* is not my wish." Sophie drew in her breath. "My affections are engaged elsewhere."

"By Mr. Ogden?"

"Is it so obvious?"

"Your partiality for his company has been noted by several people."

"But not by him," Sophie said ruefully. "Netta says I might as well be a book as a human being to him."

"I don't think that is quite fair."

"It isn't. People think that because they don't see his emotions that he doesn't have any. He does. He cares deeply for those children, and for his friends."

"Who are his friends?"

Sophie shrugged. "Apart from me? The children. Mr. Raeburn, who thinks very highly of him. And some people at Cambridge who don't mind that he's odd and just like him for himself."

"As you do."

Sophie couldn't help smiling. "Oh, I do. I know he can be awkward with people he doesn't know, but he learns and improves, which is why I take him to tea at Miss Mortimer's every Wednesday. Of course, he is better when Perry is not present." She scowled briefly, then smiled again very softly. "He can be really funny, you know, and droll with a straight face. And he knows so many astonishing things, has such compassion and understanding of people, as well as literature and music and poetry, such that it would make you weep."

"You love him," Mrs. Silver said.

"I do," Sophie said proudly. "Though how would I ever know if he loved me?"

"You could ask him," Mrs. Silver said.

Sophie's cheeks burned. She felt like shuffling from foot to foot.

"He is honest, isn't he?" Mrs. Silver said. "But I think he would never…impose."

"I am more worried about imposing upon him."

Mrs. Silver smiled. "I think you will know when the time is right."

"Did you?" Sophie asked.

Mrs. Silver blinked. "Did I what?"

"Know when the time was right? You are going to marry Mr. Grey, are you not?"

"We are engaged," came the slightly wary reply.

Sophie placed the last pin from her reticule into the soft strawberry-blonde hair. "Don't you want him here with you now?"

"Not quite now. I… There are reasons I don't want him to know about this incident. Will you promise me your discretion, Sophie?"

"If you promise me yours."

Mrs. Silver smiled. "Of course I do."

"Then I'll confess to you that I have been so angry and confused, it even crossed my mind that my mother wrote that letter to herself, just to get my father's attention. It must be terrible sometimes to know he belongs to the whole village and not just to us, to her. I know she feels that sometimes and is ashamed. She does so much, you know, and I don't take nearly enough off her shoulders."

"You do well enough. Perhaps what Dr. Chadwick needs is a proper assistant. An apprentice."

"That," said Sophie, much struck, "is an excellent idea. And I don't really mean that my mother *did* send those letters."

"Of course you did not," Mrs. Silver soothed. She rose from the chair, flexed her sore arm, and walked unaided up and down the room. A little more color had seeped into her lips and cheeks. "I believe I am ready to go back now. I have a shawl in the drawing room that will cover this tear at the shoulder of my gown. Sophie? Who do you think *did* send the letters?"

Sophie shrugged. "Someone too scared or powerless to risk offending anyone? But I have no idea who that might be."

"WHERE DID YOU vanish to?" Solomon asked Constance when they were finally alone, walking back to the village. The Chadwicks had left half an hour before, the doctor being summoned by a patient, and the vicar's carriage had just passed them bearing Miss Fernie as well. "You were gone so long I began to worry."

"I just went to the cloakroom, but I ran into Sophie Chadwick, and we had a little private talk, which was enlightening in some ways." She told Solomon what Sophie had said about Ogden and Mortimer and her parents. It took her mind off the severe ache in her shoulder and arm, which seemed to have borne the brunt of her fall.

"Interesting," he said, though in discontented tones because still all they had was possibility. "And according to Miss Mortimer, Miss Fernie was forced out of her position as teacher because she was embezzling the school funds. No one knows this, apart from Miss Mortimer and the vicar, who managed her removal and her pension between them without scandal."

"Then she surely bears a grudge against them," Constance said, gripping Solomon's arm tighter in her excitement. "Which would explain Miss Mortimer's letter, in a spirit of *how dare you judge me?*"

"But the vicar didn't get one."

"The vicar didn't *say* he got one. Perhaps I shall speak to him again tomorrow. Perhaps she's saving Mr. Raeburn for a particularly nasty letter."

"Or perhaps he doesn't matter to her," Solomon said thoughtfully. "It's Miss Mortimer she must feel betrayed her, because they grew up together as friends of a sort."

"Then why Mrs. Chadwick? The Keatons? Nolan the blacksmith?"

Solomon shrugged. "Perhaps she got a taste for the letters after sending Miss Mortimer's. She is very much the judging sort, from what you have said."

And she might well have shoved me down the stairs. "Yes… But can you imagine her defending the ignorant Nell Dickie by writing to the Keatons? Or telling Nolan off for scolding the rowdy children in his shop?"

"She might feel scolding the children is her business alone," Solomon said. "And I suppose it's possible her letter to the Keatons was about something else entirely. We only suspect it was to do with Nell Dickie."

"I should have another talk with Mrs. Keaton, too."

"I feel I am leaving you in the lurch here with everything still to do," Solomon said. "Why don't I wait another day? We might even solve this tomorrow, and we can return to London together."

Constance sighed and rested her cheek against his arm. "That would be good. But your mind would be on David. I could come with you to London."

"In the middle of the case? Would that be fair?"

"No," Constance said, slightly miffed that he had argued so swiftly against it, even though he was quite right. "You need to make sure David is still safe, while I try to penetrate this village soup of gossip and accusation. Do you think Mortimer is a violent man?"

"Violent?" Solomon sounded startled, and uneasy. "I could

more easily imagine his lashing out in temper than troubling to compose anonymous letters that he would surely find ridiculous."

"What if that was the point? Some kind of joke that he began just to annoy his aunt, who keeps him on some kind of financial leash?"

"And the other letters are just covering fire, as it were? That we have been reading too much into?" Solomon rubbed his chin. "You might have something there, only I don't see what his letter to his aunt has achieved for him."

"Neither do I," Constance admitted. "So why did he keep sending them to others? Did Mrs. Chadwick annoy him by thrusting her daughter under his nose?"

"It hardly appears to annoy him," Solomon said dryly.

The village was quiet, with only a few lights still showing behind curtains and shutters. In the long nights of winter, Constance supposed, a person could probably flit more easily between houses, pushing malicious notes under doors. No one would see, concerned as they were with keeping themselves and their homes warm and dry.

Even the Goose taproom, though it still had a light, was quiet. The innkeeper came through to lock the main door behind them, and they made their way up to bed. Constance felt suddenly very tired, and her arm throbbed.

"Knock on my door before you leave in the morning," she said.

Was that disappointment in his gaze? More than anything, she wanted the comfort, the sweetness of his embrace, but in such intimacy she would never be able to hide the pain in her arm or the bruising that had no doubt formed colorfully by now. And if he knew, he would not go to David as he needed to do.

He halted at her door and took her into his arms. His lips felt cold on hers, and then warm, almost burning. "Goodnight."

"Goodnight."

CHAPTER TWELVE

CONSTANCE WOKE BEFORE he even touched her bedchamber door. It was not yet fully light, and her arm protested sharply enough to make her wince as she threw herself out of bed and staggered toward the door, which she wrenched open at the first brush of his fingers.

Without hesitation, she cupped his cheek and kissed his mouth. "Safe journey," she whispered. "Write if you cannot come back."

"Of course."

Even in the gray gloom of the morning, she could see in his eyes that he did not want to go. That made her ache and rejoice.

"Let's get married, Solomon," she blurted, and his face lightened like sunrise.

He kissed her back and then he was gone, leaving her to slip back into her room before the inn staff caught her in her nightgown.

For some reason, her heart felt bright and hopeful. She washed in cold water and dressed before opening the shutters and letting in the lightening gloom. She imagined she heard the train puffing its way out of the village, carrying Solomon to London.

Fetching her notes on the case from the desk drawer, she spread them out across the bed and updated them with what they had learned last night—including the fact that someone, probably either Miss Fernie or Peregrine Mortimer, had pushed her down the stairs. She would tell Solomon when he returned. And in the meantime, she would take more care.

She reread the letters that had survived, along with what they had been told about the others. Had they been properly written by hand, or even spoken face to face, they could hardly be called spiteful or nasty. In fact, they were almost polite, except for the *you will pay* bits at the end, which had a certain element of parental warning about it. Like *it won't get better if you pick it* or *don't make faces because if the wind changes, you'll stay like that.*

A parental-style warning to adults? Or children reflecting their words back at them? Kindness. Responsibility. The injustice of false accusation. There was nothing inherently wrong in any of that, so why communicate it in such a way?

Someone with no power, as Mr. Raeburn had said, or someone who feared the consequences of speaking out? Against the lady of the manor, the local shopkeepers, the blacksmith, the doctor's wife. What on earth did they have in common? Who had somehow been wronged by all of them? Or at least witnessed their wronging of someone else?

Miss Fernie might imagine herself wronged, but in fact, she had stolen. *She* was in the wrong. But she had denied receiving any letter. She might have lied, of course, but Constance didn't particularly want to visit her alone to ask more forcefully.

Then there was Mavis Cartwright, whose illegitimate daughter was the vicar's maid. Would Mavis not be a traditional target for moral outrage? The children certainly did not appear to respect her, which was probably learned from their parents. Perhaps she was worth talking to again.

Though neither Mavis nor her daughter had pushed Constance down the stairs. If that was related to the matter of the letters, then it was either Miss Fernie or Peregrine Mortimer. Neither of which seemed right.

There were more facts to collect. Someone had sent these letters, and however polite they were, however moral the intention, the nature of the act was malicious and frightening. Good people had been upset and made fearful of their neighbors.

Suspicion had been sown, and in such an atmosphere, ill feeling could easily get out of hand. Constance had already been pushed down the stairs.

Her stomach rumbled. She gathered everything up off the bed and put it back in the desk drawer before she went downstairs for breakfast.

"Which house belongs to Mrs. Cartwright?" she asked the innkeeper's wife.

"Mavis? First in Green Lane behind the square," came the answer. "But you're more likely to find her in church. Haunts the place, she does, poor old thing."

Constance returned to her room, donned her hat and coat, and sallied forth to church. She hoped she would find Mavis there, for it struck her that the woman might be more inclined to tell the truth—whatever that might be—in God's house.

In fact, she sat in the same pew as before, or at least knelt there, clearly praying. Unwilling to interrupt her, Constance walked quietly around the church, admiring a stained-glass window and enjoying the sense of timeless peace generally found in churches. She could understand why a troubled soul would come here so often.

When the figure in the corner rose from her knees to her seat, Constance walked toward her, though she gazed up at the vaulted ceiling in an admiring kind of way.

"Good morning," she said, as though noticing Mavis for the first time—then, as the other woman jumped to her feet, "Don't let me disturb you."

"You're not. It's time I got on, anyway. I'll come back later."

Constance sat down next to the place Mavis had been occupying. "Do you know all about the church and its history?"

"Not really. Mr. Raeburn is most knowledgeable, though."

"Then I shall ask him. Actually, it's quite fortuitous I ran into you here. I had been going to call on you later."

Mavis blinked. "You had?"

"Indeed. Knowing the village as well as you must..."

"Idle tongues…" Mavis began, bridling visibly.

"Oh, not idle," Constance said, hoping she looked suitably shocked at the very idea. "I'm sure you know—because everyone else seems to—that Mr. Grey and I have been asked to look into the matter of some unpleasant letters sent anonymously to various people in the village."

To her relief, Mavis sat down again. "Mrs. Chadwick. That's why the doctor brought you."

"Yes, but it isn't just Mrs. Chadwick who has received one. I believe you were the late Mrs. Mortimer's personal maid? Did you know her daughter well?"

Redness mottled Mavis's face. "Miss Jessica? Yes, of course. Lovely girl, she was."

"Pretty? Good-natured?"

"Oh yes. I was always surprised she didn't marry."

"Were they a kind family to work for?"

"Oh yes." Mavis slid her gaze free. "The kindest."

"But they wouldn't keep you on," Constance said delicately, "once you had your baby?"

"Well, they couldn't really, could they?" Mavis gave a quick glare, shifting on the pew. She seemed to catch sight of the altar and the cross behind it and groaned. "I sinned, but I won't add to it in this place. They had to turn me off because of the father."

Constance caught the other woman's rather desperate gaze. "The father of your child?"

Mavis closed her eyes. "Mr. Mortimer," she whispered.

Of course. Miss Mortimer had never married because she had been repelled by her father's faithlessness, his adultery even with his wife's maid…

"You couldn't say no to the master," Mavis said. "No one did. But I should have. I should have had the strength and I didn't. But you mustn't think the mistress turned me off with nothing. I got a pension and the right to live in the Green Lane cottage. Miss Jessica never took that away, though she must know. Everyone knows."

"It must be hard in a small community like this," Constance said gently. "When everyone is aware of your business."

Mavis shrugged. "It's old news and no one can say I haven't repented. Mrs. Raeburn even took my innocent Alice on. She'll be fine."

"And you?" Constance asked.

"Me? I'll be fine too."

"No one is unkind to you? No one casts up your past?"

"No point, is there?"

Constance resorted to bluntness. "Then you have never received one of those anonymous letters?"

"Course not. Not one can say I don't know my own sin!"

"Who doesn't?" Constance asked, watching her carefully. "Who is too full of their own righteousness?"

Mavis sniffed. "Not for me to say."

"I don't mind saying. For the greater good, you might nod or shake your head. Miss Fernie?"

Mavis didn't answer, but then, she didn't need to. Her wildly flaring nostrils said it all.

"Miss Jenson?"

Mavis shook her head.

"Young Mr. Mortimer?"

Mavis's lip curled. "The apple didn't fall far from the tree there. Old Mr. Mortimer to the life, he is. But he knows he isn't righteous. He just doesn't care."

"Mrs. Chadwick?"

A vehement shake of the head.

"Sophie Chadwick?"

A puzzled frown, a shrug, and a half shake.

"Edgar?"

"He's a child!"

"Children can see things in very black-and-white terms."

"And in that they are right," Mavis declared.

"Hmm. Tell me, in your opinion, would it ever be right to send an anonymous letter of accusation? Frightening people?"

Constance watched the expressions chase across Mavis's bewildered face. She had been judged for most of her life since she had conceived her daughter, even though servants were all too often powerless to deny their masters. But she seemed singularly incapable of judging. What Constance had imagined might be scorn for others was merely the armor protecting Mavis from the constant slights she felt she deserved.

SOLOMON, HAVING SERIOUSLY considered going first to the Silver and Grey offices, got the hackney to set him down in front of his own house.

Jenks emerged as usual as soon as he entered the house. The butler betrayed no surprise, merely took Solomon's hat and coat. "Your guest is in the sitting room, sir."

Solomon regarded him. "You know it isn't me."

"I have been with you for more than two years."

"And so I should know better than to ask if you've told anyone else your…suspicion."

"You should, sir."

"Then I shan't. Thank you, Jenks." Solomon strode forward, then paused, saying awkwardly, "How is he?"

"I could not say. He eats."

"It's a start," Solomon said. "Any…unusual visitors?"

"None at all, sir. One moment." Jenks vanished into his cubbyhole and emerged with a thick pile of letters in one hand. "These arrived while you were gone. I took the liberty of keeping them for you."

So David had still to earn Jenks's trust. As Solomon had to earn David's. He smiled crookedly, took the letters, and went in search of his brother.

David was already on his feet in the middle of the room, facing him like a mirror image. "I thought I heard your voice. Do you want your house back?"

Solomon glanced around the room. His brother had not brought many changes, apart from several pieces of paper strewn across the sofa and the floor around it.

"Not yet," Solomon said, walking forward and bending to pick up the nearest sheet of paper. "The case in Surrey is not yet concluded. I came back to be sure all was well."

"Did you think I might have bolted?"

"Yes."

To his surprise, David's eyes lightened. "I almost did. The walls were pressing in on me. I went out, meaning to lose myself in London and take the first ship that would have me on its crew."

"What changed your mind?"

"You. Me. Fear, probably. And…and the fact that I remembered a name."

Jenks appeared then with a tray of breakfast and coffee. While David hastily gathered up the strewn papers, which showed drawings rather than writing, Solomon glanced at the one in his hand.

Constance gazed up at him, her expression of both humor and challenge so familiar that it caused his heart to jolt. Her enigmatic smile glinted in her eyes and curved those fascinating lips so that he almost touched them. The artist, who could only have been David, had caught the extra little upward quirk of her mouth, the precise tilt of her head…

"She told me you have talent," Solomon said, dragging his gaze back to David, who was watching him tensely. The last time David had been in London, she had gone to his lodgings to persuade him to see Solomon.

David grimaced. "It passed the time on long voyages."

And in effective house arrest, no doubt.

"Will that be all, sir?" Jenks asked.

"Yes. Thank you, Jenks."

Solomon, who had not yet broken his fast, heard his stomach

rumble. He set the sketch of Constance on top of the pile David had gathered on the sofa, and he and his brother sat down at the dining table.

"You remembered a name," Solomon reminded him. "Whose?"

"The captain of the ship where I saw the merchant die. He was Captain Blake. Jordan Blake, I think, and his ship was the *Mary Anne*. Does that help?"

"It should do. Well done. There's been nothing in any of the newspapers I've seen about Chase's murder, let alone about identifying a culprit, so we should still have time to find out enough to clear you."

Deep in thought, it took Solomon most of his substantial breakfast to realize that he did not feel remotely uncomfortable in his brother's presence. He was glad he had come.

As CONSTANCE WALKED away from the church, deep in thought, she suddenly became aware of Miss Fernie marching along toward her on the other side of the street. The shock was enough to snap her back to the present, for after last night and the stairs, she could not afford to let her attention slip.

She had to think herself back to the old days, to childhood, when she had to be aware of everyone around her, every movement, every sound.

Though her breath froze and her stomach lurched, she managed not to miss a step, and even to lift her hand in a friendly wave. But Miss Fernie marched on, apparently not noticing her, though Constance was sure she did. The woman had her nose in the air and wore an expression of contempt that was almost…hatred.

Constance felt it like a slap, the echo of those hands striking her full in the back, hurling her into the abyss. Shaken, she actually looked over her shoulder to make sure Miss Fernie was still walking away from her.

This was more than a moment's malice in return for too many questions. This was utter hatred.

What did I do or say to her?

Nothing to inspire such contempt. And yet an upright, godly woman would hold her in contempt—many already did. She saw it in the eyes of reformers and other respectable women who believed themselves to be so superior to her and the girls she cared for.

Was that it? Did she recognize Constance's name? She had spoken of family in London with whom she corresponded, but ladies were not meant to acknowledge the existence of women like Constance, let alone write to each other about them. Still, something had caused that hatred, whether Constance's profession or the questions she had been asking—had she come too close to the truth? Was Miss Fernie indeed responsible for the letters? Or someone Miss Fernie loved?

Who *did* Miss Fernie love?

On impulse, Constance turned in at the doctor's gate and rang the bell. Recognizing her, Nora the maid let her in at once and showed her into the parlor. "I'll just tell Mrs. Chadwick you're here."

The wait gave Constance a couple of minutes to pull herself together. She wasn't sure why she felt quite so shaken. After all, in the grand scheme of things, Miss Fernie was not the scariest human being she had ever encountered.

Emmeline Chadwick swept into the room, wiping her hands on her apron, which she quickly threw off and tossed over the arm of a chair. "Good morning, Mrs. Silver. Forgive me, I was just in the still room, mixing some herbal potions for Charles. Would you care for some tea?"

Constance found she was glad of it, though she had to wait for the ritual to take its course before she could ask the questions she needed to.

Eventually, with the door closed behind the maid, she said, "Tell me about Miss Fernie."

"Miss Fernie? She's a stuck-up old thing, but mostly harmless. Why?" Emmeline's eyes widened. "You don't suspect *her*, do you? Of sending the letters?"

"It crossed my mind, though not from evidence or any real motive that I can distinguish. Just…ill nature."

Emmeline passed her a cup of tea. "I confess I have not seen that side of her. Sophie and Edgar never cared for her much as a teacher—she did not actually teach them much they didn't already know—but I never found her ill natured."

"Perhaps it is just me she dislikes… Though you clearly have nothing against her, is it possible she bears a grudge against you?"

"I can't think why. She is Charles's patient, of course, but she is very rarely ill, and I can't think of any occasion on which I neglected her or made her wait…"

"Made her wait?" Constance repeated, distracted by the oddity of the phrase.

Emmeline looked down at her tea. She looked suddenly very tired, as if all the lines around her eyes had deepened and let her skin sag. "I have to do that sometimes. For Charles's sake. If he drops dead of exhaustion, there is no doctor to make *anyone* well. Sometimes I have to make difficult decisions, and sometimes I make the wrong one."

Constance set down her cup. "Are we talking about Jenny Gimlet?"

"Richard came to the house, desperate for the doctor. His mother had sent him. I said Charles would come in the evening or the following morning. Richard shouted at me that it had to be today or Jenny would be dead. But when Charles came back from delivering the Lance baby…he was utterly exhausted, asleep on his feet. I couldn't send him out again. I fed him and made him go to bed instead. And in the morning, he went up to Dravenhoe—the Gimlets' farm. Jenny was not quite dead, but she didn't live much longer."

And Emmeline had been living with the guilt ever since.

"If the girl was so very ill," Constance said gently, "would she not have died anyway?"

"I will never know. And neither will any of the Gimlets." Emmeline swallowed and shook her head. "Charles said no one could have saved her, but he *would* say that to me, wouldn't he? Someone else thinks differently, knows it was my unkindness."

"Your kindness to your husband," Constance corrected her. "We all look after our own first. It's human nature. Would Miss Fernie have known about this?"

"Not at the time. The Gimlets are rather beneath her notice, except when Richard mimics her, which he does rather well. I suppose word would have got around the village, though. Nothing is secret here. But if she cared at all, I can more easily imagine her defending me, not sending me glued-on, anonymous letters."

Constance shook her head. "Something has bitten her, but it might not be the subjects of those letters. Who are her friends in the village?"

"Miss Mortimer and Miss Jenson, I suppose. And the vicar and his wife. Everyone else is beneath her, even Charles and me. She only tolerates us."

"Then the Keatons are not her friends? Nor Mr. Nolan the blacksmith?"

"Hardly."

Then certainly not the Gimlets nor the Dickies, Constance thought. "Is she defensive of the children she once taught?"

"More critical. She will not have it that Mr. Ogden is more learned or a better teacher."

"Because he comes from a lower class? She does not regard that as a mark of his success, his strength of character?"

A hint of color seeped into Emmeline's face. "No one could deny his scholastic achievements. Nor should they try."

"But you do not approve of his friendship with your daughter?"

Mrs. Chadwick waved one impatient hand. "It is not really a

friendship. She is fascinated, besotted, because she has never met anyone like him. That is not a basis for lasting love and marriage."

"Forgive me, but neither is cheating at cards and raking around the country."

"Of course not! Who on earth behaves so?" Constance held the other woman's gaze until Emmeline laughed uneasily. "Mr. Mortimer? I feel sure you are wrong!"

"He most certainly cheats. For the rest, he is young yet, but I would not leave my daughter alone with him. May I ask you about another village scandal?"

"Which one?"

"Miss Mortimer's father and her mother's maid?"

"Oh, that must have been before our time."

Constance left it there, wary of stirring up a scandal that had quietened to all but the older residents.

⋙✦⋘

SOLOMON ENTERED THE Silver and Grey offices to find Janey grinning at him.

"Ha! Welcome back! Where's herself?"

"Thank you. In Surrey still. I can't stay long. Have you anything to report?"

"Well, according to the constable forced to stand outside the Crown and Anchor, poor sod, there were two men seen running away from there after the murder. One sounds like your double, the other's another sailor, but no one knows who he is. The peelers've been asking around for someone called Johnny."

Solomon swore beneath his breath—Janey's language could be catching—for Johnny was the name David had gone by before he remembered his own identity. Someone in the Crown and Anchor must have recognized him and given the police that name.

"I can't find anything about the other sailor," Janey continued. "None of the working girls can help me. Lenny's been looking into Herbert Chase, the dead cove. He left a list of his investments, going back ten years. Seems he was the up-and-coming man for a while, and then began to lose it all through bad investments—whatever that means."

Solomon went to his desk and snatched up the closely written paper on his desk.

"This is good," he said. "The sailor *and* the list."

"Can we get more money, then?" Janey asked cheekily.

"Probably," Solomon said, without paying much attention, for a handful of words on the list of Chase's past investments jumped up at him. *The Mary Anne, cargo vessel, London, 1842-1850.*

The *Mary Anne* was the ship David had been on when he had seen Chase "die" the first time. And if Chase had been the owner, or part owner, it certainly explained his presence on board.

"I'm going to St. Catherine's," he said, stuffing the list into his pocket, "to see what else I can dig up. I might have something more for you and Lenny to do before I go back to Surrey."

"You got other letters," Janey growled. "I only leave you the ones you *have* to deal with."

"So you do," Solomon agreed, sitting down at his desk, more to pacify her for a few moments than because the letters interested him. His mind was already dashing ahead to his own records at St. Catherine's, and to who among his staff and acquaintances might have relevant information. He rifled through the letters at high speed, took one out and told her to mark the appointment in the book, then came across one from his man of business that brought him to a halt. It was about a house for sale that the solicitor felt sure would suit.

Solomon blinked at it. Had he really forgotten that he and Constance needed somewhere to live together? Far too much had been pushed out of the way to accommodate cases recently. Or to avoid the appearance of overeagerness or unwanted pressure. And it was not making them happy.

He folded that letter and stuffed it in his pocket, too. "The rest can wait," he told Janey. "All else is well?"

"Course it is."

"Then I'll see you in an hour or two."

CHAPTER THIRTEEN

EMMELINE HERSELF ESCORTED Constance to the front door. There was a small table in the hall with writing materials and a pen, presumably for the use of callers who missed the doctor and did not wish to confide in his wife or his maid. Constance had noticed this both times she had called. Now, however, three letters lay in a neat heap at the side.

It struck her that they had been too often distracted by the personalities in this case to concentrate on the practicalities.

She halted and turned to her hostess. "Tell me again how your letter was delivered. When and where did you first see it?"

"It was there, where these letters are now, when I first came downstairs that morning."

"And were you up early?"

"About eight of the clock, I suppose. Charles had already gone off on a call to one of the distant farms."

"And how did it get on to the table? Did someone leave it there?"

"It had been pushed under the door. Nora—our maid—picked it up and put it there."

"Do you know what time that was?"

"Well before seven. The letter was on the floor when she came downstairs, so she picked it up and put it on the table. Charles saw it there when he went out about half past seven."

"And none of you saw or heard anyone approach the house who might have delivered it during the night or very early that morning?"

Emmeline shook her head.

"What time did you all go to bed the night before?"

Emmeline rubbed one finger across her forehead as though trying to dredge up the details from her memory. "Charles and I went up around ten, I think. Sophie was still in the parlor, reading something. We had to tell Edgar to put out his candle in his room. Sophie nodded off in the parlor, reading, but she was in bed by midnight, she says."

"And the letter was not here by then?"

"She would have seen it and put it on the table, but she didn't. It was Nora who picked it up."

So, at some time between midnight and seven in the morning, someone had pushed the note under the front door.

Constance nodded her thanks and wished Emmeline good morning.

Continuing on her way, she at last found the village constable at home. He opened the door in his shirt sleeves, and his jaw dropped.

"Constable Heron?" she asked brightly. "I wonder if I might have your help."

His long, rather lugubrious face colored beneath his whiskers, and he mumbled something incomprehensible. Only the fact that he stood back told her she was being invited in.

He directed her into the small room on the left that was furnished with a desk at its center, and two chairs, one on either side of it. Mumbling an excuse, he bolted while she sat in the visitor's chair and reappeared a few moments later buttoning his coat.

"How can I help you, ma'am?" he asked more coherently.

"To be honest, I am not quite sure. My name is Constance Silver, as you probably know. I suspect you also why Mr. Grey and I are in Sutton May."

"Matter of unpleasant letters. Not against the law, to my knowledge, but not neighborly either."

"Exactly," Constance said, pleased that there would be no

territorial disputes between them. "Dr. Chadwick asked us to find out who has been sending them, with a view to—er…discouraging the practice."

Heron nodded. "And have you? If they ain't broken the law, I can't really help. Though I could have a word, in an unofficial capacity."

"That might well be useful—once we know who did it. At the moment we are rather struggling, not having the local knowledge that you do."

Heron nodded again, in a sage kind of a way.

"I was wondering if you had much trouble with the local children?" Constance said.

His eyes widened. "The *children?*"

"Oh, I don't mean serious trouble," Constance assured him. "More in the way of mischief or rowdiness, playing jokes on people who might not appreciate it, rushing around dangerous places like the blacksmith's shop."

Heron scratched his head. "Some of them's a bit wild. The Dickie boys'll cheek you soon as look at you, and draw the others into their games too, given half a chance." He ruminated on that for a bit. "Hid one of Mr. Gimlet's hens once, but they brought it back next day. Might have pinched an egg or two, but no one could prove it."

"Did Mr. Gimlet make a fuss?"

"No. He had a word with Hen Dickie and it never happened again. They're not bad kids. In fact, they're all better behaved since Mr. Ogden took over the school. There was a lot more mischief before that—like they'd been cooped up too long. Children need to run about, don't they? And Miss Fernie was quite the dragon, kept their heads down with no breaks, even on sunny days and snowy ones. The children used to *explode* out of those school gates like stampeding cattle, run from one end of the village to the next until I grabbed a couple of them and people yanked their own indoors. Haven't seen that in a year or two."

"So, Mr. Ogden has been good for the children's behavior?

Do the parents think so?"

"In general, yes, I'd say so. Plus, they *go* without a fuss instead of slipping away somewhere else, and even the Dickies see the sense in learning, since their oldest lad's doing very well in his schooling, by all accounts."

"I have heard rumors," Constance said delicately, "that the Dickies are not strictly honest."

Heron shrugged. "They get the blame of it. I never caught them at anything. Mostly keep themselves to themselves—though Hen can be a handful after a night in the Goose."

"Then the rumor that Mrs. Dickie stole a shawl from the Keatons' shop is untrue?"

Heron shifted in his chair. "Never proved one way or the other."

"Did you charge her with the theft?"

"I never had anything to do with it, just heard the gossip like anyone else. The Keatons banned her from the shop, but they never pressed charges."

"So no one searched her or her house? No one ever saw her with the shawl?"

"She might have sold it in Guildford when she went to the market there. But..." He scowled. "It's my belief it was never taken in the first place. Otherwise, Keaton would have pressed charges against her."

"You don't like Mr. Keaton?"

"Don't know him—he doesn't come from round here."

"But he has lived here for, what, twenty years?"

"Seventeen. The shop was Corner's then."

Constance let that one be. "So you think the Keatons lied about the theft?"

Heron looked shocked. "Oh no! I reckon she made a mistake, had already put the shawl away and forgot. She probably discovered after she'd barred Nell, and didn't want to admit it. So Keaton gets to play the generous-hearted shopkeeper, though no one stole anything in the first place."

"Would he not rather be known as the sharp shopkeeper who cannot be stolen from?"

"Yes, which is what makes me think nothing was stolen in the first place."

Which could well be why someone chose to defend Mrs. Dickie with an anonymous note to the Keatons about bearing false witness.

"Are the Keatons generally well liked in the village?"

"Good source of gossip and can get you anything you want to buy at a fair enough price."

"Then no one bears a grudge against them?"

"Excepting Jimmy Nolan, who wanted to marry Faye Corner before Keaton muscled in."

Constance raised an eyebrow. "Did he indeed?"

"Never married anyone else, neither."

"Then Mr. Keaton and Mr. Nolan do not get on?"

"Doubt they like each other much, but I've never had to separate them on a Saturday night, nor May Day on the green. Mind you, I don't fancy Jimmy's chances in a fight now with just one hand."

Constance stared at him. "One hand?" she repeated, utterly confused.

The constable's face relaxed into a grin. "I'm talking about *Jimmy* Nolan. He's the younger brother of *Matt Nolan*, who's run the smithy alone since Jimmy's accident."

"Ah, I see!"

"Don't know who'll be blacksmith after Matt," Heron said, stroking his mustache in a thoughtful kind of way, "'cause *he* never married, neither, and got no family. Neither brother's been lucky in love, come to think of it—poor old Matt had his heart set on Mavis Cartwright when he were young. I know you wouldn't think it now, but she were a pretty little thing thirty years ago…"

Constance sat up straighter. "Nolan the current blacksmith wanted to marry Mavis?" It was a connection, though she couldn't quite see how it helped.

"Oh, yes. They were engaged and all before…" Heron trailed off, blinking rapidly, as though remembering he was talking to a stranger.

"Before Alice was born," Constance supplied, her thoughts racing. Could Alice be Nolan's child and not the late Mr. Mortimer's? And how did that make any difference to the matter of the letters?

Could Jimmy, the Nolan she'd never met, be responsible for the Keatons' letter? Or Matt, the current blacksmith, bearing a grudge against both Keatons on his brother's behalf?

After all these years? Unlikely, but some event she didn't know of *could* have brought it all back. Miss Mortimer's father had—probably—ruined Mavis, his old love, which gave him a motive for that letter. Though Constance couldn't imagine what he had against Emmeline Chadwick… Or why he would pretend to have received a letter himself if he had not. Except to throw Dr. Chadwick off his scent.

This was getting ridiculous. With an effort, she turned back to the matter of theft, and the one thief she knew of, who was looming altogether too large in her mind: Miss Fernie.

"Have you ever arrested *anyone* for theft in Sutton May?" she asked the constable.

"Couple of strangers on market days."

"Do you get many complaints of theft?"

Heron shrugged. "Things go missing from time to time—not often, by any means, just occasionally, over the years—but it was always felt the things were just…lost."

Like the silk shawl in the Keatons' shop.

"People don't steal from their neighbors in small communities like Sutton May," Heron said.

Because everyone knew everyone else's business and it was too easy to be caught? Or was that too cynical a way of regarding a law-abiding village?

"What sort of things have been lost?" Constance asked. "Apart from the shawl and the Gimlets' hen." *And the school funds embezzled by Miss Fernie.*

"Oh, just little things. A small wooden box of Mavis Cartwright's. A *Book of Common Prayer* from the vicarage. Miss Mortimer lost a bracelet years ago—that was probably the most valuable, but she reckons she probably left it up in London. That was a *long* time ago, mind you, just before the old squire died. Must have been thirty years ago and more. I wasn't even a constable then, just a child, but I recall it being talked about."

Not exactly a plague of thefts over thirty years, and she could not really see how they might be related to the anonymous letters, except in so far as Miss Fernie was a known thief.

"Has anything ever gone missing from the school?" she asked on impulse.

"Not that I ever heard." He frowned. "Why?"

Constance smiled ruefully and rose to her feet. "I don't honestly know. I think I'm just clutching at straws. But thank you for your time and your help, Mr. Heron."

The constable jumped to his feet to accept her offered hand and bowed as far as he could with the desk between them. "My pleasure, ma'am. You'll let me know before you go making accusations, won't you? Just in case of trouble…"

His sudden anxiety was not lost on Constance, though she merely replied, "Of course. Good morning!"

From the police house, she walked on to the Keatons' shop, which she found surprisingly empty.

"Good morning, ma'am. How are you today?" Mr. Keaton greeted her so professionally that she had no idea whether he was pleased to see her or not. There was no sign of his wife or of any other customers. As though he saw her looking, he added, "You have caught us at our quiet time, after the morning rush and before the afternoon surge. Are you looking for anything in particular?"

"Just information again, I'm afraid. We are trying to establish a more definite delivery time for the letters, which could make identifying the culprit a bit easier. Your letter was pushed under the shop door, was it not?"

Keaton nodded.

"Do you have a separate entrance to your house?"

"Yes, by means of the outside stairs round the corner."

So the shop was by far the easier to access. "And you found the letter when you opened the shop in the morning?"

"Well, my wife found it when she opened the door to Mavis Cartwright, who cleans the step and the windows for us each morning."

"Does she?" Constance didn't know why she was startled, except that Mavis's name had been mentioned several times this morning. No doubt the woman's pension didn't stretch very far and she would need some kind of work. A bit of a comedown from a lady's maid at the manor to a village shop cleaner.

"Has done for years," Keaton said, watching her.

"I see. What time does she come?"

"About a quarter to eight, so that we can open at eight o'clock."

"An early start for you all, then. So Mrs. Keaton found the letter at about a quarter to eight or so?"

Keaton nodded.

"Could it have been put there the previous evening?"

He appeared to think about that. "Well, it wasn't there when I locked the shop at ten o'clock."

"You are open so late?"

"Oh, no! I was at a church meeting and tried the door on my way home. My wife had left it unlocked, so I had a quick look around the shop to make sure all was in order, and then left, locking it behind me. There was no letter underfoot."

"Why had Mrs. Keaton left it unlocked?" Or was her husband simply blaming her?

Keaton shrugged. "She is a little forgetful sometimes."

Like forgetting she had put a shawl away and accusing Nell Dickie of stealing it?

"There is little danger of theft in the village," Keaton said quickly. "Our neighbors are honest."

"Apart from the Dickies?"

Keaton colored slightly. "It was of no moment and no harm was done. Faye had been doing some work in the shop during the evening and come up to the house by the internal staircase in the back."

The explanation was not really necessary, so Constance moved on. "I believe I saw your children coming home from school yesterday. Twins, are they not?"

"They are," Keaton said proudly.

"They must be a handful—double the trouble, as I have heard it said. Mr. Grey is a twin."

"Is he? Ours are no trouble at all."

"Do they enjoy school?"

"They do."

Something in his voice made her look at him more closely. "Are they academically inclined?" she asked.

"They're bright. Paul is clever enough to expand the business in many new and profitable directions."

"Forgive me, but you don't seem pleased."

Keaton gestured with one hand. "Of course I'm pleased. And proud. But he doesn't need his head filled with *unnecessary* learning. University is not for him—how would we afford that?"

"I believe there are scholarships for the cleverest. Was Mr. Ogden himself not such a recipient?"

"We have no need of scholarships and universities. Ogden earns a pittance for all his degrees and hard work. Paul will be a gentleman."

Again, Constance let it go. "And your daughter?"

"I have been persuaded to allow her one more year at school. After that, she will learn more from her mother."

"Who are their best friends in the village?" Constance asked.

Keaton blinked. "They are friends with all the children. Though perhaps they are better friends with each other. Being twins."

Or being forbidden from playing with the poorer children. "Then there is no one they dislike? No one they have fallen out with?"

"Nothing serious enough to upset them. Why are you so interested in the children?"

"Feelings run high over children," Constance said. "I am really crossing off possibilities in my mind. We have to consider everything."

"Then I gather you are no closer to finding the culprit?"

"We know more than we did," Constance said vaguely. Though it was a pity she could not see the relevance of that knowledge.

⤜⤜⤜※⤛⤛⤛

SOLOMON, HAVING QUIZZED his staff and many business acquaintances on the subject of Captain Jordan Blake of the *Mary Anne*, found himself outside a modest house in Bloomsbury. There may or may not have been a maid, though it seemed to be the lady of the house, dressed to go out, who opened the door to him. No doubt she was the married daughter with whom Blake apparently lived.

She looked surprised.

"Mrs. Tanner?" Solomon touched his hat and offered his card. "My name is Grey. I was hoping to speak to Captain Blake."

"What about?" she asked suspiciously, glaring at the card. "He doesn't keep well, which is why he's living with us."

"I understand you are his daughter? Perhaps you would be so kind as to ask if he is able to receive me? I am particularly interested in his days as captain of a ship called the *Mary Anne*."

"Well, I'll ask him," she said dubiously. "Come in for a moment."

She left him in the hall while she opened a door on the right toward the back of the house.

A small maid and a boot boy poked their heads out of what was no doubt the kitchen and watched Solomon with blatant curiosity.

Mrs. Tanner returned. "He says he'll see you. Come in. Ring the bell when you're ready to leave and the servants will show you out. I have to be elsewhere. Don't tire him out."

Solomon bowed to her retreating back and walked into the room she had just left.

Captain Blake did indeed look like an invalid. Huddled in a chair by the fire, his legs covered by a tartan rug, he wheezed when he spoke, and his face was beset with lines of chronic pain.

Solomon bowed and went forward to offer his hand. "Captain Blake? Thank you for seeing me."

Blake dropped Solomon's card in his lap in order to grasp his hand with thin fingers.

"Mr. Grey." He gestured to the chair on the other side of the fireplace, but Solomon brought it nearer, while avoiding blocking the heat from his host.

"Your daughter tells me you don't keep well."

"Master of understatement, is my Elsie. I'm dying, Mr. Grey. Lungs are shot. A tumor, they tell me. Doctor says it's not the sea air but the smoking is the cause. Something gets you in the end, eh? Elsie said you were asking about the *Mary Anne*?"

"I am."

"Why?"

"I'm investigating the death of the owner, a Mr. Herbert Chase."

"Chase is dead?" Blake's eyes had widened with genuine surprise, if no obvious grief.

"He was murdered earlier this week. Which must seem odd to you, considering he also died seven years ago aboard the *Mary Anne*, according to witnesses."

"Must have been a different Chase."

"Not according to my witness. Captain Blake, what took place on that ship?"

The captain gazed past him and slowly shook his head. He sighed. "Nothing good. I left the *Mary Anne* after that voyage, swearing secrecy to Chase—it was the only way he'd let me out of my contract. I kept my bargain. But I suppose it doesn't count if he's really dead this time."

"I suppose it doesn't."

Blake leaned forward, peering at him. "I know you, don't I?"

"It's possible, though I don't recall it. I am a ship owner."

"A ship owner who investigates murder?"

"I have many strings to my bow. So, I believe, did Herbert Chase, and not all of them were legal."

Blake wheezed out a bitter laugh. "Not remotely. We had a hold full of spices on the *Mary Anne*, enough to make everyone's fortunes. I genuinely didn't know it was stolen—from several different merchants, I found out later. I doubt Chase had paid for any of it. He had legitimate partners in the venture, one of whom was known to me. That's why I sailed for Chase. I don't know if he ever meant to *buy* the spices. At any rate, I didn't suspect a thing until that night Drayman stole a couple of pocketsful."

Blake reached for the glass of water beside him and swallowed. He kept hold of the glass.

"What was Chase's plan?" Solomon asked. "To give his partners an expected share of the profit and keep the rest for himself? Having spent nothing on acquiring his cargo in the first place?"

"Something like that. He was a greedy little... Anyway, Drayman was a lot more savvy than me."

"Who was Drayman?"

"Just a rough seaman with a nasty temper and a bad reputation. I only took him on because one of my men was ill and useless and I didn't think he'd last the voyage home." His eyes fixed on Solomon and began to widen. "That's who you remind me of! The sailor who was ill! What was his name? Johnston or something..."

"It wasn't me," Solomon said, "though I might know who you mean. He does look a bit like me."

"Only around the face. Perhaps it's just the—Johnny. That was his name. Decent man, but he had brain fever. He lasted until Marseilles, where we left him at the hospital to die. I should have checked back on him, but I never did. I was too busy trying to break my ties with Chase."

"Because you had discovered the theft. Through Chase's fight with this sailor, Drayman?"

Blake nodded. "Chase caught Drayman with his pockets full of saffron and pepper. Like most thieves, Chase hated to be stolen from, and he was furious enough to attack Drayman. I could have told him that was a mistake without at least three other men to watch his back. Drayman disarmed him and beat him unconscious with his own club. He looked dead by the time I got the club off Drayman and we managed to get him locked up. That was when Drayman told me the whole cargo was stolen. I didn't believe him at first, but Chase actually confirmed it."

Blake's lips twisted. "No, he wasn't dead. He came to when he was carried below. In a hell of a state, though. Broken ribs and shoulder, blood everywhere... He said we shouldn't hand Drayman over to the law because it would draw attention to the cargo, and the fact that it was stolen. Drayman wasn't going to keep his mouth shut. I was in a bad position."

"Because no one would believe you didn't know," Solomon guessed.

Blake nodded. "And Chase was quite prepared to swear that I did if I opened my mouth. I'm not proud if it, but I didn't dare speak out. We reached the agreement that I would remain silent and break all ties with him and the *Mary Anne*. Then we separated Drayman from his spices and, without paying him for the voyage, bundled him into a ship sailing back east. We pretended Chase was dead and we were saving Drayman from hanging. But it was undoubtedly a rough ship with a bad captain and a worse reputation. I daresay Drayman deserved it. What Chase deserved was another matter. He certainly got a nasty beating, but the law never touched him."

"What happened to Drayman? Did you ever hear of him again?"

"I never saw him. But Chase did track me down about a year ago to tell me he'd seen Drayman down by the Pool of London. He wanted to make sure I was keeping my word about silence. I was already ill by then and didn't much care, except I don't want my family thinking bad of me when I'm gone."

Blake began to cough, and Solomon rose to take his glass before it spilled all over him. When the paroxysm stopped, Solomon offered him the glass back, but Blake waved his hand weakly toward another bottle. Sherry. With a sizeable tumbler beside it. Doubting it could do a dying man much harm, Solomon poured him a glassful and brought it to him.

Nodding his thanks, Blake said huskily, "Chase wasn't doing so well either, when he came to see me. He'd risen high in the business world and was falling fast. Unsound investments, he said."

"Very unsound," agreed Solomon, who had discovered a great deal from Lenny Knox's list and from his own inquiries.

"At any rate, he left me alone."

"Do you think it's possible Drayman caught up with him? Would he have borne a grudge for the lie that he'd killed Chase?"

"Oh yes. And for us keeping his pay and the spices he stole from the original thief. You think Drayman *did* catch up with him?"

"At the Crown and Anchor," Solomon said. Or was that wishful thinking because it put David, with his unstable mind and memory, in the clear? "I don't suppose you know where Drayman can be found?"

"Some dockside brothel, I shouldn't wonder. Men don't change much, as a rule." Blake lifted the glass to his lips and drank it all down, then lay back and closed his eyes as if waiting for some ease.

Solomon rose again and took the empty glass from him. "I'm sorry. I've tired you out with bad memories."

"Will you make it right?"

"Yes," Solomon said. He owed the captain for taking David to the hospital in Marseilles.

CHAPTER FOURTEEN

MISS MORTIMER WAS next on Constance's list of people to see, not just about the delivery of her letter but about the missing bracelet. She didn't know if the two were connected, but they both seemed odd and out of place. Although few and far between, the missing items were remembered by the village constable, even from childhood. Surely that said something?

She found herself curiously reluctant to go up to the manor house. After last night, it had become a place of danger in her mind, and she had long ago learned to avoid those. At the back of her mind lurked the uneasy thought that if Peregrine Mortimer had pushed her down the stairs because she'd caught him cheating at cards, what might he do to his aunt in order to inherit her fortune more quickly?

Did she prefer to think of the culprit as Miss Fernie so she didn't have to face him again? She had grown too used to being *safe*, to having her bodyguards in footmen's livery. And she missed Solomon.

How had he found David? Was his brother even still in the house, or had he bolted again? Part of her wished they could just forget the trivial matter of these foolish letters and concentrate on the more serious crime of this murder and keeping David safe.

But something in Sutton May was *not* trivial. The letters were surely symptomatic of something much nastier building behind them, something very dangerous. Someone, whether a genteel old schoolteacher or an entitled young rake, had pushed her down the stairs.

Outside the Keatons' shop, she hesitated. Then, deciding it would be quicker to borrow the inn's gig to go to the manor, she turned back toward the village square and the vicarage.

Mr. Raeburn might be reluctant to talk about his flock, but she doubted Mrs. Raeburn felt the same restrictions.

Alice the maid admitted her at once, though she asked her politely to wait while she found out if the mistress was at home— the fiction by which ladies could avoid receiving those they did not wish to see.

Most vicars' wives, apart from a few reforming zealots, would have avoided Constance like the plague. Mrs. Raeburn received her at once with a welcoming smile, so if Miss Fernie *had* somehow discovered Constance's identity, she did not appear to have blabbed it. Yet.

"Mrs. Silver." Gliding toward her, with her hand out-stretched, Mrs. Raeburn glanced beyond Constance's shoulder, and her smile drooped slightly. "Mr. Grey is not with you?"

"Mr. Grey was called back to London on urgent business. But I expect him back this evening, or tomorrow at the latest." Constance, though more used to identifying physical attraction in men, was not blind to the signs in women. She knew a spurt of irritation with Mrs. Raeburn, even found herself examining her hostess's charms with an anxiety she was appalled to recognize as jealousy.

"I do apologize for taking up your time again," she said hasti-ly. "I know vicar's wives tend to be kept as busy as their husbands."

"Oh, I have no appointments until the Christian Women's Circle meeting this afternoon. We organize the May Day Fair every year. Do sit down. Does your investigation prosper? Or must you wait for Mr. Grey's return?"

"I would not waste my time—or Dr. Chadwick's—in wait-ing."

"How very independent you are!" The remark did not seem

to be entirely admiring. "Is it true you are betrothed to Mr. Grey?"

"Indeed I am." *So keep your eyes on your own husband.* Constance tried and failed to laugh at herself and turned swiftly to business. "I have just been talking to Constable Heron, and he mentioned a few items in the village that have been inexplicably lost over the years."

"Really?" Mrs. Raeburn sounded only vaguely surprised and not terribly interested. It was not, clearly, the sort of gossip she enjoyed.

"One of them, apparently, was a prayer book from the vicarage."

"Ah!" Memory clearly dawned, followed swiftly by annoyance. "Yes indeed. It was a lovely little book, bound in leather with gold tooling, engraved with my husband's initials. The pages were edged with gold leaf, too. I gave it to him as a gift, on our first Christmas at Sutton May."

"It sounds very beautiful. He must have been delighted."

"He was. He treasured it. We were both really annoyed when we could not find it anywhere."

"When exactly did it disappear?"

"Oh, it must have been at least three years ago now. Maybe four. Certainly, between one Sunday and the next."

"Then he only used it during the Sunday service?"

"Oh no, he kept it in his study to consult also. But if he couldn't lay his hands on it at once, he would use one of the others that were to hand. A vicarage tends to collect several Bibles, prayer books, psalm books, and hymnaries... At any rate, he only noticed it was missing when he was looking for it on Easter Sunday. We couldn't find it in any of the likely places, and he had to take another to church that day. Later, of course, we searched all the *unlikely* places too, but it never turned up."

"Did you report it to Constable Heron?"

Her eyes widened. "Why would we do that?"

"In case it had been stolen."

"Who would steal the vicar's prayer book?"

His favorite prayer book, Constance thought. Was that the reason behind the theft? "I don't know, but it is always a possibility. Anything can be stolen, with or without reasons you or I might recognize. In this case, I imagine it was quite a valuable book, in terms of money."

"It was not cheap," Mrs. Raeburn agreed, her expression softening. "But I wanted to give him something special to mark his arrival here. Sutton May is an excellent living." She shook her head. "But I really doubt it was stolen."

"Then what do you think happened to it?"

She shrugged with an air of helplessness. "I really don't know. It was not a large book, so I suppose it might have got knocked off the study desk and landed in the wastepaper basket. Alice could have emptied it without noticing."

"Alice was with you then?"

"Oh yes. She was quite young when we took her on, when we first arrived here. To be honest, we were not sure we could afford the luxury of a parlor maid."

And young maids, especially those with less-than-perfect backgrounds, could be paid less than their more experienced sisters. More to the point, Alice's mother, Mavis, had also lost something.

Of course, servants generally got the blame for anything lost or stolen, but in this case, Mrs. Raeburn seemed to bear no suspicion of malice in her servant.

"Or Luke could have dropped it in the street, I suppose," she continued. "Although I would have expected someone to bring it back to him if that were the case. Unless it was a market day."

The day that strangers came into the village. "I suppose," Constance said without much hope, "you cannot recall who visited you or the vicar during that week? Or whom he called upon, perhaps with the prayer book in his pocket?"

"Oh, goodness, no. You really think someone stole it from him? I thought you were interested in Mrs. Chadwick's nasty letter—surely the two cannot be connected?"

"They are both unusual events," Constance said, feeling slightly foolish. "But no, I don't know if they are connected at all."

She did not stay long after that, since Mrs. Raeburn seemed more interested in Solomon than in gossiping about the village, and Constance did want to be too pointed in her questions about Miss Fernie. When she rose to take her leave, Mrs. Raeburn rang the bell for Alice to show her out, and they exchanged civil goodbyes.

As the maid helped her back into her coat, Constance said, "Alice, do you recall a box of your mother's that went missing a while ago?"

Alice's hands stilled, then dropped as Constance turned to face her. "I do," she said. "Pretty little carved box with a sliding lid. You had to find the hidden catch to open it. I loved playing with it, but Mam always put it back on the mantelshelf because it was one of her favorite things."

"She valued it particularly, then?"

"Oh yes, Miss Mortimer gave her it when she left the manor."

"Did she?" Constance was aware of her heart beating suddenly faster. "Your mother must have felt the loss of it then. What happened to it?"

Alice shrugged. "We never found out. It must have got knocked into the fire, or into something else that was thrown away."

"Did she have many visitors around that time?"

Alice's eyes dropped, then lifted with a shade of defiance. "She don't have many visitors at all, ma'am."

Because she was a fallen woman. Like Constance. Only Constance had found a way to thrive in the city, flaunting her sin, and had grown rich, while Mavis Cartwright cleaned the village shop and spent all her free time in church, atoning for what had probably not been her fault in the first place.

"She is a good woman," Constance said abruptly.

Alice smiled suddenly, like the sun coming out. "She is, ma'am."

SOLOMON FOUND HIMSELF, with some reluctance, at Scotland Yard. Although his instinct had been to personally pursue Captain Blake's information about the sailor Drayman, to go looking for him among the dockside stews and alehouses, he did not have the luxury of time.

For one thing, the letter about an available house was burning a hole in his pocket. For another, he was uneasy leaving Constance alone for long in a village seething with undercurrents of ill will. As it was, he would struggle to catch a train back to Sutton May this evening.

So he had decided to take a chance on the police doing the work—and not arresting him either *as* the fugitive or for harboring him. In this particular case, he could not afford to be fobbed off on Constable Napier. It had to be Inspector Omand.

Accordingly, glad of his decent suit and overcoat—which would have been disastrously out of place in the dockside dens of vice—he squared his shoulders and walked into the teeming building as though he expected to be served immediately.

And he was. The sergeant on duty sent a minion scurrying for Inspector Omand. To Solomon's relief, because he didn't have time for another round with the hostile Napier, the messenger came back to conduct him straight to Omand's office.

To get there, he had to walk through an open office of desks, from one of which Constable Napier stared at him in open disbelief. The man was about to stand up and no doubt cause a scene, but fortunately Omand appeared in the doorway at the end of the room, coming forward to meet Solomon with hand outstretched.

There was nothing Napier could do in the face of his superior's obvious welcome.

"Mr. Grey," the inspector greeted Solomon as they shook hands. "A pleasure to see you again—I hope! Come in and sit down. I'd offer you tea, but it's pretty nasty by this time of the day."

Solomon assured him that tea was not required and sat down on the hard visitor's chair, placing his hat on the desk in front of him. "Perhaps your constable told you I was interested in the case of Herbert Chase?"

Omand blinked. "Actually, he did not."

Napier, of course, had his own agenda, which seemed to consist largely of outshining his rough old inspector. Omand, a man of amiable demeanor, was both shrewd and experienced, but Napier found him slow and plodding. Which was far from the truth.

"No matter. I have some information that you may not have come across and probably should be made aware of. You know that Chase was a merchant losing money hand over fist?"

"Indeed."

"And not quite the clean potato."

Omand inclined his head.

"I understand that Chase was seen in the Crown and Anchor drinking with a sailor who left before him, and then shaking off a second sailor who tried to talk to him and left after Chase."

Again, Omand nodded, though since some of this information came from David, it might well have been new to the inspector.

"I have a suspicion," Solomon continued, "that I know who the first sailor was. Unfortunately, I am involved in another case in the country and don't have time to confirm or deny it, but I want you to know who I think it is. His name is Abel Drayman and he was once a sailor on Chase's ship, the *Mary Anne*. Back in 1844, the *Mary Anne* brought back a large cargo of stolen spices from China and the East. Chase and Drayman had a very physical disagreement that ended in Drayman's being hustled onto another ship heading out of Marseilles in order to avoid being charged with Chase's murder. Chase, of course, was not dead, but it kept the matter from authorities who might then have poked into the cargo's origins."

"But Drayman was afraid to go home," Omand said thoughtfully. "So he bore a grudge."

"A large one, I imagine, by the time he learned that Chase had never died in the first place. He is not, I understand, a gentle man. When Chase saw him in London, it certainly alarmed him."

"So Drayman and Chase met in the Crown and Anchor? Would Chase not have known better than to meet such a person there?"

"My guess is he had little choice. He certainly dressed to blend in."

"Blackmail?" Omand guessed. "Either Chase wouldn't or couldn't pay, or Drayman always intended to kill him. What of the second sailor? An accomplice?"

"A convenient scapegoat, I believe. Though I suspect he raised the alarm faster than suited Draymen."

"Which is why they both ran. The second sailor should turn himself in for questioning."

"If I ever see him," Solomon said politely, "I shall pass that on. I shall be going out of town tonight or early tomorrow, though, so I leave it all in your capable hands. I imagine you can find a missing sailor far more quickly than I."

"If he's even in the country. I don't suppose you have any clues as to where to begin looking?"

"In dockside brothels, according to his old captain," Solomon said, rising to his feet and offering his hand once more. "Whose name is Blake, and he stays with his daughter in Bloomsbury. Thanks for your time, inspector. Good afternoon."

As he retraced his footsteps through the outer office, he felt Napier's malevolent eyes on his back. It made his flesh crawl because there was no reason for it.

Was that the nature of whatever hatred swirled in Sutton

May? Unprovoked and reasonless prejudice? It bore thinking about.

In the meantime, he had a house to view.

WHEN CONSTANCE DROVE the inn's gig up the carriageway to the front of the manor house, she felt quite safe. Until the notion entered her head that she was being observed from behind those rows of windows, which made the hair on the back of her neck stand up.

As she climbed down from the gig and handed the reins to the groom who had run round from the side of the house, she was very aware of the aching bruises on her arm and stiff shoulder. Was there real malevolence in this house? Or was she just fanciful because of the incident last night? If she was right that Miss Fernie had pushed her, then she was perfectly safe at the manor house today.

Miss Mortimer and Miss Jenson were discovered in the drawing room, arranging daffodils in separate vases and arguing. Constance was glad to see no sign of Peregrine Mortimer at this stage, since she wanted to speak to the ladies first.

The pair halted their argument at once to welcome Constance with gracious and apparently genuine smiles.

"No Mr. Grey today?" Miss Jenson inquired.

"He has gone to London for the day," Constance said, slightly surprised that they didn't already know. She sat in the offered chair and regarded the two expectant faces before her. "I've been speaking to Constable Heron, who told me about items that have gone missing over the years."

"What items?" Miss Jenson asked.

Miss Mortimer frowned. "He hasn't become involved in the matter of Faye Keaton's wretched shawl, has he?"

"Oh, no. He is not talking about crime, as such, just about

things that have got lost. He mentioned a bracelet belonging to you, Miss Mortimer."

Her eyebrows rose. "Did he? How on earth did he know about that?"

"Then you remember the bracelet I mean?"

"Of course I do. It was a twenty-first birthday gift from my father, and really quite valuable. I couldn't believe I had been so careless as to leave it in London."

"Is that what you did?"

"I must have, for I never found it in this house or in any of my bags."

"Did the staff of your London house not find it?"

"The house and servants were not ours, merely hired for the Season. My father wrote to our man of business, but the bracelet was never found."

"When was this exactly?"

"Oh, thirty years ago at least! Not long before he died."

"Could you describe it for me?" Constance asked.

"It was a double circle of tiny diamonds, the two strands connected by a ruby. A rather beautiful thing. I was touched that my father had taken such effort over a gift for me."

As a mere daughter? "Was the bracelet much admired in the village?" Constance asked.

"To be honest, I had not many occasions on which to wear it here."

"Then who did see it?"

"I wore it to dinner with the Lances at Chettering—that would be the parents of the current Lance crop. The old vicar was there—long before Mr. Raeburn's day—as was Helen Fernie."

Miss Fernie again.

"I understand Mavis Cartwright was your mother's maid. Did you have no personal servant of your own?"

Miss Mortimer's face seemed to close up. "No, not then. Mavis served both of us. If you want the truth, I did not want her to leave us."

"It appears to be something of an open secret why she did."

Miss Mortimer's chin went up. Her eyes turned arctic. "I won't have you judge her."

"I?" said Constance before she could help herself.

"You suspect she stole the bracelet in revenge for being dismissed."

"Actually, I thought you might have given it to her," Constance said mildly. "In compensation for her being dismissed."

Miss Mortimer blinked rapidly, then gave a crooked smile. "She would not take it. Because my father had given it to me. I gave her a little box instead. She had always admired it."

"Then you always knew who the father of her child was?"

"Everyone knew," Miss Mortimer said wryly. "One cannot keep secrets in Sutton May. There is no point in judging my father, either. Even I gave up on that. He had been brought up to think he could take what he liked, and he never saw his infidelities as betraying my mother. Nor even ruining girls like Mavis. A little money and a few presents over the years and his conscience was perfectly clear."

"Do you still see Mavis? Or Alice?"

"That would not, alas, be proper."

Constance could not tell if she was serious. "Who does visit Mavis?"

"The vicar, of course. A few of the charitable ladies."

"Like Miss Fernie?" Constance asked.

"I shouldn't be surprised."

Miss Jenson snorted. "As if poor Mavis has not suffered enough!"

"You don't care for Miss Fernie?" Constance said quickly.

"No, I do not," Miss Jenson retorted. "She has all the compassion of a-a fish!"

"Yet she visits a woman spurned by much of the village," Constance said, "and she has not been sent a letter to remind her to be kind."

"You really think that is the main purpose of the letters?" Miss

Mortimer asked.

"Yes, I think it is. The letters say nothing about old sins, so far as we can judge, only about odd instances of mistake or temper…"

Miss Mortimer shook her head. "I really cannot see Helen's sending letters in such a way."

"Oh, I don't believe she sent the letters," Constance said. "I did wonder if the two things *might* be connected, but…" She stood abruptly. "I need to go home and think."

What she really needed was to go over everything with Solomon. Missing him was an ache that never quite went away except when he was with her.

"Goodbye," she remembered to say to the old ladies, who were looking both amused and baffled by her haste.

She hurried down the stairs, thoughts rushing through her head while she tried to grasp some important, elusive idea that would explain everything.

Stairs.

Her neck prickled. Instinctively, she grasped the banister and glanced behind her.

Peregrine Mortimer smiled at her from the landing.

Her heart lurched, for it was an ugly smile and there was no one around to see what happened next.

CHAPTER FIFTEEN

S OLOMON BARELY NOTICED the snarled traffic, so eager was he to show Constance the house he had just seen. For the first time, he had felt at home in a strange house, and was sure Constance would feel it too.

When he alighted from the hackney at last at the Silver and Grey office, he realized it was dark. Janey was locking the front door.

"There you are," she said. "I'd about given up on you. You going back in?"

"Where are you going?"

She stared at him. "Home? You all right, guv? I mean sir?"

Solomon extracted his watch and read it by the light of the streetlamp. He swore under his breath. "I've missed the train back to Sutton May."

"So you have. And I'm missing me dinner. You sleeping in there or back at your own place?"

For a moment, stupidly, he felt lost. He had been looking forward to dashing back to Constance, to telling her the latest about David and what he had set in motion. To telling her about the house…

He shoved aside what he could not change. "Sorry, Janey. Take a cab home." He shoved some coins in her hand at random and set off for his house. And his brother.

"Abel Drayman," he said abruptly, striding into the room where David was dining.

David dropped his fork with a clatter. "I remember him!" He stared at Solomon. "I think…it was him, not me, who killed Chase, the merchant?"

"I think he killed him both times. Could it have been Drayman that Chase was drinking with in the Crown and Anchor?"

"I didn't see his face. His back was to me, and then I was so fixed on Chase that I didn't look. What made you think of him?"

"I found your Captain Blake." Solomon cast himself into the chair opposite his brother. Oddly enough, the place had been set as though Jenks had expected him home for dinner. "It was he who took you to the hospital in Marseilles. He thought you would die but was too taken up with Chase and his own problems to find out."

David shrugged. "It doesn't matter. I don't mind."

"It does matter. You were ill with brain fever, David. The scene you witnessed had such a nightmare quality not because you were mad and imagining things but because you were sick and fevered. That was the illness that deprived you of your memories for so long."

"I am not mad," David stated.

Solomon poured wine into both their glasses. "You are not mad. You were never mad."

David raised his eyes. "Remembering you, pretending to be you… That was just…loneliness."

"Missing your family. As we missed you. But worse because you were alone and unsafe." And suffering… Imagining that suffering was unbearable. To both of them.

David picked up his glass and drank a large mouthful. "How was Captain Blake?"

"Not well, and somewhat ashamed. I promised him I would put it right."

"How will you do that?"

"By finding Drayman. I have—er…delegated that task to the police. I doubt they will call here to tell me what they discover, but don't be alarmed if they do. Either Jenks will deny you or you can pretend to be me."

David gave an unexpected shout of laughter. "Like the old days."

And suddenly it *was* like the old days. Just a little.

CONSTANCE KEPT WALKING, although every nerve urged her to run.

She tensed, gripping the banister hard, for his arms and legs were longer than hers and he could get close enough to push or kick and she would have no chance of fighting back with elbows or heels. Her only chance was to cling to the rail with her hand and get close enough to the bottom for least damage…

Or she could call out.

Which would reveal her fear, and she had learned long ago never to do that.

"Allow me to show you out," Mortimer said behind her, his voice dripping with sarcasm. "Did my aunt offend you so much that you storm out before she can even ring for a servant? It's how things are done in a gentleman's house, you know."

So it was to be a verbal attack. *That* she could deal with.

She kept descending the stairs. "I daresay she trusted me not to steal the silver in my rampage through the premises."

His footsteps sounded behind her. "But then, she doesn't know your name."

Meaning Miss Mortimer did not *recognize* Constance Silver's name? Which meant that her nephew did. No doubt Miss Fernie, yet again.

"My name is hardly secret," Constance said. Only three steps to go now. He wasn't going to hurt her.

"And yet you expect to be received like an honest woman?"

She reached the foot of the stairs with relief and turned to face him. "I *am* an honest woman. What are you, Mr. Mortimer?"

He brushed past her, not to help her retrieve her coat and hat, but to riffle the little pile of letters on a sturdy table.

"I am her nephew and her heir and she will not receive you again."

The sight of his picking through the letters made her remember that she had not even asked Miss Mortimer what she meant to about the delivery of her anonymous letter. She was not thinking straight enough or clearly enough.

"Were you here when she received the anonymous letter?" Constance asked abruptly.

His gaze flew to hers, not in guilt or irritation, but in sheer surprise. He had expected a retort to his taunt, not a change of subject. "Yes. It was just before the end of my last visit."

"How did you know about it?"

He curled his lip. "Are you accusing me of sending it?"

"No," Constance replied impatiently. "I want to know when and how you saw it. Were you looking for post directed to you, as you are now?"

"Yes, as it happens." A frown tugged at his handsome brow. "I noticed it because the direction was written in such an odd way, in capital letters all of the same size. She never receives letters like that."

"What time was this?"

"Time?"

"Of the day," Constance said urgently. "Was it first thing in the morning?"

"No, it was about this time, round about tea, when the latest post is usually fetched from the village by one of the grooms."

That was different. The other letters had been slipped under front doors during the night, or very early in the morning. "Did you take it directly to her?"

"No, for she had guests to tea. She read it later. And so did I by the simple means of walking into her sitting room and looking. I make a point of knowing everything that goes on in my aunt's life. I protect her."

"Do you?" Constance said. "What do you think the letter referred to?"

"Taking responsibility for Hannah Jenson," he said contemptuously. "It would have been the simplest matter for *her* to leave an extra letter among the post as though it were nothing to do with her."

"The same could be said of you. Who had tea with your aunt that day?"

"Lord, how should I remember? The same old faces. It was a Wednesday, when they all come bleating for free food."

"You won't make a very bountiful lord of the manor, will you, Mr. Mortimer?" She walked to the hall stand and donned her own coat while he gazed at her with dislike. She placed her bonnet on her head without tying the ribbons. "Good afternoon."

She drove back to the inn, her head still buzzing with thoughts and excitement, mostly because Solomon might have come back.

He hadn't, as she quickly discovered. Hoping he would be on the last train, she went up to her room, lit the candles, and spread out her notes again, adding what she had learned.

The first anonymous letter had been delivered to Miss Mortimer before or during her tea party on a Wednesday afternoon. There had then been a gap of a week before the Keaton letter, and the Nolan letter, both of which had been delivered either during the night or first thing in the morning. And then nothing—that Constance knew of—until Mrs. Chadwick's letter last week. A gap of more than two weeks.

Had the writer meant to give up the practice and then been unable to help themselves? Only the death of a child had set them off again. And that letter too had been delivered during the hours of darkness, when the sender was less likely to be seen.

Who had the legitimate business to be out and about at night? Not children, whatever her original suspicions. Those walking home at night, from the Goose or from church meetings. People who lived alone without spouses or servants to notice their going out at such odd hours.

And the matter of the missing items... Was she right that they were thefts? Was she really understanding the reasoning behind them? It was not truly her or Solomon's business. They had been hired to find the sender of the anonymous letters.

Solomon...

Her watch told her it was time for the last train from London. She rose and went to the window, opening it a crack until she was sure she heard the familiar rumble of wheels on the railway track, the engine's distinctive whistle...

Her window looked out onto the courtyard and the street beyond. Several men of varying degrees in life, both singly and in groups, did pass through the arch into the courtyard, but none of them were Solomon.

No one came upstairs or knocked on the door.

Until someone did and she actually jumped. "Come in."

It was the maid, asking if she wanted to have supper downstairs or in her room.

"Here in my room, I think," Constance replied.

She told herself it was good he had stayed in London, that he needed time with David as well as time devoted to his brother's problem. Unthinkable that they allow him to hang...

She began to pore over David's case in her mind until it became confused with Sutton May and letters, and she knew she was too tired to think anymore.

Solomon...

SHE WOKE TO daylight, and the peace of the countryside, apart from the soft knocking at her bedchamber door.

Blinking blearily, she threw back the bedclothes, feeling without success for her dressing robe. Giving up, she decided to simply hide behind the door and staggered across the room.

She unlocked the door and opened it a crack, peering around it.

Pleasure caught at her throat, depriving her of words, even his name. She opened the door wide, still hiding behind it, and he slipped inside, shut and locked the door, and took her in his arms.

His kiss was unexpectedly fierce and hungry, and she wallowed in it. He still wore his overcoat, and even his tall hat, which made her want to laugh, and his bold caress deprived her of breath and thought. Throwing her arms around his neck, she kissed him back with everything she felt and yearned for, and grew dizzy with delight. Her nightgown had vanished when her back landed on the softness of the warm bedsheets.

Her mouth was still fused to his and she didn't even think of resisting. Love, intense and inevitable, surged and claimed them. Even so, there was tenderness in his urgency and her own fierce response.

This was how it should always have been since the first time. Without words or doubts, without *self*-doubts and even thought. Sheer instinct, sheer feeling, the giving and receiving of joy.

It could not last at such intensity, and it didn't. But God, it was necessary and wonderful and more than she had ever dreamed, even after the first time.

They held each other bonelessly, recovering their breath.

"At least your hat fell off," she said unsteadily, and they both began to laugh.

She helped him out of his coat, and then the rest of his clothes, until they could be skin to skin at last. And then, it all began again, this time with slow and leisurely worship.

SOLOMON HAD NOT intended their reunion to be quite so urgent, but the sight of her, the feel of her yielding in his arms, returning his passion… Well, for once in his life, he'd abandoned thought and control and gloried in the result.

By the time they were ready to talk, all their personal issues, the inexplicable distance he had been unable to fix, had been solved without words. He was hers, and she was his.

"I saw a house I think you will like. And I applied for a special license."

She had been lying draped over his chest, but at this she levered herself up, her warm, sleepy eyes brightening with excitement. "Really? Tell me!"

"No, I want you to see it for yourself without my influence." He hauled himself up against the pillows and settled her against his shoulder, his arm around her. "Tell me first about the case."

"I think I've found a thief, and it's not Nell Dickie. I'm sure whoever wrote the letters must live alone, because apart from Miss Mortimer's, they were all delivered during the night or very early in the morning. How is David?"

"I think I know who the culprit is, but I've left Inspector Omand to find him so that we can try to prove it." He told her what Janey and Lenny had discovered at the Crown and Anchor, and their list of Chase's investments, then moved on to Captain Blake and the story of the *Mary Anne* and its stolen cargo.

"That must set David's mind at rest, at least. You don't suppose Omand will call at your house if and when he finds this Drayman?"

"Well, he might," Solomon said. "I could hardly tell him not to. So we had better finish here quite quickly, if we can. Jenks already knew David was not me, so I can't rely on Omand's failing to notice the differences either. I suppose," he added reluctantly, running his fingers through her hair, "we should get up and dress. After you've told me about your thief..."

Oddly, it was only as he rose from the bed at last that he noticed the bruises on her arm and shoulder, and caught her around the waist.

"Did I do that to you?" he demanded, staring in horror.

"No, of course you did not! I forgot all about them..."

"What happened?" He skimmed a gentle hand over the soft, discolored skin. "Those look nasty."

"Oh, they look worse than they feel, although I admit it was sore at the time. I fell downstairs at the manor."

He knew there was more, but forced himself not to tense.

She examined the bruises. "It was slightly swollen just after it happened—"

"Which was when?" he interrupted.

Her gaze lifted to his. "The card party." She turned, sliding both arms around his neck and pressing her cheek to his. "I couldn't tell you. You wouldn't have gone to London."

"I wouldn't have," he said, pulling back to search her face, "and you wouldn't have hidden it if you had merely tripped. Constance—"

"I was pushed. When I was returning from the retiring room. Someone had put out the lights and lay in wait. I fell only to the half landing, twisted my ankle slightly, but landed mostly on my elbow and shoulder. Sophie Chadwick saw me fall and ran up to me. My attacker fled down another staircase."

"Who?" he demanded. Sick anger had closed around his heart and kept squeezing until he recognized fear as well. And guilt because he had not even noticed. He had been so absorbed in the case, in David's, in his own feelings at parting from Constance, that he had not seen her pain. Not even this morning in the grip of his desire.

"I am indebted to Sophie," Constance said, "for noticing that Miss Fernie and Peregrine Mortimer left the drawing room shortly after I did. It was because of Mortimer she came after me, afraid I didn't know that he ambushes women alone."

His fingers curled into fists, and she caught one in both her hands.

"I don't think it was Mortimer. I did, at first, but I don't believe he is violently inclined. He was just never taught to keep his hands to himself, and enough women must have welcomed his attentions."

"Then you think it was Miss Fernie? Really?"

"I know she is the same age as Miss Mortimer, but she's fit and strong. And angry."

"And dangerous, it would appear. Why on earth would she push you? Because she feared you suspected her of writing the letters?"

"I wondered that, but no. I think she recognized my name and made her judgment."

"A fallen woman," Solomon said slowly.

"It still counts if you're pushed."

"Don't," he said painfully, resting his forehead against hers, closing his arms around her. "How *dare* she?"

"There is some kind of bond between her and Miss Mortimer. Bonds of childhood and shared experience. Thinned and even betrayed at some points—Miss Mortimer did remove her from her school post, after all—but still there. In Miss Fernie's eyes I insulted Miss Mortimer with my presence, with pretending to be respectable."

She shrugged. "I'm guessing. But it makes sense. Think about it. Miss Fernie is a vicar's daughter, related to a powerful, aristocratic family who gave her Seasons in London. She still visits them occasionally, and writes, which must be how she heard my name—and, I think, passed it on to Mortimer so that he would tell his aunt. Judging by our conversation yesterday, he has certainly learned something against me and wishes to forbid me from his aunt's presence."

There was no point and no time to voice his outrage, because Constance didn't pause for breath, so eager was she to share her theory.

"Miss Fernie's family has been generous to her, yet she lives alone in Sutton May, in a little cottage, as if she is no more than an ordinary village schoolteacher. Why? Why has she no companion, like Miss Mortimer has Hannah Jenson? Why does she not live with her family?"

"Because she doesn't want to be a poor relation? Because she is unpleasant and they don't like her?"

"Both of those, probably. They are happy enough to write to her at a distance, even have her to stay for a week or two, but I'll bet they lock up their silver and jewels while she's there."

Solomon blinked. "You believe she is the thief that no one in Sutton May acknowledges? Is that not rather a leap without evidence?"

"Possibly, but I'll bet the evidence is there. We already know that she embezzled from the school." Her eyes gleamed, and he wondered irrelevantly if she had any idea how beautiful she was, so animated, with her red-gold hair tumbling around her naked shoulders. "She was in the Keatons' shop when the shawl vanished. She must have had many opportunities to steal Miss Mortimer's bracelet. She visits Mavis Cartwright and could easily have taken her pretty box—she might even regard that theft as just punishment for Mavis's committing adultery with Miss Mortimer's father. She is on all the church committees and visits the vicarage frequently. She must have had many opportunities to take the vicar's prayer book."

"I allow all that to be true," Solomon said, "but it could be equally true of anyone. We have never even met half the people in the village."

"I *feel* it is her," Constance said stubbornly. "Remember also when we spoke to the children, they said she chased them out of her garden, *furious mad*. Would not their old teacher handle such incursions better? Even be pleased to see the children? She doesn't want anyone near her house."

"Then no one calls on her?"

"Inside the house, she can control where they go. Keep doors shut. Keep things out of sight. But people peering in windows? Who knows what they might see?"

Solomon regarded her with some unease. "Pure speculation. And no, I will not creep about her garden, spying through her cottage windows."

Constance grinned and totally disarmed him by kissing his lips. "Yes, you will. We'll go together."

CHAPTER SIXTEEN

CONSTANCE STROLLED THE village streets with her arm in Solomon's. She could hardly believe the difference in her mood since he had returned. From feeling unsafe and oppressed by the village atmosphere and desperately uncertain both about the case and her future with Solomon, she was suddenly lighthearted and confident.

Because they had stopped overthinking and over-considering each other and returned to instinct, to the basic fact of love, physical and otherwise. This intimacy, this closeness, made her both deliriously happy and determined.

Solomon's doubts did not upset her. She enjoyed his challenges, his arguments, because they helped clarify her thoughts, and even if he didn't quite agree—yet—he was listening. He always listened.

They walked past the school, empty of children because it was Saturday, though someone was working in the garden behind the house. Ogden. And some feet away, a woman kneeling on the grass. Sophie, no doubt.

"We don't know whether she is at home or not," Solomon pointed out as they came to Miss Fernie's neat little cottage.

"Which is why we have to wait until we see her leave."

"If she is so unhinged, she could have written the letters too. She lives alone and would have had every opportunity."

Constance shook her head. "They're too...*polite.*"

He didn't dispute it. "The other spinster we know who lives

alone, and has no doubt borne much scorn from the village, is Mavis Cartwright."

"I was thinking that," Constance said unhappily. "She was wronged by the Mortimers, even if Jessica gave her the box. She has to work for the Keatons in a menial role that she must resent, and they probably lord it over her, too. Nolan the blacksmith rejected her when she was pregnant. And she is powerless to fight back, except in a way that points no more fingers at her."

"What about Mrs. Chadwick? What grudge could she possibly have against her?"

"I wondered about that. Especially as there's a gap between most of the letters and Mrs. Chadwick's. Perhaps she just felt strongly about the death of the Gimlets' daughter, imagined her own grief and helplessness if Alice had died in such a way. I'm sure everyone in the village must know that Richard Gimlet tried to fetch the doctor the day before, and his wife didn't pass on the message until the following day."

"So she creeps around the village in the dark, delivering her anonymous scolds," Solomon said. "Except for Miss Mortimer's letter. How did it get into the pile of mail in the front hall of the manor?"

Constance sighed. "That, I don't know. I can't imagine her going near the manor. Unless she gave it to one of the servants to deliver."

"Then why don't we walk up to the manor now and discreetly question the servants?"

"Because we might miss Miss Fernie going out."

"The thefts, if there truly were any, are not our primary concern," Solomon reminded her. "If we solve this today, we can go home tomorrow and concentrate on keeping David out of prison."

"Tomorrow is Sunday," Constance objected.

"So it is. And on Sunday, Miss Fernie will most definitely go to church. As will the rest of the village."

Constance began to smile. "Who won't then catch us trespassing and peering in windows. You are not just a pretty face, are you, Mr. Grey?"

"I have always said so."

"Then by all means, let us go the manor house kitchen."

QUINTIN OGDEN LEANED against his bare apple tree and watched Sophie plant the last of his summer-flowering bulbs. He liked to watch her, for her movements were graceful as well as quick and efficient. He found the combination rather beautiful. Like Sophie herself.

Patting the earth, she glanced up and caught his gaze. "What are you smiling at?"

"You." He stepped nearer and stretched down a hand to help her up. "Thank you for the bulbs."

She accepted his help. He liked that too, for even through the thick gardening gloves, her touch warmed him. She smelled good, like flowers and grass after rain. Her breath gave a little hitch as she looked up at him, and he knew an urge to kiss her. He didn't, because that would be imposing after her kindness.

She turned away, dropping his hand. "What is the time, Quint?"

He consulted his slightly battered old watch. "Ten minutes past two."

"I had better go. I promised my father I would look in on the Gimlets."

Obediently, he began to walk toward the path that led to the front gate. "How will you get there?"

"Walk, of course."

The strength of his desire to go with her took him by surprise. Being a shy and humble man, he could see no reason why she should want his company, and yet she often did. For example, she had had no real reason to come today. Despite the gift of the bulbs, it was not a charitable visit, and he knew her mother didn't like him.

But then, her mother liked Peregrine Mortimer, so her judgment was flawed.

"Should you have an escort?" he asked, trying to give her a way out and yet hoping she would say yes.

"No," she said, and his spirits sank.

Now that he knew her, he was lonely without her. She calmed his spirit and spoke of interesting things, argued sensibly, and made him think. And she made him smile, just by the sound of her own laughter.

Well, he had the children's work to mark.

"I don't need an escort," she explained. "But I would welcome your company, if you'd like to come."

He smiled. "I would."

She smiled back, her color just a little heightened. "You had better fetch your hat."

He could not be bothered with hats, but she was right. People were less critical when one behaved according to rules he never quite saw the point of.

"I'll wait for you at the gate."

Re-entering his cottage, he hastily washed his hands, wiped a smut of soil off his cheek, and fetched his hat and slightly worn gloves. Another hour or two in Sophie's company was more than he had dared hope for.

But when he left the house again, she was outside the gate, talking to Peregrine Mortimer.

His happiness evaporated. She didn't like Mortimer, who frightened her in some way, and yet, like most people, she felt compelled to be polite to him. Which meant choosing him over Quintin because of his rank and his relationship to Miss Mortimer, as well as her parents' wishes. In truth, Quintin didn't understand any of that, but he accepted it.

Disappointment and a dislike of confrontation almost caused him to turn and go back inside. But he would stick to the offer he had made until told otherwise. He walked up the path and opened the gate.

Sophie smiled at him as he joined her. He thought there was relief in her eyes. He pulled on his gloves and waited.

"Oggie," Mortimer mocked as he always did, as though Quintin was one of his own pupils and Mortimer the teacher. "Where are you off to this fine, wintry morning?"

"I'm escorting Miss Chadwick to the Gimlets' farm."

Mortimer laughed. "Don't be silly. What use are you as an escort? If you must go, Sophie—though I have never seen the attraction of mud and pig swill—I shall take you. Run along, Oggie."

Defeated, Quintin nevertheless refused to retreat until Sophie stated her preference. But it seemed she wouldn't have to. Mortimer simply took her hand—she had changed her gardening gloves for finer ones—and began to pull it through his winged arm.

Misery swamped Quintin. But he had no time to dwell upon it, for Sophie snatched her hand free of him, moving instinctively closer to Quintin.

"No, sir! I have chosen my escort."

"Oh, Oggie doesn't mind," Mortimer said. "Do you, Oggie?"

He did mind, of course. More than anything, Quintin minded the way Mortimer reached for her again, and the fear in Sophie's face.

Without conscious thought, he stepped between them. "Miss Chadwick minds. She said no."

"*What* did you say?" Mortimer thrust his face into his, forcing his ugly gaze onto Quintin's, which was almost painful. He was a bully. Quintin had seen that from the first. But he had been dealing with bullies all his life, on his own account and then on behalf of his pupils.

Quintin held the gaze, and was ready for any violence, though he doubted it would come. "I believe you heard the lady."

Mortimer's mouth was ugly too. "Send the half-wit on his

way, Sophie. He doesn't seem to understand he is *de trop*."

Sophie's hand curled around Quintin's elbow. Which would make it difficult to fight with both hands. Neither of them spoke.

Abruptly, Mortimer spun around and stalked off.

"Oh, well done, sir," Sophie breathed. "Thank you."

And Quintin felt he was walking on air, the happiest man alive.

IT WAS A pleasant day for a walk, especially in Solomon's company. They walked arm in arm, and sometimes, since there were few people about, hand in hand. For Constance, it was one of those breathless hours of happiness that made everything else worthwhile. She wanted to think the best of everyone, and so began to wonder if she was wrong about the missing items being thefts. After all, they spanned more than thirty years, and the numbers concerned were hardly high over such a period.

As for the letters, they were undeniable, but they were not so very threatening, were they?

And Solomon was happy, too. She could feel it in his relaxed posture, in the way his arms swung as he walked. What were the odds, she asked herself in wonder, of her finding such a man, such a friend, such a lover? Such a husband…

She was smiling as they approached the manor house, her mood quite the opposite of the fearful wariness with which she had last come here. This time, they did not walk up to the front door, but skirted around the side of the house to the kitchen garden.

Here, maids were making the most of the wintry sunshine and hanging out washing. A footman was leaning against one of the clothes poles, idly watching and flirting, though he sprang to attention quickly enough when Constance and Solomon strolled past his line of vision. The maids dropped curtseys.

The footman strode toward the visitors. "Sir, madam, may I show you to the front door." It wasn't really a question, but Solomon chose to answer it.

"Actually, no, thank you. You may be the very man we are looking for."

"Me?" The footman was little more than a boy and looked distinctly alarmed.

"You don't need to worry," Constance reassured him. "You've done nothing wrong. As you probably know, we are trying to solve an upsetting puzzle for Miss Mortimer."

"I heard it was Mrs. Chadwick's—er…puzzle," the footman replied with more than a hint of insolence.

"Then it seems you don't know quite everything about your betters," Solomon observed. "Oblige me by looking at this envelope, addressed to your mistress. And yes, she did give it to us to investigate. Do you remember it?"

The footman peered at it, rubbing his knuckles against his cheek. His uncertainty might have been due to memory, or to concern over what his employer truly expected of him.

"Yes, I do," he said at last. "It was on the hall table about a month back—maybe more. It was at the top of the post pile I took up to her."

"Why do you remember that one in particular?" Solomon asked. "Doesn't Miss Mortimer receive many letters?"

"Yes, she does, but not with writing like that. Even the letters from children aren't all in capital letters."

"I see. Is it your normal duty to take the post up to Miss Mortimer?"

"Yes, unless Miss Jenson or someone has taken it up in passing. Since I was on my way up, I did it."

"Can you remember the time of day?" Constance asked.

"Teatime. Well, after tea, since she had callers."

"Can you remember who those callers were?"

"I didn't look. Mr. Larkin and Betty the parlor maid showed them in. I just hung the coats up and carried the tea tray."

"Hmm. So they were all front-door callers," Constance said, wondering how to ask if Mavis Cartwright ever visited the back door.

"Of course."

Solomon said, "Did anything else unusual happen that day? Around that time?"

The lad began to shake his head, then stopped suddenly, his eyes widening. "Actually, yes, the vicar was sent for! So he must have been among the guests." He grinned, pleased with his feat of memory and deduction.

"Who sent for the vicar?" Solomon asked.

"Old Mrs. Flowers. She was dying again."

"Again?" Constance asked, startled by the similarity with David's story of the murder at the Crown and Anchor.

"She thinks she's dying regularly and sends for the vicar. Give him his due, he always goes to her, and she's never died yet."

"How did he receive this summons? Did some family member come to the manor house?"

"No, there was a note to the vicarage. Alice Cartwright, the vicar's maid, brought it."

Alice... "By the back door?" Constance asked, her heart beating suddenly fast.

He scratched his head. "No idea. I was stationed outside the drawing room door when Betty brought the note in."

Curiosity had brought the two maids over to join the conversation.

"Betty was showing out Miss Fernie," said the first maid, "when she caught sight of Alice scuttling up the path. So Alice just gave Betty the note and waited outside while Betty ran up for the vicar's instructions."

"Did Betty leave the front door open?" Solomon asked.

Constance almost wished he hadn't.

"She did," the second maid said. "I know, because I was polishing that big mirror in the hall that someone had breathed on, and the wind howled in!"

"Thank you," Constance said. "You've all been very helpful."

Almost blindly, she turned away, heading back the way they had come.

"Alice," Solomon said, catching up with her easily. "Not Mavis but Alice, resentful on her mother's behalf?"

"I hadn't thought of it, but... I suppose it makes sense. She could easily have darted inside without the maid's noticing and left the letter on the hall table with the others. Her grudge against the Mortimers must be huge. And against Nolan for rejecting her mother and failing to give her the respectability that would have saved them both from scorn. Mrs. Chadwick, the Keatons... Just examples of unkindness from apparent leaders of the community?"

"And it would explain why the vicar and his wife are the only prominent people in the village who didn't get a letter. The vicar visits Mavis, is kind to her, tolerates her haunting the church at all hours, and he and his wife employ Alice."

"All true..." Constance shook her head. "No, I still think it's Mavis, though perhaps with Alice's connivance for this first letter. A matter of luck, perhaps, if Mavis met her scuttling up to the manor house. But I don't see how Alice could creep in and out of the vicarage at night without being seen or missed. She'd surely be far too tired, for one thing. There's a cook employed there too, and I daresay the vicar can be up and about at all sorts of odd hours. Mavis answers to no one, and if she is seen in the street, everyone assumes she's on her way to or from the church."

Solomon considered. "Maybe you're right. If so... Do you think Alice knows what her mother is about? Could they be allies? They must be close, after all. For years it must have been the two of them against the world."

Constance cast him a sardonic glance. "What, like me and my mother?"

"You stand by each other," Solomon said.

"We don't conspire together and never have. On the other hand, my mother and I are not everyone. They *could* be in alliance." She sighed. "I suppose we should go and visit Mavis and see what she says."

Solomon took her hand. "You don't want it to be Mavis."

"I think she has suffered enough. I don't want to add to the village's scorn for her."

"And yet we can't allow her to continue writing such letters," Solomon said gently.

"No. No, we can't, of course." She clung to his fingers. "Am I right, Solomon? Are we right? I'd hate to accuse her of something else and be wrong."

"Then let's go back to the inn and look at everything again."

ALICE'S HALF DAY was on a Saturday, and she always spent it with her mother. At least it kept her out of the church for a few hours.

Not that Alice disapproved of churchgoing. She could hardly do so and work for the vicar, who was a kind, if distant, man. Besides which, his fiery sermons gave her hope that the true wrongdoers in her mother's past would face their punishment on Judgment Day.

Over the tea that her mother always tried to make into a special meal for her on Saturdays, Alice said, "That Mrs. Silver was asking me about your missing box."

"What box?" her mother asked in surprise.

"The little carved one with the secret catch that Miss Mortimer gave you."

"I thought she was interested in letters, not boxes."

"So did I. Maybe she's just a general nosey. Though what Dr. Chadwick's thinking of, setting her and Mr. Grey on us, I don't know."

Mavis picked up a slice of bread and butter. "I don't think she's a nosey. But she is curious, by nature. I rather liked her."

"You like everyone."

"Well, their inquiries are nothing to do with us."

"Then why," Alice asked, when she had swallowed her mouthful of boiled egg on bread, "are they interested in your lost box?"

Her mother brightened. "Perhaps they found it."

"I heard her asking Mrs. Raeburn about the vicar's lost prayer book, too."

"I didn't even know he'd lost one."

"Oh yes," Alice said. "Lovely book. Mrs. Raeburn gave it to him, so it meant a lot. So did your box to you, though I never understood why. You always stick up for the Mortimers."

"For Miss Jessica. She's no more to blame than you are."

Alice gave up and devoted herself to tea while she gazed restlessly around the room. A large pile of newspapers lay in the dark corner next to the fireplace.

"Why do you always have so many newspapers?" she asked irritably.

"Mrs. Keaton lets me take the old ones that are unsold. I use them to light the fire." Mavis wriggled uncomfortably in her seat. "And they're useful when it's really cold. Keeps the frost off the windows."

"Does it?" Alice asked. She had a much smaller but similar pile of newspapers in her tiny attic bedchamber, but she used them quite differently.

CHAPTER SEVENTEEN

W ITH A NOD to the respectability of the house, Solomon and Constance separated for the night, though with a considerably warmer and longer farewell than of late.

Solomon did not even mind—much. A cold wash helped. The rest of him was happier than at any time since their first night together. They were about to finish another case, and David's problem seemed likely to be solved just as soon as Abel Drayman was found.

And most of all, Constance would be his wife. They would make their own home.

He lay awake for a while, going over the Sutton May case in his head, but his mind kept straying to the personal until he drifted off.

In the morning, they went down to breakfast separately. The sight of Constance, her eyes dancing with humor and excitement, only made him more determined.

The church service was at ten o'clock. They left the inn just after half past nine and strolled along the road past the school and Miss Fernie's house. Sure enough, she hurried past them in a dark blue wool dress and coat with a matching hat. Not quite lady of the manor, but much more stylish than the usual village schoolteacher. She carried an old prayer book and kept her eyes straight ahead as if she did not see or recognize either of them. When Solomon touched his hat, her nostrils flared, but that was her only reaction.

Constance and Solomon strolled on a few more yards, then turned back to view the procession of most of the village toward the church. They crossed the road and, a few minutes later, entered Miss Fernie's garden.

It was a sizeable cottage compared to Mavis Cartwright's or the one attached to the schoolhouse. Even walking down the path, Solomon could see good-quality curtains and a well-proportioned front parlor with its fire banked and a guard on the hearth.

Constance looked behind her and to either side, then peered blatantly in the parlor window. "Pretty."

"Can you see anything there that shouldn't be?" he asked, moving toward the window on the other side of the front door.

"Not obviously, no. But then, this is where she would receive visitors."

"Dining room," he said, peering. "Decent table and four chairs and a sideboard. Good carpet. Let's go around to the back."

Behind the dining room was a kitchen, old-fashioned but functional.

"This looks like a storeroom," Constance said eagerly at the other back window. "All the stolen things could be in here."

"Or it could be her parents' old furniture and things she cannot bear to throw out."

She grimaced. "Spoilsport. We might need to break in."

"Last resort," Solomon said, though it would not be the first time they had broken into someone's property in the pursuit of a case. It just seemed more reprehensible when the victim was a little old lady living alone.

On the other hand, this particular little old lady might have pushed Constance down the manor house stairs.

He stood back and regarded the upper windows that were built into the eaves—presumably these were bedrooms. Solomon eyed up the lower and upper windowsills, and the drainage pipe from the guttering. Then, after handing Constance his hat, he leapt up onto the kitchen sill, discovered a decent foothold, and climbed up, holding on to the pipe and the upper sill alternately and scrabbling for footholds. With difficulty, he hauled himself onto the upper sill and, feeling like a Peeping Tom, forced himself to peer in the window.

It was not a bedroom, but another parlor, and a rather cozy, feminine one, too. A fire also burned in this grate beneath a handsome mantelshelf. Above it was a portrait of a young woman in ball dress. She wore an old-fashioned, high-waisted gown and a tiara in her hair. She was not particularly pretty—there was a certain hardness about the eyes and mouth—but it was a face of character, and it bore a strong resemblance to Miss Fernie's. Her left hand rested on her right shoulder, showing off a glittering bracelet made of two strands of diamonds with a ruby at the center. The artist had made it seem that the light reflected off the diamonds and onto the lady's face.

Solomon glanced down at the ground quickly and almost lost his hold on the stone. Constance's anxious face was turned up to him.

"What did Miss Mortimer's bracelet look like?" he asked.

CONSTANCE STUCK SOLOMON'S hat on the end of a tree branch and clambered onto the windowsill with some difficulty.

"Don't come up," he said in alarm.

Naturally, she ignored that, for she had to see. On the other hand, he had a point. Climbing in a crinoline was no easy matter. Since her arms and legs were shorter than Solomon's, she found it easier to shin up the pipe, as she had often done in her reprehensible childhood, until Solomon reached precariously for her hand and helped her jump across the windowsill beside him.

He was scowling, but didn't waste his breath on pointless remonstration.

Secretly glad of his hand at her back, she gazed straight ahead.

The portrait and the bracelet gleamed at her through the glass.

"The bracelet," she murmured, "looked just like that. According to Miss Mortimer's description."

She gazed around the rest of the room, which was furnished with a comfortable, upholstered chair, a table set for one with a tall-backed dining chair, and a couple of smaller tables with ornaments, knickknacks, and a vase.

One of the little tables was draped with fringed silk cloth.

"Could that be the Keatons' stolen shawl?"

"It could," Solomon said grimly. "Look at the round table by the fireside chair. I suspect that is the vicar's prayer book."

It was certainly a small book bound in burgundy leather with elegant gold tooling, the page edges also gleaming with gold leaf.

"All those years ago," Constance said slowly, "she must have stolen Miss Morton's bracelet to wear for her London Season. Or even just to wear to have her portrait painted. Why on earth would she bother when she has to hide it away? She'll never bring anyone here. No one will ever see it. The parlor downstairs is where she takes her guests. Do you suppose all of these things are stolen?"

"Possibly."

An intricately carved, small wooden jewel box stood on top of the shawl-covered table, presumably the one Miss Mortimer had given Mavis Cartwright. Perhaps the bracelet was inside it.

"Why would she take that?" Constance demanded. "Why would she take any of those things? Just for spite?"

"Who knows? I have known an otherwise very fine person who seemed *compelled* just to take things. As if he couldn't help it. But this is...like a shrine to her cleverness, her fantasy. She must have plenty things of her own in that storage room downstairs. This is her secret pleasure. A portrait that can never be admired, surrounded by things she must hide. Can you climb down again?"

That was another good question. Having come this far on the false courage of sheer curiosity, the journey back made Constance's stomach quail. She wanted to close her eyes and beg

Solomon to somehow get her down again, but that was just too poor spirited for her to live with.

Heart in mouth, she launched herself from the sill to the pipe. Her hands and feet scrabbled for purchase and she slid painfully almost half the way down before recovering some measure of control. She reached the bottom with her dignity mostly intact and regarded the front of her skirts and coat with some disfavor. They were covered in dirt, and crumbs of paint and rust, with several pulled threads if no actual holes.

She shook out her skirts, brushing furiously with her equally grubby gloves, which had the leather scraped off a couple of fingertips. *Better than my skin.*

"Are you hurt?" Solomon asked. "Your arm…?"

She flexed it very carefully. "I didn't feel it until now."

"I could just have told you what I saw."

"I know. I wanted to see it for myself."

He helped brush off her skirts with his bare hands. "Well, you were right about Miss Fernie, whatever her reasons. The question is, what do we do about it?"

"Break in and take it all back?"

"We don't even know what is stolen and what is not. We need confirmation."

"Or divine guidance," Constance said flippantly. "Let's go to church."

He brushed something off the brim of her bonnet then rescued his own hat from the tree branch. "Are we decent enough?"

"You are," she said, inspecting him. "I will probably be forbidden entry if Miss Fernie and Mortimer have been spreading their gossip."

He crooked his elbow, she took his arm, and they departed Miss Fernie's garden as if they had every right to be there in the first place.

Even walking very briskly to church, they had missed a chunk of the service. From within came the village voices raised in hymn singing. Solomon opened the heavy door as quietly as possible and they slipped inside.

It was hardly a large church to begin with, and it was already full, the congregation squashed together on the pews and even standing at the back. Several heads turned to see who was so late, including Miss Fernie's near the front. Those who stood at the back—farm laborers, from their dress—shuffled along the wall to make room for Constance and Solomon.

While they all stood singing, Constance had little chance of recognizing most of the congregation, but several of them were certainly children, all singing lustily. Only when the hymn finished, and they all sat, could she begin to see more of the faces.

Nearly everyone she knew in the village was present. The two Mortimers and Miss Jenson at the front, along with the Lance family, Mrs. Raeburn and Miss Fernie. All the Chadwicks were in the row behind, along with the Keatons. Some of the upper servants were scattered among the better-to-do villagers. Mrs. Gimlet and her son were there. And at the back a gaggle of the lesser folk, who included Mavis and Alice Cartwright, clearly sticking together despite the strict observation of hierarchy.

Ogden was not present. Nor were any of the Dickie clan.

The vicar climbed into his pulpit. *Sermon time.* Mavis's gaze was avid, almost frightened, as if she knew he would preach against the anonymous letters and was already acknowledging her wrong. What on earth had possessed her to risk what was left of her reputation? Was it somehow for Alice? Or was Alice actively involved? And how should the matter be resolved for the greater good?

Silver and Grey was contracted to lay their findings before their employer, Dr. Chadwick, although it was possible the fee would be shared with Miss Mortimer and perhaps the others who had received letters. He and they must surely decide how to proceed. It was hardly a matter for the law but... Would they be kind to poor Mavis? Or isolate her further? Would Mrs. Raeburn dismiss Alice?

Had the letters even done any good? Would Miss Mortimer

leave the rents unchanged? Would Mrs. Chadwick ever again delay a message in order to look after her husband? Would Nolan control his anger against the rowdy children? Would Mrs. Keaton stop blaming her poorer customers for anything she mislaid? Or for anything Miss Fernie stole from them…

The vicar began to speak, beginning with a welcome that pointedly included strangers, causing several heads to turn once more to the obvious newcomers at the back. He made a couple of local announcements and read the banns for a wedding. Constance felt her heart lighten as she sought and found Solomon's hand. His fingers closed around hers.

By the time she returned her attention to Mr. Raeburn, he was closing his Bible after reading a short passage. *"Let he who is without sin cast the first stone,"* he repeated in a serious voice, leaning forward from the pulpit to gaze around the congregation, making eye contact with as many as he could. "Can anyone in the world claim that? Can anyone in this church today? God knows I cannot. Can you?"

Mavis bowed her head. Several people shifted in their seats, causing a mass creaking of wood.

The vicar straightened, his whole face suddenly fierce. *"Judge not, lest ye be judged!"* he thundered. *"For with what judgment ye judge, ye shall be judged. And with what measure ye mete, it shall be measured to you again. And why beholdest thou the mote that is in thy brother's eye, but considerest not the beam that is in thine own eye?"*

The whole church suddenly felt electric, as though it had been struck by a divine thunderbolt. The vicar certainly knew how to seize and maintain the attention of his congregation. A baby began to cry. One of the smallest boys Constance had seen in the schoolroom turned his face into his father's arm.

"Oh, it is a very human fault," Mr. Raeburn allowed. "But one we must at all times be aware of. If our neighbor sins against us, by all means we must seek redress, through law or simple discussion. If we see wrong, we are duty bound to speak out, with quiet and human compassion. What we should *not* do"—his voice began to rise again, and the small boy clutched at his father in anticipation—"what we must *never* do, is hide behind a veil of secrecy and spout our own flawed judgments in ways guaranteed to frighten and wound far beyond the original slight, real or imagined. Such a course is cowardly and vile and *must* lead to tragedy for both recipient and sender. It is always the way! The sender of such letters—and yes, you all know of what letters I speak!—goes against God and will be damned for all eternity to the fires of hell!"

Having reached his bellowing crescendo, the vicar again swept his gaze around his congregation, who were staring at him largely open-mouthed.

Constance knew how they felt. Mr. Raeburn was quite the orator and, unlike his usual mild manner, in full flood he was positively scary, tugging at all the emotions, but mostly guilt and fear.

Mavis was clearly drinking it all in, but she showed no alarm. Or even shame, for once. It was as though she were distracted by the vicar's sermon, rather than racked with guilt. Beside her, Alice was glancing uneasily around her neighbors—to see if they were looking toward her mother? Or just wondering if one of them had sent the kind of letter so abhorred by God and the vicar?

"Unless," Mr. Rayburn said, the moderation of his voice so much more moving after the previous haranguing, "the culprit not only desists but repents. And that is what we all must pray for… If we truly repent, God forgives our sins. We should do no less."

Several of the congregation were nodding gravely in agreement and looking about them much as Alice was. Mavis appeared to be more focused on her own sin, which seemed to be habitual for her. Her gaze hovered between the vicar and her own hands. Occasionally, as the vicar continued his theme of redemption through prayer, her lips moved as though in silent plea.

She prayed all the time, Constance thought, yet still felt herself unworthy of forgiveness. So why had she turned to the letters to point out the faults of others? Because no one would have taken her quiet remonstrance seriously? Because she lacked the courage to say it in person?

Such self-flagellation was beyond Constance. The woman had to allow herself what happiness she could find.

Someone else was gazing toward Mavis. Constance noticed because, on the left of the aisle, he was looking to the right and slightly behind, so she could see his face. Nolan the blacksmith, who had once been engaged to Mavis and jilted her when her shame became apparent. Did he too have suspicions? He must have known her very well at one time, have watched her change from whatever bright and promising young woman she had been into the scorned, timid spinster who brought up her child alone in guilt, her only comfort in the church. Did he recognize her as the same girl he had once loved? Or did he know only that she had told him off by anonymous letter? Had that always been in her character?

Judging by his expression, Constance doubted it. For a moment, his habitual scowl vanished. The fierce eyes softened and displayed something like pity. Or more than pity. Constance didn't know him well enough to tell, but there was no accusation there. He had forgiven her everything, perhaps even felt still the regret-tinged love of his youth.

Did *she* know that?

The next instant, the frown returned, and he faced the front once more.

Someone brushed past Constance's skirts—the man with the scared, small boy, who was still sniffing and wiping his tear-stained face on his sleeve while his father led him outside by his other hand.

An innocent casualty of the vicar's fierce sermon, and certainly not the one he had been aiming for. But then, there were a few such innocent casualties of this whole business. In trying to keep them safe, Nolan had frightened some of the children and even put them at risk. And hadn't Nell Dickie had her youngest with her when Mrs. Keaton accused her of stealing and threatened her with arrest? Mrs. Chadwick had been short with Richard Gimlet and delayed passing on his message.

Those circumstances were what had led Constance and Solomon to consider the children as the senders. Perhaps it had even been the effect of the injustices on the children that had inspired Mavis, without her foreseeing that the vicar's sermon would be quite so terrifying.

Even though the vicar's sermons were frequently terrifying, by all accounts… Who would know that better than Mavis?

With unspecific unease, Constance thought of Mavis's avid face listening to the vicar's sermon, focused and surely in agreement. God knew *she* had been judged too much…

So why was she judging Miss Mortimer? Or Mrs. Chadwick? She did not really fit as the judgmental spinster anxious to exert a little power…

Well, every situation, every person, was different.

But Mavis is obsessed with her own sin. Not with other people's…

The expression on Nolan's face bothered Constance. There had been no suspicion in it, none at all.

Am I wrong? Are we *wrong?*

Why had she been so certain? Because Mavis lived alone and could move freely at night, and so could deliver the letters more easily, and because she was a powerless spinster with a grudge, like the woman in the previous case the vicar had come across.

Only Mavis didn't seem to bear any grudges. Rightly or wrongly, she accepted her sin and the scorn of the village as her due for falling… Was it Alice after all? Her mother's only defender, furious with all those judgers with their own eyes full of "beams," as the Bible put it?

Alice did not live alone. She seemed happy and proud of her position in the Raeburns' household, and the only real opportunity she'd had to deliver one of the letters was when she had gone to the manor house in search of the vicar.

But even so, how could she have known in advance that she

would have that opportunity? How could Mavis? Alice must have expected to go to the back door like all servants and never have got near the post in the front hall. To hand the letter over to one of the manor servants would have been to give herself or her mother away. Pure luck had left the front door open. And the maid polishing the mirror in the hall had said nothing about seeing Alice, only feeling the draft. Alice had waited outside.

Which brought Constance back to the drawing room guests. Mr. or Mrs. Raeburn? The vicar would have to be positively evil to preach a sermon like that against something he himself had done! He was not evil. Neither was his wife, although recalling the way she had monopolized Solomon, Constance considered the possibility with unkind relish before discarding it. No one at the vicarage lived alone.

Miss Fernie? The stealing proved her to be considerably subtler than Constance had initially given her credit for. But she had pushed Constance down the stairs for her sin. Not cut out print from a newspaper and sent her an anonymous letter. That was not her way.

Which left only the Chadwicks. The doctor, probably, had been too busy to attend a tea party, but Mrs. Chadwick and Sophie had almost certainly been there…

According to Peregrine Mortimer, *"It was a Wednesday, when they all come bleating for free food."*

And Sophie had borne that out. *"I take him to tea at Miss Mortimer's every Wednesday."*

Constance's heart gave a thump and seemed to stop.

She tightened her grip on Solomon's hand so convulsively that he winced. Her thoughts and other people's words and faces raced through her mind, fading out the vicar's voice and those of the congregation as the ritual prayers continued.

I know who did it. This time I do know. The vicar has not been honest with us…

ABEL DRAYMAN CAME to with the sound of voices in the next room and the sense of danger flexing his limbs. Though he felt awful—mixing gin and rum did that to a man—he sprang up from the bed with silent speed and didn't even feel dizzy until he stood facing the door with his knife in his hand.

Then he did reel slightly, but at least he knew where he was—in one of the back bedrooms of his favorite brothel, where Rosie let him sleep sometimes. There were signs of her presence all around, half-full perfume bottles, skimpy gowns and under-clothes. Her robe was not hanging on the rusty hook on the door, so she must be wearing that while she talked to her visitor in the next room.

"Look, I ain't seen him," Rosie whined more loudly. "You got no cause to come round here bothering my friends."

"We're not bothering your friends, are we, Rosie? Or you."

Drayman's flesh crawled. He knew a peeler when he heard one. Instinctively, his eyes sought the loose plank in the floor, beneath which he'd hidden his good fortune from Rosie's prying eyes.

"I only want to know when you last saw Drayman."

Drayman cursed beneath his breath. They knew his name, whether in connection with the thefts around the docks, or worse, the croaking of Herbert Chase. He had to get out of here. How long would Rosie be able to keep them out?

"Not for ages," she was saying. "Must've been months ago. Or was it…?"

Drayman dropped down and used his knife to ease up the floorboard, trying not to make any sound louder than Rossie could talk over.

"Wait, no, I tell a lie!" she exclaimed. "I saw him just a week ago. Or was it two? Hey, Mags! When was it Abel turned up here, middle of the night, drunk as a wheelbarrow? Was it last

Tuesday? Or the one before?"

"Abel who?" came the muffled answer from another room across the passage.

Drayman grinned as he set the plank aside and loaded up his pockets with what he'd hidden in the floor cavity—a fair bit of money and a few pieces of gold jewelry. He thought briefly of leaving Chase's gold watch. It might get the rozzers off his back by setting them on Rosie instead. But when it came down to it, the watch *was* solid gold, and he needed it. He crammed that into his pocket as well and crept over to the window.

"Anyway, I told him to bugger off, he can't come round here bothering me in that state and expect to stay here for free. Free! I asks you now, inspector, is that fair or reasonable? No, it ain't, so I told him not to come back."

There was another peeler waiting outside the building, his back to the wall, looking for a fight. Drayman wasn't ready to give him one. To the side of the window frame was a narrow, secret door that opened to the next room. Drayman took it and closed it behind him.

One of the whores was snoring her head off on the bed. Drayman ignored her and crept toward the door. On the hook there hung a dirty white cap and a moth-eaten velvet cloak. Grinning, Drayman crammed the cap on his head, swung the cloak about his shoulders, and left the room. The door to Rosie's outer room stood open to the passage. He could still hear the peeler asking questions as he strolled along the passage away from him, swinging his hips as he went.

Then he bolted down the stairs and left by the secret back entrance, avoiding all the traps set for the unwary and unknowing, where he hung the cloak and cap on a spike. From there, it was easy to escape into the dank warren of narrow allies and steps and passages where the rozzers would never find him.

On the other hand, he had to consider how they'd got onto him in the first place. He'd been lying low, on account of the Chase trouble nine years ago, and used a different name until he'd actually seen Chase, most definitely alive, and knew it was all for nothing.

The bastards had sent him off on that vile ship without pay or even the spices he'd taken as his share of Chase's loot. And they'd behaved as if they were doing him a favor! He'd been afraid to go home, even missed the death of his old mum. Chase and Captain Blake had fooled him.

There was no point in getting angry about that again. He'd seen to Chase this time, all right. And relieved him of all he was carrying. He had the feeling that was how the rozzers knew his name. Because there had been another man from the *Mary Anne* at the Crown and Anchor that night.

Johnny, who'd not been right in the head. Or he was delirious with fever. Drayman hadn't really cared which at the time, but he'd clocked Johnny in the Crown and Anchor. He'd seen him look in a puzzled sort of a way at Chase too, though he'd paid no attention to Drayman.

But later, when he'd been going through Chase's pockets, it was Johnny who'd come out and seen him. He'd shouted and the peelers had come running, and both Johnny and Drayman had it away on their toes in opposite directions.

They must have caught Johnny, who'd have bought his own life with Drayman's name.

In which case, Johnny was the only proof they had. Drayman would be happy enough to do away with him too. If he could find him.

✦

CHAPTER EIGHTEEN

THE REVEREND LUKE Raeburn was quite pleased with his sermon. Several of his flock looked suitably chastened, which had to be good for many reasons. Abigail, his wife, wore an expression of approval. On top of which, Mrs. Silver and Mr. Grey, who'd had the discourtesy to arrive late and now stood at the back of the church with the tail end of the laborers in their Sunday best, were watching the congregation as well as listening. Their attention was diverted, for now, but it was time to end this before they got to the truth and turned the whole community upside down.

Having blessed his flock, he made his stately way down the aisle, aware of the respectful gaze of everyone he passed. He was not being arrogant to believe he had done good work in Sutton May. As he reached the door, which the verger opened for him, he glimpsed Mrs. Silver again, still watching him with an expression that drowned his self-satisfaction in unease.

It was as if she could not look away and yet she was thinking of something else entirely—stricken, yet busy in her mind.

Had he misjudged? Sometimes, he got carried away by his own oratory and said more than he had planned to. To him, such moments came from God, and he delighted in them. But had God made him speak words that defeated his main objective?

In the cold, fresh air of the porch, he recalled his own words while he prepared to greet his departing parishioners. He could find nothing that betrayed the truth. No, there had been no letters for more than a week, and now there would be no more at all. Dr. Chadwick's investigators would have to give up and go home, and Luke and everyone else could move forward.

Bother Chadwick! He had told the doctor not to drag strangers into this…

Miss Mortimer and Miss Jenson made their slow way out of the church, escorted by young Peregrine. Smiling, Luke shook hands with them all and exchanged a word with each before they moved on either to churchyard gossip or to their carriage, according to their various moods. Luke greeted the rest of his congregation by name, exchanging a word with each. He knew them all so well now, it was almost mechanical, yet his interest was always genuine as he asked after various ailments and family members, troubles and joys in their lives. They were his flock and he would always look after them.

As well as his family.

Abigail and the children had stopped just inside the door, where Mrs. Silver and Mr. Grey were lingering as though determined to be the last to leave, as they had been to arrive. Abigail, bless her, ushered the strangers out before her. She had never been immune to a handsome man, and she had certainly noticed Grey, who was certainly *different* from anyone else she knew.

As a young man, her "noticing" of other males had made Luke unbecomingly jealous. Older and wiser now, he accepted it as part of *her*. After all, she only ever looked.

He took Mrs. Silver's hand. "How lovely to see you this morning. I'm only sorry you could not find a place to sit."

"Oh, we were happy to stand, and we learned much from your service. I wonder if we might speak in private?"

His heart jolted. He reminded himself that they were curious people, were employed to be so, and that he should not be surprised. It did not mean his sermon hadn't worked. It just meant they would finish investigating every avenue before they left. Hopefully tomorrow or the day after.

"Of course," he replied, smiling. "Abigail will take you to the vicarage while I finish here and join you in a few minutes. If that suits?"

"Indeed it does."

In fact, there was little for him to do in the church, and the cold had scattered his flock back to the warmth of their own homes. Or the Blue Goose taproom. But he needed the moments alone to rearrange his thoughts.

Or, at least, he imagined he did. In fact, by the time he closed the church door and strode up to the vicarage, he realized he had already thought everything out to perfection. All that was required was for him to repeat his previous assertions, with added reassurance.

Abigail had done exactly the right thing, showing their guests into the study, where she stayed drinking hot chocolate with them until he arrived. She then poured him some chocolate of his own and whisked herself out of the room.

It was a cozy, friendly scene of the kind Luke liked best.

Cradling his cup in both hands, he smiled faintly. "I take it you wish to discuss your inquiries?"

"We do," Mrs. Silver confirmed.

Luke did not quite like the way she thrust herself forward into the lead, as it were, while her betrothed was present to speak for them. But if he noticed, Grey seemed content to let her.

Mrs. Silver set down her cup and saucer. "I almost accused an innocent woman of sending those letters, a woman who had already been accused of much that was not, in my opinion, her fault. Can you imagine how bad we would have made her feel by my mistake?"

"I suppose it is a risk of your—er…profession," Luke replied, hiding his triumph. He was right. He had retaken control of the situation.

"It is. And we hate making such mistakes, but in this case, we did not have all the facts, did we?"

"I suppose you can't have," Luke said calmly.

"Sir, did you receive one of those letters?"

That was not what he had expected. He played for time by sipping his hot chocolate—which was, in fact, lukewarm. "I have already told you I did not." He transferred his gaze to Grey, who surely had the superior understanding. "Look, I believe the matter has been dealt with. You heard my sermon. There will be no more letters. Together with the alarm engendered by your inquiries, we have put the fear of God into the sender, who will repent and sin no more."

"I think you are right about all of that," Mrs. Silver said. "Except the sermon bit. That was as much to mislead us as to persuade the sinner to repent, was it not? Please, vicar, show us your letter."

His stomach tightened. Holding Grey's steady gaze became increasingly difficult.

"We know who sent them," Mrs. Silver said. "We just need to be sure."

And so he had snatched defeat from the jaws of victory… Or was the woman lying? Grey clearly believed her. Luke would have to throw himself on their mercy and hope they had some.

He placed his cup deliberately in the saucer on his desk. "I destroyed my letter. To be honest, I was somewhat ashamed to receive it."

"Why?" Grey asked, speaking for the first time since Luke had come in. "Were you ashamed because its accusation was true?"

Luke swallowed and nodded. "They were all true in their way."

"Did it accuse you of frightening the children with your fiery sermons?" Mrs. Silver asked.

Luke nodded slowly. "I get carried away. I believe my enthusiasm comes from God, but that is no excuse for delivering his words the way I did. The sad thing is, I did not even notice the effect on the children, until it was pointed out to me. I did take more care, but the damage will take some time to work out. Especially as I *had* to be a little more dramatic today. Poor Archie

Smith had to be taken out again, even though I said nothing about the tortures of hell."

"Children have imagination," Mrs. Silver said, though it didn't seem to be an accusation. "But it was that frightened child leaving that suddenly let me see the truth. All those letters were to do with the children."

Uh-oh...

Grey began to speak, looking not at Luke now but at Mrs. Silver. "Mrs. Chadwick kept back a message carried by Richard Gimlet about his sister's sickness. The boy was so angry, no doubt, because he felt *he* was the cause of her death. He hadn't been clear enough or forceful enough with his message. When, in fact, Mrs. Chadwick had merely been looking after her exhausted husband, and the poor child would have died anyway.

"Nolan endangered and frightened children by the way he chased them from his shop. We noticed one child scurrying to the other side of an older sibling as they approached the smithy. Nell Dickie had her youngest with her when Mrs. Keaton threatened to have her thrown in prison. Miss Mortimer... If she puts the rent up, all the tenants will suffer. Some might have to leave and put laborers out of work too. The children of all those families would be included in that suffering."

Mrs. Silver looked oddly relieved. "Exactly. And who knows the children best? Who hears their problems through chatter and stories in the classroom? Who defends them?"

Luke sighed. He had tried and failed. She had struck the truth and all three of them knew it. "I wish it had been me."

"But," Grey said, "it is Mr. Ogden."

SOMETIMES, MAVIS COULD not bear the emptiness of her little cottage. She decided to avoid it for a little after church, by taking a walk away from the village, with the vicar's sermon still ringing in her ears.

As she walked past families going home to enjoy their Sunday meals together, she tried not to feel oppressed with loneliness. Her own family had disowned her when she was pregnant with Alice. Unable to endure the shame, they had moved across the county and vanished from her life. Then there had been Alice, of course, her one earthly joy and comfort.

Although she tried not to, she missed Alice, and she missed her old dream of family and husband and a place in the village…among people she had imagined were her friends. It was, of course, the price of sin, and she did find comfort in God and prayer. And Mr. Raeburn was kinder than the previous vicar had been.

She took the quiet path toward the manor woods and walked more briskly in an effort to shake off her mood of self-pity. She appreciated the beauty of the countryside and the wonder of God's creation. A clump of bright-yellow daffodils made her smile, as did the chirping of the birds and the feel of the wind against her cheek…

She had almost reached the wood before she became aware of the steps behind her. She thought at first it was children—they followed her up the street, sometimes, making fun of her behind her back because to them she was just a funny old woman whom their parents and grandparents didn't speak to. Even Alice didn't know how much the scorn of the children hurt her.

She turned to face them. That usually sent them scampering off, because they were not bad children, but her jaw dropped in shock. No children. Just the very large figure of Matt Nolan.

They had not spoken in nearly thirty years. It had been strangely easy in the community this size to ignore each other, even at church. She was not used to looking at him, to taking in his ageing face, his beard, his scowl. Poor Matt, he was still not at peace.

She dropped her eyes and stood aside, waiting for him to pass her.

Instead, he halted. "Mavis."

Her gaze flew back to his. "Matt," she whispered.

He swallowed, and it came to her with astonishment that he was nervous. More than that, had he followed her out of the village just to speak to her?

"Have I done something wrong?" she asked.

He squeezed his eyes shut for a moment. "No. I doubt you ever did. A proud and hurt young man is too free with his judgments."

She felt her eyes widen. He had been listening to the vicar. Words choked in her throat. *I was too timid when I should have been strong. I should have died rather than hurt you, hurt us...* "It was all a long time ago," she managed.

"Too long." He swallowed again. "May I walk with you, Mavis?"

Mavis blinked. There was no one around. No one was making fun of her. Matt was not.

She couldn't speak, but she nodded once, and they moved on together.

SOLOMON HAD KNOWN the moment Constance solved the case. In church, her hand had gripped his to the point of pain, and she had gazed unseeingly ahead while she tested it in her mind. He had watched the excitement and the sadness grow and knew she had found the all-important truth.

Not Mavis or Alice.

Well, their motive had never seemed quite *enough*, although their guilt was certainly possible. It just wasn't true.

Maddeningly, there had been no opportunity to learn Constance's thoughts because they were surrounded by people. Even at the vicarage, Mrs. Raeburn hadn't left them alone for a moment, and Constance herself had turned uncharacteristically quiet. So Solomon felt his way to the truth through her questions and the vicar's answers.

Ogden.

Solomon's stomach twisted in protest, for he rather liked the eccentric teacher and had instinctively trusted him. He thought himself a good judge of character, and yet he knew Constance was right. He too could see it all now.

"You guessed the sender," Constance said to Raeburn. "But you like him, admire him, even. You helped to choose him and probably feel responsible for him in some way. Moreover, you know that on the whole he is good for the village, especially the children. So you kept your own letter away from us—perhaps it gave more away than the others—and you sent us deliberately on the wrong track with tales of a previous and no-doubt-mythical case involving a powerless spinster with grudges."

"Actually, that was all true," Raeburn said with dignity. "I knew none of *our* spinsters were guilty, so you would never find anything that could lead to an accusation."

Solomon said, "Did you forget that Alice came to fetch you from the manor house on the day Miss Mortimer received her letter?"

"Alice?" Raeburn blanched. "Dear God… In fact, I did not know about Miss Mortimer's letter until you mentioned it today. She never confided in me. Well, there's a lesson in humility. I am very glad you refrained from accusing poor Alice. Or her mother."

"It was a near-run thing," Constance said ruefully. "I was too eager to finish this case for personal reasons. But your sermon today was for *us*, too, wasn't it? Perhaps partly to discourage anyone else from sending similar letters, but mainly to convince *us* there would be no more, that you had it all in hand and we might as well leave."

"You could not stay forever," Raeburn said apologetically.

And possibly, Solomon thought, the vicar was eager to have him removed from Mrs. Raeburn's vicinity. In truth, Solomon was not averse to that either.

Raeburn drew a deep breath. "Look, my friends, I will gladly admit that I should have been more open with you from the outset, and perhaps I should have acted sooner to stop the letters. In truth, I thought Ogden had seen the error of his ways already, for he is not a stupid man, and I have never known him to repeat a mistake. Only then there was Mrs. Chadwick's letter. But I truly believe there will be no more. I shall speak to him, of course, to be sure he understands…

"There is no malice in Quintin Ogden, you know," he added. "He is a good and caring man, as well as being the cleverest teacher we are ever likely to attract to Sutton May. He just reasons differently from you or me. By nature, he is honest, disastrously so on occasions, and he has learned by hard experience that such honesty can offend and work against him and against whatever he is trying to achieve."

Raeburn spread his hands in a gesture of helplessness. "As far as the letters are concerned, he merely thought he had solved every problem of offense and danger to get his point across, without realizing the havoc he would cause."

Constance nodded as though she understood. "To him, it made sense."

"He had to speak to defend the children," Solomon said, "but he could not risk his position, his livelihood, by offending those who had appointed him, namely you and Miss Mortimer. Nor could he defend the children at all if he was dismissed from his post. So the letters seemed a perfect solution at first. Especially, I suspect, when you toned down your sermon in response. He decided his method was successful and tried it on Nolan and the Keatons."

Solomon shook his head because he still could not quite grasp Ogden's reasoning. "Yet from what you say, he is clever enough to have realized that those letters to Nolan and the Keatons had no effect at all. So why then trouble Mrs. Chadwick with one? Was that not unnecessarily cruel when she was already punishing herself? She is a kind woman who has no hold over him. Couldn't he have spoken to her instead?"

"Not when he wants to marry Sophie," Constance said. "He couldn't risk alienating her parents further."

"*Does* he want to marry her, though?" Solomon asked.

"Oh yes," Constance said, "though he might not be fully aware of it just yet. The question we have to answer is, what do we do about our knowledge?"

Raeburn met her gaze. "Are you not all for second chances, Mrs. Silver?"

Solomon tensed. Was that a jab at Constance's past? He would not have her insulted by anyone.

But she smiled. "I gather Miss Fernie has been talking to you."

The vicar grimaced. "Miss Fernie is one of those I was addressing on the subject of self-righteous judgments. I make no charges against you, Mrs. Silver. Nor would I. I merely point out that we *all* deserve a second chance. At least in matters that do not break the law of the land."

"Will Dr. Chadwick agree?" Constance asked. "Especially if Ogden and Sophie want to marry in the teeth of parental disapproval. And the doctor is clearly upset about the letter on his wife's behalf."

Raeburn steepled his fingers under his chin. "I understand you have an obligation."

"And we also believe in second chances," Solomon said. "But we have to lay the truth before Chadwick and see how he wishes to proceed. This is not a matter of the law; it is a matter of village respect. And I suspect few would understand or forgive Ogden. But Chadwick is not a vindictive man, and I believe Ogden could put matters right with an apology."

"To everyone concerned?" Raeburn asked doubtfully.

Solomon met his gaze. "Does everyone concerned care? Nolan doesn't. Nor do the Keatons, or not beyond gossip rights, in my opinion. Providing Ogden understands his error, I don't see

why a doctor and a vicar—those most given to confidentiality—
cannot make things right with Miss Mortimer and let the matter
of the letters sink into the annals of village folklore."

"*Mr.* Mortimer must not be told," Constance said at once.
"He hates Mr. Ogden and would cause trouble if he could."

"Then we shan't let him." Raeburn rose from his chair. "Are
you going to the Chadwicks' now? Perhaps I should accompany
you."

DR. CHADWICK LOOKED forward to a rare Sunday meal with his
family. Barring emergencies, he thought he might just have the
day to himself.

For once, they all gathered by the fire in the parlor after
church, with warming drinks to hand—why were churches
always such wretchedly cold places?—and he thought again how
lucky he was. Emmeline was smiling faintly, her trouble over
Jenny Gimlet's death and the letter eased, at least for the
moment. Edgar was laughing over some banter with his sister.
Sophie…

Sophie was looking particularly happy. She was quick to smile
these days, and today her eyes positively sparkled. His daughter
was a beautiful girl, but one with her feet on the ground and
kindness in her heart. Like her mother.

Chadwick felt an ache in his heart, a happy, appreciative ache,
for his family was precious to him. He wished he had more time
to enjoy with them. Sophie would surely marry in a few years
and be gone. Edgar was growing up so fast. There should be
more days like these.

The sound of the front door knocker interrupted his thoughts
and his heart sank. Everyone heard it, though they all pretended
not to. They carried on chatting while Nora's footsteps sounded
hurrying up the passage from the kitchen…and back again.

Nora's head appeared around the door. With a sigh, Chadwick rose to his feet to deal with the inevitable medical emergency.

"Mr. Ogden is here, asking for you, sir."

"Oh!" Sophie jumped to her feet too.

"He says he's not ill," Nora added.

Chadwick brightened. "Show him in, then, Nora."

Ogden was a slightly awkward young man, though Chadwick never held that against him. In fact, Chadwick approved of him, for he had brought Edgar forward in leaps and bounds, academically speaking, and encouraged a change of attitude to school and to other people.

"Greetings, Mr. Ogden," Chadwick said cheerfully, going forward to shake his hand. "Come and sit down. Cup of tea? Glass of sherry?"

"Oh, no thank you." Inexplicably, Ogden's hands were shaking.

So was the rest of him. The man was intensely nervous. He sat down on the edge of the chair Edgar vacated for him and cast a quick glance around the room. His eyes rested briefly on Sophie, who seemed to be glowing as she returned to her chair.

"I have something to tell you," Ogden blurted. "And something to ask you. I've tied myself in knots working out which to do first, but this is the only honest way." He wiped the palms of his hands on his trousers, then clasped them together tightly in his lap, perhaps to hide their trembling. "It's about the letter."

"Letter?" Sophie repeated, clearly startled.

"Well, letters, plural. The anonymous letters."

Chagrin flickered in Sophie's face, and then a sort of resigned amusement. No, this was not what she had expected.

Emmeline was frowning. "You know something about the letters?"

"I know everything about the letters," Ogden stated. "I made them and I sent them."

"*What?*" Chadwick sprang to his feet again.

Color surged into Emmeline's cheeks and Chadwick went to her, dropping his hand to her shoulder in comfort. Sophie's face was suddenly white. Edgar stared at his teacher, almost fascinated.

In Chadwick, fury warred with sheer disappointment. He knew an urge to strike the younger man.

"Why?" he barked. "Why would you do such a nasty thing? And to my wife…!"

"I'm sorry," Ogden said desperately. "I was wrong, misguided, and I truly never meant to cause you pain."

"She was already in pain," Sophie said hoarsely. "How could you, Quintin?"

The utter misery in the young man's eyes disarmed Chadwick into silence.

It was Edgar who said clearly, "I don't understand."

"I'm not surprised," Ogden said. "I don't understand it myself now. I've tried to teach you and the other children to *do as you would be done by*, to see things from each other's points of view. And yet *I* forgot to. I saw only Richard Gimlet's pain, and wanted to stop any other such tragedy…" He shook his head, almost violently, and seemed to force himself to meet Emmeline's gaze. "I was blind. I knew you for a kind lady, and I knew Sophie's— um…Miss Chadwick's affection and admiration, and yet I still thought I could do good by such means. I never thought of your being hurt or frightened by it."

"How could you *not*?" Chadwick exploded.

Ogden's hands twisted. "I don't know." He swallowed convulsively. "I am quick in some things, slow in others. It's just the way my mind works, though I strive to make it better… I—I don't want you to be hurt or frightened anymore, Mrs. Chadwick, and I thought you wouldn't be if I told you. And you knew how sorry I am, how appalled with myself, not just for yours but for the others. I thought I was standing up for the children, making things better… Totally misguided, you see."

"Totally," Emmeline said faintly. She took a deep breath.

"Thank you for telling me this, Mr. Ogden. I am shocked. But…oddly, it does make me feel just a little better."

"Jenny's parents don't blame you either," Ogden said. "I know, because I spoke to them about Richard." His Adam's apple wobbled as he swallowed. "I asked you to return to kindness, Mrs. Chadwick, but you never left it. I did."

"Oh, Quint," Sophie whispered.

Chadwick sank back down onto his chair. Well, he thought numbly, that was that problem solved, and without the aid of his expensive investigators from London.

"There is more," Ogden said in a rush. "I think I also wanted you to be more receptive to Sophie—er…to Miss Chadwick's wishes and stop leaving her alone with Mr. Mortimer, who is not a good man. Neither am I, of course. But I do love her, and you had to know everything before I asked you for her hand in marriage."

Chadwick's jaw dropped. A stunned silence echoed around the room.

"Oh, *Quint!*" Sophie said again, in what sounded like sheer frustration.

Which was when the parlor door opened again and the vicar walked in, followed by the expensive investigators from London.

CHAPTER NINETEEN

CONSTANCE SAW AT once that they had walked into a fraught moment. Everyone in the room was staring at Ogden, who seemed curiously resigned.

Mrs. Chadwick roused herself to welcome them, and everyone else followed suit as though pulled by the puppet strings of civility.

"Forgive the intrusion," the vicar said. "I suspect we are too late to avert the storm."

"Mr. Ogden," Chadwick said furiously, "has just simultaneously confessed to a heinous crime and made my daughter an offer of marriage!"

Constance's lip twitched, an involuntary gesture caught by Sophie, who stared for instant before a rueful, conspiratorial sort of humor touched her eyes.

"Have I done the wrong thing again?" Ogden asked humbly.

And Sophie choked out a laugh, throwing out her hand to him. He caught it eagerly.

"No!" Mrs. Chadwick exclaimed. "Sophie, you have just heard... You cannot throw yourself away so young on such a-a..."

"A what, Mama?" Sophie said. "A good, clever man who occasionally makes mistakes? Show me anyone who does not."

"Mistakes!" her mother repeated, flabbergasted.

"Do we take it," Solomon interrupted, "that Mr. Ogden has just tried to rectify his mistakes by confessing to them?"

"And proposing marriage in the same breath," Dr. Chadwick said. "*I* take it you are aware of what he has done? All of you and Sophie—"

"Oh, Sophie didn't know," Ogden said. "I didn't have the courage to tell her until now. But it had to be done." He looked from the vicar to Constance and Solomon. "How do *you* know?"

"Constance worked it out," Solomon said. "Once she realized that children were the motive for all the letters. And you had the best opportunity, being able to wander about at all hours of the night—and being taken each Wednesday to tea with Miss Mortimer."

Mrs. Chadwick's eyes widened. "You sent a letter to *Miss Mortimer?*"

Ogden shifted in his seat. "It seemed a good idea at the time."

"Well now," the vicar said, "shall we all sit down and discuss this?"

With the same focus he seemed to bring to his teaching, Ogden followed the conversation about his letters and the subsequent arguments for and against dismissing him for it. He did not contribute, though he seemed puzzled by the vicar's defense of him, and by Constance and Solomon's explaining the advantages of forgiveness and silence to Chadwick.

"Sounds fair to me," Edgar pronounced. "*We* always get two chances at school, and Mr. Ogden owned up *before* he was found out. Besides, school will be terrible if he has to go. We might get *Miss Fernie* back."

"Maybe, but it isn't up to you," Dr. Chadwick said, scowling. "It is up to your mother. And the others who received the letters."

Everyone gazed expectantly at Mrs. Chadwick, who took a deep breath. "I am inclined to forgive him. He meant no malice, and I believe him when he says he would never go down such a misguided road again. But I am not the only one who received a letter. Miss Mortimer…"

"I shall ascertain Miss Mortimer's wishes in the matter,"

Raeburn said smoothly. "But I believe she will think as Mrs. Chadwick does."

"But she'll tell Perry," Sophie said, appalled. "And he will *persecute* Quintin mercilessly!"

"I don't believe she will. Miss Mortimer and Miss Jenson have ways of keeping their own secrets."

"And you should know," Sophie added defiantly, "that there is no way in the world I would *ever* marry Perry Mortimer. Not even if he asked me, which he assuredly will not."

"You don't know that, Sophie," Mrs. Chadwick began. "You are too young."

"In this case, I believe she is right," Constance said. "It is he who is too young. None of his intentions would appear to be honorable at this point in his life, and I believe he sets his matrimonial sights on the aristocracy."

"Even so, Sophie, consider," Mrs. Chadwick pleaded. "A poor schoolteacher…"

"A poor physician," her husband reminded her gently, and she turned quickly to look at him.

"You will allow this?"

"I would allow an engagement—of some months—if it is what Sophie truly wants."

Ogden's intensity was painful. Constance had never seen anyone in such an agony of uncertainty. "Did I ruin it, by doing what I did?" he asked hoarsely. "Is marriage with me what you want, Sophie?"

Sophie met his gaze, her color fluctuating as the silence stretched. "No."

His gaze fell. Everything about him seemed to slump in total defeat.

"No," she repeated. "You didn't ruin it, though I'll confess you took me by surprise. And yes, marriage with you is what I want."

Happiness seemed to blaze between them. Over their heads, Constance met Soloman's gaze in a quick, all-too-brief moment of understanding. Happiness seemed to be infectious.

It was time to go.

"Well?" she said, when they were once more in the street, arm in arm. "Shall we go home and be married? There might be a late train."

"I have one more thing to do. And no, you shouldn't come. I doubt she would let both of us over the door."

SOLOMON'S FINAL VISIT of the day was to Miss Fernie.

When he knocked on the door, she was clearly upstairs, no doubt in her secret parlor of stolen treasures, for he heard her footsteps descending before she opened the door. Her eyes widened in astonishment, then darted to either side, no doubt in search of the absent Constance.

"Mr. Grey."

He removed his hat and inclined his head. "Miss Fernie. I trust you'll forgive this intrusion on the sabbath, but there is something I must discuss with you."

She opened the door wider. "Come in."

He was led, of course, to the front parlor, where the fire still blazed merrily. Obviously, she did not need to economize on winter warmth.

"Please, sit," she said politely, although she did not offer refreshments. When he had taken the chair she indicated and she had sat on the opposite side of the fireplace, she said, "Have you come about your betrothed?"

Solomon raised his brows. "I have not. I'm afraid I have come about you."

She blinked, uncomprehending. "Me? I have already told you everything I know about these foolish letters, which is nothing at all."

"Oh, we are no longer concerned with that," Solomon said

with an airy wave of his hand. "The matter is dealt with. But during our investigation, another matter came to light which is, sadly, criminal."

"In Sutton May?" she said incredulously. "Then I would look no further than the so-called schoolteacher. This is what comes of raising common people out of their class."

Solomon sighed and held her gaze. "Miss Fernie."

Rather to his surprise, color seeped into her thin cheeks. "Well, what is it?"

"A matter of thefts committed over decades. A bracelet, a carved jewelry box, a *Book of Common Prayer* valued by the vicar…"

"I have heard of all these. They were not stolen but mislaid."

"Then what," Solomon asked, "are they doing in your up-stairs parlor?"

Her pursed lips parted in shock. She stared at him but recovered quickly. "I rather think the question is what were *you* doing in my upstairs parlor? Breaking and entering is a crime I shall be most happy to report to Mr. Heron!"

"Really? For the record, I did not enter but merely climbed up and looked through your window. We can, of course, go down the road of formal accusation and counteraccusation, and let the law sort it out. Miss Mortimer might even save you by claiming she lent you the bracelet for that really rather good portrait above the fireplace."

"She did!" Miss Fernie gasped.

"No, she didn't. Nor did Mavis Cartwright lend you the jew-elry box. Why on earth did you steal such things? You, who already has so much more."

Miss Fernie glared at him, half lifted one hand in dismissal, then dropped it and stared into the fire instead. "None of my family gave *me* beautiful things. My uncles and cousins were rich, and yet they thought their duty to us done by allowing me to stay in their home during a few London Seasons, attend a few parties with them in my provincial clothes. Jessica always had lovely gowns and jewels to shine in and she never even *thought* to lend them to me."

"So you took the bracelet for your own Season, had your portrait painted in it, and never gave the original back. What of the box?"

Her lips twisted. "Jessica would have *given* that Jezebel the bracelet! And she did give her the box. I saw it every time I called on Mavis, until all I could think was that she did not deserve it."

"And the vicar," Solomon said quietly. "Did the vicar not deserve his beautiful prayer book? A gift from his wife?"

"The vicar is a good man," she said sulkily. "But Abigail Raeburn is a silly, worldly woman who saw fit to dispute with me at the Christian Women's Circle."

"And the shawl you stole from the Keatons' shop?"

She shrugged with impatience. "She can be too sharp, Faye Keaton, imagining she and I are equal because she has a little money now."

Solomon leaned back in his chair. "They're excuses, aren't they? Reasons to justify what you did because you knew you were in the wrong."

A shudder shook her, but she said nothing.

"Are they the only things you took over the years?" he asked.

Slowly, she shook her head. A tear formed at the corner of her eye and trickled down her winkled cheek.

"I can't help it," she whispered. "It just comes upon me, and I *have* to take them. And then I make the best of them, because after all, I can't give them back, can I?"

"Why not?"

She blinked at him.

"I had the same kind of problem with an employee of mine once," Solomon said. "He described it as an illness, and I think it is—brought on, perhaps, by unhappiness at a life that isn't going according to your dreams. But that does not mean you can't make it right."

"How?" she demanded, gulping as though for air.

"Give them back. *Sneak* them back, if you have to. Make it a game, and smile at your friends' happiness in finally finding the things that mean so much to them."

"I could…" She frowned and sat up straighter. "I could!"

"No," Solomon said, holding her gaze once more. "You *will*. Because that is the only agreement I will make with you, and I will find out. I can sympathize with your compulsion. But you were quite prepared to let Nell Dickie take the blame for your theft—while her frightened child was with her, too. There is no excuse for that. Nor for pushing Mrs. Silver down the stairs at the manor house, and I *will* prosecute you for that with great pleasure if you do not begin today returning your stolen goods. *And* if anyone in this village suffers an unexplained accident, *everyone* will know where to look."

He rose abruptly because pity had dissolved once more into anger.

Miss Fernie opened her mouth to speak, but Solomon raised his hand. "Your opinion of Mrs. Silver does not matter to me. You do not know her. But know *this*—her compassion is all that prevented my bringing Constable Heron with me today and charging you with *everything*. Do you understand me?"

She was trembling, and he was not sorry for that either.

"Yes," she whispered.

"Then we have a bargain?"

"Yes."

He nodded curtly. "Good," he said, and left the house with a massive sense of relief.

FOR WANT OF anything better to do, David punctuated reading Solomon's books with sketching the view from the window, and remembered faces from his past. Then he read everything new on Solomon's desk. He didn't understand all of it—much of it was to do with money and investments and ships—but his brother seemed to have fingers in many pies, and the amounts of money involved were incomprehensible.

What he did begin to comprehend was the strange, ordered, but lonely life his brother had led, especially since leaving Jamaica. There was no correspondence from friends. It was all business and charity boards, or invitations that were politely declined. And amongst it all, reports from all over the world from people Solomon paid to look out for his brother and investigate all possible sightings. Which might have been the inspiration behind the birth of Silver and Grey Inquiries with the enigmatic Constance.

David wasn't quite sure what to make of her. She wasn't like any whore he had ever met, or like any wealthy lady who had occasionally brushed past him with her nose in the air. Who was David to judge anyone's past? Or present. She looked out for Solomon and was helping David because of Solomon, and that was fine with him.

His brother's face changed when he spoke of her, when he looked at her. Which, oddly, gave David hope for himself. In the time he had spent in this house, a new sense of freedom had begun to grow, in bizarre counterpoint to the knowledge that he was trapped indoors.

Reuniting with Solomon seemed to have freed him in a way his previous wanderings never had. He had money from the Jamaican estate. He could do something else. Whatever he liked. Perhaps even nothing, although that seemed dull.

But any future depended on his not being hanged for Chase's murder. When would Solomon be back?

In abrupt need of fresh air, he stood up and clattered downstairs—then froze, for Jenks the manservant stood in the hall conversing with a middle-aged stranger who looked right at him.

Jenks turned in his usual unhurried manner and inclined his head respectfully. "Sir, Inspector Omand of the police has called."

For an instant, David felt sick. It was all over.

And he didn't want it to be. He had *more* than freedom now. He had his brother. And hope and life.

Pretending to be Solomon was an old skill. Pretending to be adult Solomon, a man he barely knew, was something else entirely. But in for a penny…

He forced his feet forward, using Solomon's elegant saunter. And Solomon's accent, which he had only practiced once in front of the mirror. "So he has. Good afternoon, inspector. What can I do for you?"

Inspector Omand had a kindly face, but David didn't let that fool him. He also had extremely shrewd eyes.

The policeman took off his hat. "Sorry to interrupt on a Sunday, sir. I was just passing and thought you might like to know that we tracked Drayman down to a brothel that's more than half rookery."

"Then you have him?" David's heart drummed with excitement. Was that it? Was he cleared?

Omand grimaced. "Sadly not. He bolted, taking his ill-gotten gains with him."

"Damn."

"Well, at least we know he's guilty of something. And we can find him again. Just thought you'd like to know, but I won't keep you. Good day, Mr. Grey."

"Good day."

Omand departed, and as Jenks closed the door behind him, David breathed a massive sigh of relief.

"Did I fool him?" David asked.

"You almost fooled *me*," Jenks replied.

But David's brain had jumped back to Drayman on the *Mary Anne*—on shore, hiding from a set of ruffians. Catching his breath, he ran up to the front door and wrenched it open.

"Inspector!"

Omand, who was several yards away, swung back in surprise and, as David strode out, hurried back to meet him.

"Inspector, where exactly is that brothel you found him in?"

CONSTANCE AND SOLOMON caught the evening train back to London. Dr. Chadwick accompanied them to the station and waved them off.

"Thank you," he said ruefully. "I think."

"Ogden's a good man," Constance replied. "And with Sophie, I believe he and the school will thrive. And you'll still have her in the village with you."

"That is a good point," he allowed, and bowed over her hand. "And I do thank you. Goodbye, Mrs. Silver."

Solomon handed her up onto the train and she walked forward. Through the window, she could see Solomon talking quickly to the doctor before they shook hands and he climbed aboard.

"What was that about?" she asked when they were seated side by side and alone, and the train was puffing noisily out of the station.

"I suggested both he and the vicar make Miss Mortimer understand her nephew's habits are unacceptable. She is the only one who can influence his behavior, since she holds the purse strings."

"I should have thought of that…"

"I also mentioned Miss Fernie. I don't want her pushing anyone else downstairs."

"Well, making her return the stolen items, which she will inevitably do as secretly as she took them, should keep her occupied for a while. I do think I was a bit of an exception for her. She can tolerate fallen women like poor, remorseful Mavis, but she's never encountered a brazen jezebel before."

"Constance," he said.

"What?"

"Shall we be married and go off on a wedding journey?"

"Haven't we already agreed to that?"

"It's a lady's privilege to change her mind. Besides, I meant now. As soon as I receive the license. And find a house."

"What if it needs work?"

"Then we'll get someone to do the work while we're away."

She slid her hand into his. "That is a good idea."

"I thought so."

Weeks alone with Solomon, without anyone else's problems and puzzles to think about… The idea was intoxicating. To enjoy his full, unadulterated attention—and to give him hers. She *needed* that. But…

"There is still the small matter of David and the murder of Herbert Chase."

"We are almost there," Solomon said.

CHAPTER TWENTY

I T WAS LATE by the time they reached Solomon's house, but Jenks still appeared as soon as they entered. More interestingly, so did David, though from the top of the stairs.

"All quiet, Jenks?" Solomon said quietly.

"Apart from one visit from Inspector Omand, which went very well. I'm sure Mr. David will explain all."

"Thanks, Jenks. Don't wait up any longer."

Constance thought Solomon would rush to his brother to be sure he was not badly affected by the police scare, and certainly he wasted no time, but he took Constance's hand before striding to the stairs and hurrying up. That inclusion warmed her, erasing a concern she hadn't even acknowledged.

For his part, David looked more alive than she had ever seen him. The fear had vanished from his face, and he looked even more like Solomon, his eyes blazing with excitement.

"I know where he is," he blurted as soon they reached him.

Solomon led the way into the sitting room. "Drayman? Did Omand's men find him?"

David grimaced. "And lost him again." He dropped in the nearest chair, then, remembering his manners, sprang back up again and waited for Constance to sit first.

She did, as though she hadn't noticed his lapse. "Then how do you know where he is now?"

"Because I know Drayman," David said at once. "It was a trick he played in Sicily—ran from his enemies to his mistress's house, then bolted as soon as they approached, and when they'd torn the place apart looking for him and given up for pastures new, he simply went back there."

"And she let him stay?" Constance asked.

"I doubt he gave her any choice. He's not a pleasant man."

"People rarely look in the same place twice," Solomon said thoughtfully, perching on the arm of Constance's chair. "So where did the police find him in London?"

David fished a scrap of paper from his pocket and handed it to Solomon. "I wrote down everything he told me, because I don't know the place at all. Apparently, it's a brothel and a rookery full of thieves and cutthroats and fugitives."

"Then it's also full of traps for the unwary and the police," Constance said grimly. "I hope they got out safely." She peered over Solomon's arm to read what David had noted down.

"Do you know it?" Solomon asked.

"I know *of* it," Constance said. "Dangerous for strangers, but the girls have some protection there at least. It doesn't stop their clients being scum of the earth." She looked up at Solomon. "You can't go in there. Not without an army of policeman who know how to get out again alive. I mean it, Solomon."

He was still gazing at the paper without blinking. "We don't need to go in. We need him to come out." He looked at David. "He saw you at the Crown and Anchor. He must know you gave his name to the police and that's why they're looking for him. You are the one who could hang him."

"So he'll kill me first," David said, equally casual. "I can bring him to me, but I'll need more of a reason than reminiscing over the good old days. We never liked each other."

"We need him to bring more than himself, though," Solomon said. "He needs to bring proof that he murdered Chase."

"Oh, he'll bring that along to murder me," David said cheerfully.

"It's not enough," Solomon objected. "It could be a different knife, or it could be a common blade similar to hundreds of others that might match the victim's wound. Did Chase have nothing on him that Drayman would have stolen?"

"His watch," Constance said. "You said he wore a big watch."

"Why would he wear something so valuable to the Crown and Anchor?" Solomon demanded. "Especially when he was incognito as an ordinary sailor."

"He had two," David said. "Both engraved with his name. His gold one that he kept safe, and a slightly battered brass one that he thought would fool people."

"Then that's what he needs to bring," Solomon said decisively. "Ask for gold. He'll try to palm you off with the brass one, but that doesn't matter. Someone will recognize it."

Constance stared at him. "A stranger might think you experienced in the art of criminal negotiations."

"Just negotiations," Solomon said.

"Well, we can think how to deliver this message tomorrow," she said, rising to her feet.

"What's wrong with tonight?" Solomon asked, his eyes hard and glittering with determination. "We have a house to see tomorrow."

DRAYMAN WAS LYING down, staring at the ceiling while he tried to think how to find Johnny without going to the Crown and Anchor. Not that even Johnny would be foolish enough to go back there, but someone would probably know where he was living.

"'Ere," Rosie said, invading the back room with her skimpy robe hanging off one shoulder. "Kid brought a message for you and ran off, poor little—"

Drayman sat bolt upright in one quick motion. "What message?"

"You've to go meet him at the Crown and Anchor."

"I ain't going near the Crown and Anchor."

Rosie threw up her arms. "Don't, then. It's all the same to me."

He scowled at her. "When?"

"Tonight. Now."

Drayman swore. "Who's it from?"

"How the hell would I know? Certainly not the boy." She turned to go, then swung back as her gin-raddled memory made a discovery. "Johnny, he said."

A slow smile began to curl Drayman's lips. It seemed he didn't have to look for Johnny after all. Johnny had found him, only he was too scared to come in. Not that Drayman could blame him for that. There were trapdoors and spikes and blades all over the building—Drayman had almost lost an arm once in this bloody place. "Did he say that? Good old Johnny. What else, Rosie, my love?"

Rosie gave a derisory snort. "He says he needs paying to keep you safe. And gold will do."

Drayman began to laugh. Sure, he'd give Johnny the brass watch after he'd killed him—and then the law would be off Drayman's back. It couldn't have worked out better than this.

He sobered again quickly, though. "Here, Rosie, got a job for you. You need to go out."

"I need to work if I've got two bleeding mouths to feed!" she said furiously.

Drayman didn't have to say anything, just look.

And inevitably, she dropped her gaze first. "What?" she asked aggressively.

"Fetch a couple of my lads to meet me outside..."

CONSTANCE DID NOT mind particularly that she had been given the easy job to keep her out of danger. She was quite happy to summon the police to the Crown and Anchor—and to accompany them to that less-than-salubrious establishment. Accordingly, she set off to Scotland Yard in a hackney that she instructed to wait for her.

She gave the sergeant at the desk her best smile and told her tale—a servant had overheard that the perpetrator of the murder outside the Crown and Anchor last week was there again now, and that it was Constance's duty to pass the word along.

The sergeant eyed her skeptically. "That a fact, madam? Well, you'll be glad to know we already have a police presence at the Crown and Anchor, and if any murderers turn up, we'll be sure to catch them."

Constance raised a haughty eyebrow. "I don't believe you're taking me seriously, sergeant."

He scowled back. "I don't believe you've took me seriously neither. Thank you for your information, ma'am, now please leave the matter to the police."

She waited, but he neither moved nor called anyone. "Sergeant, one tired man wilting in the cold and the rain is not going to be enough! Drayman will be with friends."

"And you know this how, madam? More overheard conversations?"

"Yes," Constance declared.

"Go home, ma'am," the sergeant said wearily.

"I wish to speak to Inspector Omand. Or failing that, Inspector Harris."

"Do you? Well, you're out of luck, 'cause they're not here. And they deserve their beauty sleep."

"Sergeant Flynn, then! Anyone who will take me seriously."

The sergeant straightened and looked her over with undisguised contempt. "Madam, return in the hours of daylight. Now please go before I'm obliged to have you removed."

"Imbecile!" Constance exploded, which was hardly wise, but she'd had enough of his scorn and his superior manliness and wanted to scream in frustration.

Two large constables were advancing upon her. She walked in the direction of the door and, while they accompanied her, told the story to them again and requested they do something about it for the sake of their careers.

They shut the door in her face while she was still talking.

Stunned, Constance was temporarily flummoxed.

It had been a long time since any man had dismissed her, and she truly hadn't expected it now, at the worst possible time, when she needed the police to save Solomon and arrest the murderer.

Well, she wasn't going to give up. She marched back to the hackney and said loudly, "Bow Street police station!"

Would the attitude at Bow Street be any better? Did she really not look respectable enough? Even at this time of night?

And then she realized that no, she didn't. She should have had a husband with her, or at least a male escort. And failing either of those, a maid or female companion. She should have taken the time to fetch Janey or one of the footmen at her establishment, for now she had lost time she could little afford. With no idea how long it would be before Drayman made his appearance at the Crown and Anchor, she wanted to drive the horses forward herself. They seemed maddeningly slow.

Arriving at Bow Street, she found something of a party on the police station steps. The entranceway was blocked by a crowd of expensive young man, all drunk as lords. They may even have *been* lords, for all Constance knew or cared. She just acknowledged with a freshly sinking heart that the harassed police constable trying to deal with them would not have time for her, and neither would any of his colleagues inside, who were no doubt gathering to arrest the crowd on the steps.

But she had to try.

"Wait, please," she ordered the hackney, and sailed up the steps wishing she had an umbrella to lay about her with. Panic was beginning to set in, because the plan that had seemed so simple in Solomon's house was falling apart because of her, and Solomon would be abandoned in danger alone.

"Excuse me!" she bellowed. And rather to her surprise, the crowd of men parted for her, although the noise did not recede much.

"Mrs. Silver!" called someone in great delight. "Have you come for the party?"

It was Lord Rawleigh, an amiable if hedonistic young peer and occasional visitor to her establishment.

"Not at a party, Rawl," his nearest companion informed him, as they both bowed to Constance with unimpaired grace and offered her their flasks. "At Bow Street."

Rawleigh frowned, looking about him in surprise. "What the devil are we doing at Bow Street?"

"Arrested, old fellow. Or at least Pinster was, and we objected, so the constable had to take us all."

For a moment, they all regarded the hapless constable in the midst of this sea of good-natured but utterly castaway young gentlemen. He had a firm hold of his prisoner—presumably Mr. Pinster—by the arm, but whenever he tried to move forward, Pinster's companions surged too and everything came to a halt. The poor policeman, red-faced in the lamplight, was clearly wishing he had never begun the procedure.

Constance, having politely declined the proffered flasks, was beginning to move past Lord Rawleigh when a somewhat outrageous idea began to form. "Why are the other policemen not coming out to haul you all inside?" she asked.

"Expect they're all busy," Rawleigh said wisely. "Good thing, if you ask me."

Busy, Constance thought, and reluctant to embroil themselves with the well-connected drunks who might damage their careers.

Rawleigh offered her his arm. "Escort you to the door, ma'am!"

Constance laid her hand on his arm and assessed her prospective army. Swigging from flasks and bottles, they sat on steps and milled around, mingling and calling to each other. A few were singing a bawdy song. Two on the steps were playing cards. Two more were climbing dangerously onto the shoulders of their companions with the apparent intention of racing, to the accompanying cheers of those nearest.

"Dashed rowdy party when there's ladies present," Rawleigh said with disapproval. "Lady Davenham shouldn't allow it."

"Goodness, you're well oiled," said his friend. "Best let me escort the lady."

Rawleigh grinned. "Not at Lady Davenham's!" he said triumphantly. "At Bow Street!" He peered at Constance. "Do you really want to be at Bow Street?"

"Actually, no," Constance said, making her decision. "I want to be at the Crown and Anchor."

"Doesn't sound the sort of place for a lady."

Constance smiled. "Not quite a lady, though, am I? All the same, I would appreciate the escort."

Rawleigh scratched his head. His friend looked thoughtful. One of the would-be racers fell off his friend's back, to roars of laughter. The constable made another effort to take his prisoner inside, and again found his path blocked.

"Can we go if we're arrested, Sammy?" Rawleigh asked his friend.

"We could come back again."

"Good idea." Rawleigh offered his flask to Constance.

This time she took it and replaced the stopper. "I think a large escort would be safest, since a friend is in trouble. In fact, the constable should be with us, too." For if he was, the police inside the station would surely be forced to follow.

"Of course it would!" Sammy said, and filled his lungs.

He and Rawleigh bellowed together, "Or-der!"

And bizarrely, the ruckus cut off like a tap.

"Rescuing a lady in distress!" Rawleigh declared.

"Hurrah!" cheered the drunks.

Rawleigh and Sammy brandished their fashionable walking canes like swords, and Constance, taking a firmer hold of

Rawleigh's arm and a very deep breath, tugged him briskly toward her still-waiting hackney.

"Charge!" yelled Rawleigh, and they all did, even the gentleman balancing a friend on his shoulder.

Several hats bounced down the steps and were crunched underfoot or leapt over. Constance's hackney driver, looking terrified, brandished his whip.

"The Crown and Anchor, if you please!" Constance commanded, and dived inside the cab. Rawleigh, Sammy, and a complete stranger piled in after her, and she heard a thud as someone else landed beside the driver.

The driver gave in to the inevitable and urged his poor horse forward at a decent clip, no doubt to prevent the arrival of anyone else to his vehicle. Through the window, Constance saw the shouldered man fall off onto the roof of a waiting Black Maria. Another cheer went up as several men dived inside it and clambered onto the roof. Pinster jumped onto the driver's box, dragging the alarmed but determined constable with him.

Someone bolted out of the police station at last.

Hysterical laughter caught in Constance's throat. *Oh dear, what have I done?*

For authenticity, Solomon dressed in David's rough seamen's clothing. Regarding himself doubtfully in his bedroom mirror, he adjusted his posture, the tilt of his head, the friendliness of his normally cool gaze. *Now* he looked more like his brother.

A shadow darkened the doorway.

David stood there, looking at him. "It should be me. *I* should go. Or we both should."

"There can't be two of us. They would know it was a trick and scarper. And it can't be you just in case the police arrest you before we have the proof."

"They could arrest you for being me."

"But I have proof of who I am and connections who can speak for me. Even in these clothes, I am Solomon Grey. This is the only way."

"You were always a stubborn little—"

"So were you," Solomon said, his lips twitching. He met his brother's gaze in the mirror. "What did we quarrel about that day?"

David shrugged. "It's always bothered you, hasn't it? I never thought it was your fault. It wasn't. Nor mine, though that conclusion was harder to reach. We can't change the past, Sol."

Only David—and Constance—had ever called him that. He swallowed. "No. And the future will be better. Once we catch this miscreant." Solomon strode purposefully to the door, snatching up David's waxed wool jacket on the way.

"Are you sure she'll bring the police?" David blurted. "*Can she?*"

Solomon smiled. "Constance can do anything."

CHAPTER TWENTY-ONE

D RAYMAN AND HIS companions lurked in the shadows surrounding the Crown and Anchor, which was far too lit up for his liking. There were no streetlamps in this dingy corner, but since the murder, there were two lanterns and a policeman placed on the rubbly little square of waste ground to the side of it.

The policeman paced miserably, occasionally thumping his hands together for warmth.

Drayman nudged his companions. "Take him inside and make sure he stays there. Then come back out." He already knew Johnny was not inside the pub, for he'd already been in to look. He'd no intention of allowing Johnny over the door either, for there should be no witnesses but his own to this murder.

Draymen's companions grunted and brushed past him, emerging into the faint light emanating from the Crown and Anchor. They did a fair job of pretending to see the peeler for the first time.

"Here, mate, what you skulking over there for? Freezing yourself to death!"

"Duty," the policeman said with a large sniff. He already had a cold.

"Ain't right, is it? Come on inside for five minutes. What's going to happen in that time? Come to that, what good's it doing the poor bugger what croaked here to have you watching the place now? You'll learn more inside. We'll help."

The man held out, but not very convincingly and not for very long. He was soon whisked inside the pub with his solicitous companions. Drayman didn't much care if they slid a knife between his ribs while he was in there, though it might be better if they didn't, considering Johnny was meant to be the murderer around here. There were other ways to keep a man inside a public house against his better judgment.

Drayman let a man walk past him and out of sight. Then he darted to the waste ground next to the pub and quickly doused both lanterns.

SOLOMON, HAVING ABANDONED his hackney, approached the Crown and Anchor on foot. He almost didn't see it, for the sky and the air were murky and only the faintest of lights emanated from the public house's windows. He had rather hoped for the presence of a policeman on watch, whom he intended to speak to on his way inside, but he must have been taken off duty. Still, Solomon doubted the police had given up on the case. From Omand's visit to David earlier today, they were still very much looking for Drayman.

And if Constance had succeeded, there were already several stout plainclothes policemen waiting inside. Like the night at the gaming club where he had first seen Constance…

Mind on the task, Grey, he chided himself, for he needed to be sharp now and aware of every inch of his surroundings. Twenty policemen couldn't save him if he let Drayman creep up too close behind him…

Instinct caused him to give the patch of waste ground a wide berth—rightly so, for surely a patch of the darkness was blacker than the rest, just in against the wall of the building?

A man-shaped figure loomed forward. "Johnny."

Damnation. This was not how he had planned it.

Solomon stopped and gazed at the man, who seemed to be

dressed in similar fashion to himself. "Drayman."

"Don't stand over there bawling my name to all and sundry."

"Let's go inside, then. Bloody freezing out here."

"That your thin African blood complaining again?" Drayman mocked.

"Yes." Solomon walked on toward the door.

"There's a rozzer in there," Drayman remarked. "It's now or never, Johnny. Want the watch? Or not?"

The best laid plans of mice and men... There was nothing for it but to swerve toward the waste ground, though Solomon moved slowly, trying to keep to David's more relaxed posture while his senses reached out, searching for the trap. His skin prickled. He could smell tobacco and humanity—but how many men?

Drayman was confident enough to have come alone. It was how he'd faced Chase and killed him. Johnny, though younger and fitter, was probably not known as a violent man.

Solomon halted several feet away. "Show me."

"Can I trust you, Johnny?"

"I keep my word. I just need to be out of this country. You can understand that. Show me."

In the darkness, Solomon could make out the other man's movement, fishing in his rustling pocket. Slowly, he drew out something that actually glittered. A watch on the end of a chain.

"It's engraved," Drayman said, holding it out to him. "But you can melt it down."

Throw it, Solomon wanted to command, but he didn't, because he needed to be close enough to Drayman to catch him. Where the devil were Constance's policemen?

As he took a wary step forward, the back of his neck tingled. Someone was behind him. He stepped aside, trying to avoid the trap for as long as possible. In the distance, some kind of riot seemed to be going on, because he could hear muffled shouts of song and galloping hooves. Hardly the saviors he was looking for. Rather, a distraction for the police that could ruin everything.

"Nervous, Johnny?" Drayman said. "You was always highly

strung, as the captain put it." He spat on the ground.

"I was ill. Talked a lot of rubbish, so they tell me."

"Seems you still talk too much. Do you want this or don't you?"

It was why he was here. But some witness, preferably a policeman, had to see Drayman giving him the watch.

"What'd you kill him for, anyway?" Solomon asked, for it had suddenly struck him that the presence behind *could* be the police he was waiting for. Or not.

"Revenge," Drayman said. "He was supposed to be dead already. I should know. I paid for it. That, and I didn't like him. Never liked you much either, Johnny."

Solomon took a step nearer.

Two more shadows emerged from the wall, on either side of Drayman. Outside of Solomon's field of vision, the riot seemed to be coming closer, the horses' hooves growing louder, along with the rumbling of wheels. *Bizarre...*

But the knife in Drayman's other hand focused his mind. The two accomplices, large and exuding considerable experience in violence, moved forward and to the side, trying to hem Solomon in. He was running out of time.

"You're trying to palm me off with the brass watch," Solomon said. "He'd never have brought the gold one to this place."

"That's where you're wrong, Johnny-boy. Finish it, lads. I'm cold."

All three of them advanced on Solomon now, forcing him to step back and adjust his position so he wasn't encircled. He tensed, ready to meet the attack—and a movement behind caused him to spin to deal with that attack first.

The darkness was almost impenetrable, and yet Solomon knew immediately. No policeman, no thug. Just his brother. Just as it used to be.

"Idiot," he breathed, facing the onslaught.

"Looby," David returned.

It had given their attackers pause, but only for an instant, for the fight was still three to two in their favor. They charged.

Drayman came straight for him, wielding the watch like a mace and the knife like a sword. Solomon sidestepped the blade and kicked him in the stomach, narrowly missing the flying watch that whizzed past his ear. The other man barged into him and they both staggered backward. David and the third man were swaying together like wrestlers. Or dancers.

Solomon recovered his balance, took an agonizing blow to his side, and crashed his fist into the man's chin. He dropped like a stone, but Drayman was on him again, seizing him by the throat, knife raised for the kill. Solomon lashed out, landing a punch, but he couldn't quite hook his foot around the man's ankles to bring him down. He had to grab Drayman's wrist to prevent the blade plunging into him.

And then the riot swerved around the corner in a blaze of light and noise. The vignette of the fight outside the squalid building was lit up like a stage. A huge cheer went up from the newcomers, some of whom seemed to be wearing silk hats as they spilled of a hackney carriage and two Black Marias, only one of which seemed to be driven by a uniformed and confused policeman.

This strange army, wielding canes and leather flasks with monogramed gold plaques, charged toward them, led by Constance Silver, her skirts billowing as she flung herself into Solomon's arms with such force that she knocked him out of Drayman's weakened hold, and they fell together.

There was an instant when she stared into his eyes, her own shining with fear and…fun?

"Are you hurt?" she whispered, which at least galvanized Solomon into action.

"He's got a knife!" Solomon yelled in warning to the men who seemed to be burying Drayman beneath them.

"No he hasn't," said the confused constable, who stooped and picked the fallen weapon off the ground. Drayman must have dropped it in shock as Constance cannoned into them.

Solomon rolled to the side and jumped up, dragging Constance with him, and reached for David, who stood on his other side, panting, but dusting off his hands as though pleased with a day's work.

Solomon gripped his shoulder, and David answered with a nod. Both Drayman's thugs lay sprawled and semiconscious on the ground. The heap of young men, stinking of alcohol, were grinning at each other. The one at the top waved an open flask.

"Who the *devil…?*" Solomon began, just as a third Black Maria sped around the corner, spilling out uniformed policemen with clubs, even before it stopped.

"Or-der!" Constance yelled at the top of her lungs, and to Solomon's amazement, the men on top of Drayman began to untangle themselves.

The policemen, finding no resistance, skidded to a halt and lowered their clubs, staring as the young men dragged themselves upright and moved aside, gradually revealing the clearly winded figure of Abel Drayman clutching the chain of a still-attached watch that glinted in the lantern light.

"Ruffian was attacking the lady's friends," one of the young men said.

Good God, it's Lord Rawleigh! And from his fatuous smile, he was three sheets to the wind. If not four.

"He was," said the first constable on the scene, marching up to his colleagues to show them the knife. "*And* he was armed with that. There were three of them."

"And that one," Solomon said, going forward to Drayman, "is the murderer of Herbert Chase. That's the knife he used, and that is Chase's watch. It's engraved."

The policeman who appeared to be in charge went to Drayman, barking a couple of orders to his men, who went to gather up the other fallen thugs. The sergeant took the watch and presumably read the engraved name, for his breath certainly caught.

He turned to Solomon. "And you are?"

"Solomon Grey." With a civil inclination of the head, Solomon presented the policeman with both the cards he'd had the forethought to bring with him. One displayed the headquarters address of his far-reaching and respected business empire. The other said *Silver & Grey.*

"There's two of you," Drayman gasped from the ground, his fearful eyes darting from Solomon to David and back.

"This is my brother," Solomon said. It gave him a little frisson of pleasure. "Mr. David Grey. He helped me apprehend Abel Drayman."

The sergeant closed his mouth.

"What on earth," asked the first constable hopelessly, "am I to do with all of *them* now?"

The sergeant frowned at the now-subdued young men who were sheepishly trying on fallen hats and passing them to each other in search of their own. "They caused an obstruction and breach of the peace and stole two Black Marias."

"And captured a murderer," Constance pointed out, "thereby saving the life of my affianced husband, Mr. Grey, and his brother." Clinging very tightly to Solomon's hand, she bestowed her dazzling smile on the sergeant. "If I were you, I'd send them home to sober up. If you need them as witnesses for the court, you can reach them through Lord Rawleigh here."

The sergeant swallowed. "Lord Rawleigh," he repeated.

"That's me," Rawleigh said, beaming. "Been to a party, you know!"

The young men laughed, and one threw an arm around Rawleigh's shoulders. "Come on, old fellow, time for bed!"

"What an excellent idea," Solomon murmured.

IT WAS RATHER later than they had intended the following day before Constance and Solomon managed to look at their potential new home. For one thing, their late and adventurous night meant they slept in, and for another, Inspector Omand had demanded statements of them.

Fortunately, he did not mention the presence of Solomon's brother at the Crown and Anchor that night, and neither did they. Since Drayman had been charged with Herbert Chase's murder, there was no point. They had the evidence of the watch and the weapon, and Solomon told Omand about Captain Blake, who would attest to the story of Chase and Drayman on the *Mary Anne*, which provided the motive.

Solomon explained that he had sent a message to the address Omand had provided, in order to entice Drayman out of his lair.

"To the Crown and Anchor?" Omand said in disbelief. "Did you imagine that would be any safer?"

"Well, yes. By the time I arrived I imagined there would be a police presence, but no one at Scotland Yard would listen to Mrs. Silver's pleas."

"No one on duty at Scotland Yard had any reason to believe a woman alone after midnight in perfect health with such a wild tale," Omand excused his colleagues. "The nearest police station would have been better."

"I shall remember for next time," Constance said gravely.

"Preferably without causing a riot of the rich and privileged," Omand added severely.

And Constance wanted to laugh again. "It was hardly a *riot*, inspector! And I didn't cause it. Your own constable did by arresting one of them. I merely helped move it on."

"Yes, well," Omand said hastily, "talking of moving on..."

There was only one nasty moment, just as they were about to leave Omand's office.

"As a matter of interest," the inspector said, "what was *your* interest in this whole affair?"

Solomon smiled. "Merely a concerned client," he said.

Their concerned client was still sound asleep in Solomon's house on the Strand, as though a huge weight had suddenly been lifted from his mind.

"Is he going to stay?" Constance asked in the carriage, on their way to view the house.

"I don't know. Neither does he. The legalities will have to be sorted out, of course, but he is owed half of the inheritance from my father, plus half of the income from the plantation, which is not huge unless you compare it with a seaman's wages."

"Will that make financial difficulties for you?"

Solomon shook his head. "No. But it will give him time to decide what to do. I have suggested he might like to study art. He is thinking about it."

"His sketches are remarkably good."

"When we have our own house," Solomon said, and Constance felt another little thrill at the knowledge they would soon be living together, married, "when we have our own home, I thought I would give David the house in the Strand, if you agree."

She blinked. "Of course I do." She hesitated, then said, "He may not stay there, Sol. He has been traveling for most of his life."

"I know. But he should have somewhere to come back to. Whether it's here or Jamaica, or both. Or neither. Look, this is the place, on our left…"

It was part of a short, residential street with an old tree growing in the middle of it. The façade of the house was oddly pleasing to Constance, and her heart beat foolishly fast as she crossed the threshold hand in hand with Solomon.

The house had been empty for some time. It smelled old and musty, but its proportions were gracious without being massive. It was nothing like her Georgian mansion in Mayfair, or like Solomon's modest dwelling in the Strand, and that pleased her. The staircase curved in a sensual, sweeping way. And there were enough rooms for them each to have a private space, bedchambers for guests, as well as a suite of their own and attic bedrooms for servants. And storage.

Constance was silent as they made their way back downstairs. They inspected the large kitchen, which needed to be modernized, and returned to the big front room.

"What are you thinking?" Solomon asked, a trace of anxiety in his voice that she had never heard before. Once, he would have hidden that.

So she returned his honesty. "I was thinking that never in my life have I had so much space to call my own…" She smiled, spreading her arms and spinning like a dancer. "To share only with you. It feels like a good house, Solomon, a welcoming house that we can fill with our own friends, our family, children…whoever and whenever we choose."

She came to an abrupt halt, sliding her arms around his waist, resting her cheek against his chest and closing her eyes while the dizziness receded.

"Could it be home?" he asked.

And she smiled again. "I think it already is."

THEY WERE MARRIED very quietly the following week at St. Mary's Le Strand church. Their only witnesses were David, Constance's mother, and, because they had been responsible for their first meeting, Lady Grizelda and Dragan Tizsa.

Constance hadn't truly expected the Tizsas to come, and she was touched that they did. Mostly, she was stunned to be married, to be no longer Constance Silver but Mrs. Solomon Grey…

She clung very tightly to Solomon's arm as they emerged from the church. And that was when the gust of cold wind seemed to blast happiness through her. Beside her, Solomon breathed and relaxed, and she knew he felt it too.

They all walked around to the unassuming hotel where they would spend the night, and where they had reserved a room for the informal wedding breakfast. After all, the entire staff of her establishment were desperate to celebrate—and they did, greeting the newlyweds with wild cheers and showers of rice.

To Constance's delight, Solomon's closest staff from St. Catherine's also appeared to pay their respects. More surprising was the presence of those she had never imagined were their friends, like members of Lady Grizelda's family, Lord and Lady Trench and Lord Forsythe Niven, and like Sir Nicholas and Lady Swan. She almost cried to see Elizabeth and Sir Humphrey Maule, and Lord and Lady James Andover. They were all part of Silver and Grey's journey.

"Are we still Silver and Grey?" Constance said suddenly to her husband. "Grey and Grey just doesn't have the same ring to it." She tried to make it a joke, and yet the sudden fear of losing what had become so dear bothered her.

Solomon put his arm around her, for that was perfectly acceptable now too. "We will always be Silver and Grey."

ABOUT THE AUTHOR

Mary Lancaster lives in Scotland with her husband, three mostly grown-up kids and a small, crazy dog.

Her first literary love was historical fiction, a genre which she relishes mixing up with romance and adventure in her own writing. Her most recent books are light, fun Regency romances written for Dragonblade Publishing: *The Imperial Season* series set at the Congress of Vienna; and the popular *Blackhaven Brides* series, which is set in a fashionable English spa town frequented by the great and the bad of Regency society.

Connect with Mary on-line – she loves to hear from readers:

Email Mary:
Mary@MaryLancaster.com

Website:
www.MaryLancaster.com

Newsletter sign-up:
http://eepurl.com/b4Xoif

Facebook:
facebook.com/mary.lancaster.1656

Facebook Author Page:
facebook.com/MaryLancasterNovelist

Twitter:
@MaryLancNovels

Amazon Author Page:
amazon.com/Mary-Lancaster/e/B00DJ5IACI

Bookbub:
bookbub.com/profile/mary-lancaster